Witness a Killing

Sue Tort

Paperback Edition

Other Books by Sue Tort:

Mumford Mystery Series

Friends Lovers Killers (Book 2)

Romance

What I Did On My Wedding Night

Thank you to my cats Dusty and Cleo.

Without their 'help and guidance' this novel would have been finished months earlier.

INDEX

Friendship is a sheltering tree

Samuel Taylor Coleridge

1

No signal.

He clambered up the ridge to the river path but still nothing, so, his injured ankle slowing him, he half stumbled, half jogged back to the iron bridge and climbed the well-trodden steps. At the top, he did get a signal, it was faint though, like a fading heartbeat.

'999 what is your emergency?'

'Police, I… we… we've found a body. A woman. She's got a head injury.'

Questions, questions. He was new to the Fens, the names of rivers, bridges, lakes, most of them had 'Fen' somewhere in the title, but exact place names?

'My name is Jude Mumford, I'm on the Fens, about 3 miles from Eaststowe. There's an old iron bridge, no, there's two bridges, one's a lifting bridge…'

'Lifting bridge?'

'Like a drawbridge, it's very wide, looks as if it might be used to get farm machinery across the river.'

He waited seconds, breathed in the view, birds in flight, hovering, diving for breakfast. Curious creatures venturing out from their frozen shelters; others skulking off to shelter after a furtive night.

As he stood, watching, waiting, he imagined the crime solving machine grinding into place. Detectives, investigators, woken from their beds, forensics grabbed, cars readied, a helicopter scrambled. Within minutes the dead body of a woman would transform this wildlife sanctuary into an active crime scene.

He heard it first, he timed it, force of habit. It took twenty-three minutes. As it neared, noise levels increased and the peaceful sanctuary transformed to a panic-stricken landmass. Wildlife scattered, spooked birds took flight, hare, deer and muntjac – alerted to the man-made intruder approaching at speed - used their wings, paws, hoofs, whatever they were gifted with, to take shelter, seek out a place of safety. In the distance a herd of dun-coloured ponies - muddied by swamp play - optimistically galloped for the hills. Only there were no hills, this was the Fens.

He knew the pilot would be watching out, looking for a sign, a frantically waving arm, anything. Today, he was the frantically waving arm they were searching for. She – the dead woman - was at the bottom of the ridge hidden amidst trees, they weren't going to spot her.

'Spud, with me.'

He made his way down the bridge steps and limped back along the river path like a car with a flat tyre. Spud looked up at his master and barked once, as if to confirm he was fully aware that something was up and that he had a role to play.

It was minutes before the two of them reached the slope that led to the lower track. Earlier that morning when Jude had tried to walk down it to see what Spud was barking at, he'd tripped and slithered down face first landing at the bottom, arms and legs splayed out like a fallen foal. This time he decided to negotiate it feet first. He turned around and spotted a man and a woman on the other side of the river. The woman held her phone skyward, capturing the helicopter and the changing contours of the landscape stippled out by the downdraft as it came in to land.

She wore a waterproof jacket, a tucked in tartan scarf, a wax hat. Apart from her obvious appetite to record an event which was none of her business, she appeared classier than her scruffy companion.

'Bloody sightseers,' he whispered under his breath. 'Please, clear the area, nothing to see here,' he shouted.

'We both know that's not true,' she shouted back.

It was no longer his job to give out orders at a crime scene.

Spud had bounded down the ridge and was at the bottom gazing at the helicopter. Jude attempted to follow his pet, grasping tufts of frozen grass, as he stepped his way to the bottom.

By the time he got there, the helicopter had landed, the engine cut and blades stilled. Three figures jumped out, two clothed head to foot in forensic outfits, the third wore a dark blue overcoat over a navy suit. There was shouting, hand gestures, pointing, then all three turned to him.

'She... she's in there...' he shouted pointing to the trees, then watched as they headed to the body site.

He stared around the reserve, its wild creatures concealed now, hidden from the intruder helicopter in their midst. It was a scene as wrong as a lorry parked in a playground, hushed of laughter without the beating hearts of children.

The navy suit approached, nodded a greeting, pulled down the knot of a pale blue tie and unbuttoned the top of her white shirt.

'I'm Detective Inspector Jones,' she said. 'I'm guessing you're the chap who called us?'

'Jude Mumford,' he stepped forward; they shook hands. 'Yes, I found her.' In the distance he could see a forensic van, a motor bike and three police cars, bumping along the heavily rutted track towards them.

'I need to ask you a few questions,' said D.I. Jones.

'Go ahead.'

'Would you like to sit down? We've got chairs.' The detective turned to the incoming vehicles as they pulled up in a semi-circle around the helicopter like a fortifying wagon train. 'At least we will have soon.'

Within minutes a pop-up marquee appeared, a table, chairs, more freshly minted forensic suits, one, two, three, four, all busied themselves carrying out their allotted tasks like worker ants, eager to safeguard the integrity of the scene and ensure the dignity of the victim.

D.I. Jones sat down on a plastic chair one side of a newly placed table. She beckoned Jude over then her eyes turned to Spud.

'He's a big one, isn't he?'

Spud, his brown and white coat blending into the natural hue of the landscape, sat down beside Jude and rested his head on the table, mouth open, ears twitching, dark eyes staring at the detective as if waiting his turn to be interrogated.

3

A laptop appeared, a pad of paper and several sharp tipped lead pencils. Without a thank-you to the young policeman who had placed them, D.I. Jones reached into her jacket pocket, pulled out a scratched glasses case and placed it on the table. She squared to the laptop and turned to Jude, her fingers hovering above the keys.

'Name?'

'As I said, Jude Mumford.'

'No middle name?'

Jude shook his head and tried to keep a straight face as he watched the detective screw up her eyes and stare first at her laptop screen and then down at the keyboard. After several seconds she sighed and reached for her glasses case, snapped it open and put them on.

She asked Jude for his personal details and started to type using just her middle finger.

'Address?' she asked, eyes still on her screen.

'2, Willow Walk...'

'Willow Walk, Eaststowe, I know it.' She made eye contact. 'Oh so you're the chap who's moved in there.' She scratched her head. 'One of the original Manor cottages that was, in the olden days.'

'So I've been told,' Jude nodded and hinted a smile.

'If you don't mind me saying sir, you're very blasé, very calm.' She leant forward and placed her elbow onto the table, arm up and twiddled her pencil through her fingers, turning it slowly as if trying to mesmerise Jude. 'Most people who find a dead body tend to be pretty shocked... bordering hysterical some of them, especially if there's blood.'

'I used to be a detective,' said Jude. 'I'm used to seeing dead bodies.'

D.I. Jones stopped twiddling the pencil, her gaze remained.

'You were one of us? Really? Tell me about it.'

Jude dragged his hand through his hair, rubbed his unshaved chin and gazed into his past. He did not tell D.I. Jones that his

4

previous life as a detective had come to an abrupt halt on the day that Spud did not eat his breakfast. He did not mention that he had gone home at lunch time to check on his pet and found his wife and his boss (who until that moment had also been his best friend) having sex on the blue and white rug his mother had bought as part of their wedding gift.

Jude's Wife: *What are you doing here?*

Jude: *Err, this is my home...I live here...*

Zac: *Mate, sorry, mate, I'm so sorry...*

Jude did not tell D.I. Jones any of that. He did mention that he had lived and worked in North London and, his voice wavering slightly, he did answer her questions and recalled places and people he had – until now – been doing his best to forget.

'Thank you,' said D.I. Jones when she had heard enough. 'Now then, this body, I believe it's a female. Have you seen her before? Any idea who she is?'

'No and no.'

'Why were you out here at this time?'

'I lost my wallet; I came to find it.'

'When did you lose your wallet?'

'Yesterday.'

'So, you were here yesterday?'

'I was, that was when I lost my wallet.'

'Why were you here yesterday?'

'I was walking Spud, my dog.' He patted Spud, who had seconds earlier, decided to lay down. At the mention of his name, he sat up again, stared across at D.I. Jones and barked as if to confirm his masters answer to the question. The detective jumped. Her eyes widened, she shook her head and muttered something before turning to Jude.

'Loud, isn't he?'

'As you pointed out earlier, he's a big dog. 'By the way his name is Spud and he's a Saint Bernard.'

5

D.I. Jones peered at Spud, then at Jude. She made no attempt to hide her confusion.

'A whatty what?'

'A Saint Bernard, the breed used to be used as a search and rescue dog in the Alps, they have an extremely strong sense of smell.'

'Is that so? Not much call for him round here then.' The detective returned her attention to her laptop. 'Just make sure you keep him that side of the table please.'

'There's no need to be scared of him, he really is a big softie.'

The detective stared at Jude over the top of her glasses.

'Give me a drug addled criminal over a dog any day...' she spoke in a whisper, as if to herself, then returned her attention to her laptop and typed for a few seconds before, with a final finger flourish, she sat back.

'That's enough of that for now.' She shoved the laptop to one side, grabbed the pad of paper and positioned it square in front of her. Pencil in hand she stared at the notepad for seconds before starting to scrawl words across the page. 'Massive, brown and white dog.'

'I take it you're not a dog lover?'

'In that you are correct sir,' D.I. Jones paused; her attention drawn to an approaching forensic suit. 'Neighbour's dog bit me when I was twelve, got bitten again when I was fifteen. Funny though...'

'Something's funny?' It was a different female voice. 'We have a body of a woman a few metres away and something's funny?'

Jude turned to watch as the two suits faced each other, tight fitting navy, versus standard issue forensic.

'This is Fearless, our forensic expert,' D.I Jones turned to Jude. 'Now she is definitely not scared of dogs,' and as an afterthought added, 'or anything else for that matter.'

'Fearless?' said Jude.

'It's what they call me.' She was masked up but her eyes sparkled like grey pools. 'Feel free to call me by my real name though.'

'Which is?'

'Fatema.'

Jude was well aware of some of the nicknames his old team had had for him and for each other, back in the old days, when he had a job.

'And who is your friend?' Fearless nodded to Spud.

'Oh, that's Spud.'

'Spud? Great name.'

Spud recognised a friend, even one fully garbed in a forensic suit. He stood up and headed to Fearless. She stepped back, both arms up in a surrender pose.

'Sorry Spud,' she said. 'Beautiful though you are this is not the time or place for cuddles.'

'As I was saying,' said D.I. Jones. 'About your dog...'

'Spud,' Jude corrected.

'Spud,' D.I. Jones stared at Jude then Fearless. 'When I said it's funny, I meant funny as in curious, because my husband, now he loves dogs, but I said to him before we got married, no dogs, and he married me anyway. Turns out he loved me more.'

'He won the jackpot that day,' said Fearless. 'Can I have a word?'

'Indeed, he did.' D.I. Jones said without a hint of embarrassment.

Jude watched as the two women headed to the marquee and disappeared inside. Twelve minutes later they reappeared. Fearless talked, nodded, gestured, pointed to the marquee, to a fallen log and then to the helicopter. D.I. Jones listened and spoke the odd word before, head down, she returned to Jude, sighed and sat down.

'You said you were here yesterday?'

Jude nodded.

7

'Were you at this exact spot?'

'Yes, I mean no.'

'Yes? No? What's it to be?'

'Well, yes, I was here, but no I was not at this exact spot.' He turned and pointed to the slope, to the top of the ridge, 'I was up there, on the path, walking along by the river. It was Spud… he was down here.'

'Aaah yes, Spud,' the detective stood up and peered over the table at Spud who was laying down again eyes closed.

As realisation took hold, Jude swallowed hard.

She had snow on her body, she was here last night.

He bent down and stroked his pet.

Spud sat up, yawned and tongue lolling to one side stared up at his master for a few seconds before sitting and staring across the table at D.I. Jones again. The detective winced and, as if mesmerised like a rabbit in the full glare of headlights from an oncoming lorry, peered over her glasses at him. Spud let out a bark, then another, the detective flinched and snapped out of her trance.

'She was here last night wasn't she?' said Jude.

'That is what Fearless has concluded. There are signs, there was light snow overnight, she's covered in it.'

'I thought as much. Spud, he came across her last night.' He turned to Spud. 'Didn't you boy?' Doleful eyes stared up at him, a wet tongue licked his hand.

'Did he indeed?' D.I Jones shuddered and picked up her pencil. 'I tell you what sir, why don't you tell me what happened.'

'It's a bit of a long story.'

'Well, I'm a very good listener,' she leaned back. 'Now, from the beginning, what happened yesterday?'

For years Jude had been on the receiving end of having to listen to emotive comments and arbitrary assumptions garbled out by a panic muddled witness and he had no intention of doing the same. He intended to make sure he recalled everything in its exact sequence, bleached of all emotion and opinion. The facts. Nothing more. Nothing less.

'Well, last night,' he spoke slowly, 'while Spud and I were out for our evening walk, we started off on the path on the other side of the river from where the victim is.' He paused, glanced across at the detective, she was busy making notes. 'And we ended up quite a bit further down the track heading away from Eaststowe.' He sighed, 'enroute we met a woman out walking her two dogs and we sort of got talking.'

'You met a woman and you sort of got talking?' D.I. Jones looked up. 'Could she be our victim?'

'Absolutely not,' Jude shook his head. 'I'd have recognised her. The woman I met was completely different, a lot younger, and she was a bit odd if I'm honest.'

'Odd? May I be so bold as to ask you to quantify exactly what you mean by "odd"?'

Jude turned away, embarrassed by his own jumbled recollection. He put his hand into his trouser pocket and pulled out a pack of paper hankies, took one and wiped around his mouth.

'Well, we sort of chatted, but she mumbled a lot, almost to herself. It was as if she were in a world of her own.'

D.I. Jones put down her pencil and grabbed a tissue from her pocket just in time to catch a sneeze.

'Excuse me,' she wrapped her coat tight around her then picked up her pencil again. 'This woman and her dogs tell me about them.'

'She was early to mid-thirties, quite scruffy, hippy looking, long light brown hair in a single plait draped over her left shoulder. The dogs, well, one was a long-tailed brown and white Jack Russell, the other a yappy brown mongrel, they growled and barked at Spud, ran around him and she did nothing to stop them. That's when Spud jumped the dyke. It's up that way.' Jude half stood and pointed in the opposite direction of the bridge.

'I am familiar with the dyke sir.' The detective returned to her notepad, the speed of her writing outstripping the speed of her typing a hundred to one. At the end of her note taking, she pointed a full stop hard down onto her pad breaking the nib of her pencil.

9

'Blast, still, plenty more where that came from,' she grinned and nodded to the pencils lying in wait for their moment in the spotlight.

Jude tilted his head slightly, tried to read what the detective had written, but it was impossible.

'No point trying to read them, I make all my notes in Welsh.' As if to prove her point she turned the pad around.

'I… I... wasn't trying to…'

'Read my notes? Well, I'm guessing that's not strictly true sir. I'm pretty good at spotting a sneaky note reader when I see one.' She sat back, crossed her arms stared at him over the top of her glasses. 'Now this woman you met, you say she was hippy looking, skinny, was she?'

'She was, and she was dressed in some sort of tie-dyed orange and green skirt and an anorak. She had a pair of binoculars round her neck, kept fiddling with them.'

'I bet she told you it was a really nice walk back that way.'

She knows her.

'She did! And I believed her! I didn't realise I'd have to walk another quarter of a mile to the bridge to cross back over.'

'That sounds true to form.'

'You know her, don't you? Who is she?'

'Her name's Saffron, local eccentric. Harmless though. Anyway, please continue Mr Mumford.'

'I headed home. I didn't want to be on the Fen at night.'

'It's a creepy place at night tis the Fen. Never know who, or what you might bump into.'

'What do you mean?'

'There's a few odd bods make an after dark appearance.' She gave a short laugh. 'Saffron for one. Some come to watch the wildlife… …others, well your guess is as good as mine as to what they get up to. Anyway sir, what happened after you jumped the dyke?'

10

'Well, I decided to follow Spud, so I jumped across but I slipped and hurt my ankle when I landed, and I strained my shoulder, but that's an old injury.'

D.I Jones continued to write, ending each sentence with a purposeful dot.

'Continue,' she said.

'To be honest it was a relief to get away from them. I walked back along the track on the other side. But as I said, I didn't realise it branched off part way and that I had to walk along the river to get back,' he cleared his throat, 'or that I had to walk the extra quarter of a mile to the iron bridge to cross back over.'

'I'm guessing you were a bit annoyed at that?'

'A little,' said Jude. 'Anyway, I was walking by the river at the top of the ridge and Spud, he was chasing up and down the slope, running around all over the place. When we got to where she was, he ran down the ridge and disappeared into the trees.'

'And?'

'And after a few seconds he barked.'

'Spud barked,' D.I. Jones started to write again. 'Once? Twice? Went barking mad?'

'I could just see him, his bum and his tail, through the trees.'

'So, what did you do?'

'I called him. There was snow in the air, it was getting dark, I was cold, my ankle hurt, my shoulder ached. I just wanted to get home.'

'And?'

'He barked again, and again after that.'

Jude swallowed hard.

Why didn't I go and investigate?

'I shouted at him to come.' He took a deep breath and held it for seconds before expelling the air in a sigh. 'Next thing he's with me up on the ridge. Wagging his tail, all excited about something.'

11

'So, none of what he did alerted you to the fact that something might be seriously wrong?'

'I didn't realise, if I'd thought there was somebody there... here...'

'Like a woman lying dead?'

'I'd have come down and investigated, of course I would.'

Why didn't I go and investigate?

'I knew he'd seen something. I thought it might be a dead hare or....'

'No need to be defensive sir.'

'I wasn't to know it was a body, was I?'

'Not without looking sir.' D.I. Jones stared over to the activity taking place around the marquee, to where her colleagues were talking, pointing, nodding, it was a few seconds before she returned her attention to Jude. 'So, your dog barked and you wanted to go home so you got annoyed with him and called him back to you. Is that correct?'

'I suppose, but put like that... look, I just wanted to get home. As I told you, I thought it was going to start snowing again, it was getting dark, I was tired, I had a long walk back and my ankle and shoulder hurt from when I fell over.'

'And as I told you sir, there really is no need to be defensive. At this stage I'm just trying to understand your involvement.'

'Look... if I went and investigated every time Spud barked at something...'

Spud told me something was wrong. Why didn't I go and investigate?

'Okay,' said D.I. Jones, 'so that was yesterday, what about this morning?'

D.I. Jones listened intently as Jude explained how the previous evening, while he was doing his evening checks he had realised his wallet was missing.

'Evening checks?'

'Every evening, I check I've got my wallet, credit cards, that sort of thing.'

'Sounds a bit OCD to me,' said the detective. 'But each to his own.'

Jude ignored her remark and instead went on to explain the reason that he had been at this particular place at this particular time on this particular morning was to search for his lost wallet.

'So what happened when you got here?'

'Well, Spud was straight down the slope again. I called him a couple of times but he disappeared and didn't reappear, I could hear him barking though. He was going mad.'

'And this time you decided to go and see what was up?'

'I had a bit more energy,' Jude nodded. 'And I'd strapped up my ankle so the slope didn't seem quite so daunting. Still bloody slipped the first time though, fell down head first, hence the...' He stared down at his clothes, his faded jeans not hiding the mud, the grass stains and damp patches making it look as if he'd been involved in a bathroom incident. 'I made a bit of a mess of myself.'

'I had noticed,' D.I. Jones said. 'To be honest when I first saw you, I wondered if you were homeless, living rough out here maybe.'

'Thanks for that.'

'You're welcome. Now Mr Mumford, would you mind accompanying me to the police station so that I can take a proper witness statement? Tidy the t's and dot the whatsits.'

Jude lifted his head and winced at the brown eyes that stared unblinking at him.

'Do you mind if I go home first?'

'I'd rather you didn't. Best get the paperwork sorted,' she said. 'As an ex-detective I'm sure you'll appreciate the need for me to get down your recollection of what happened while it's all still sharp in your brain. There'll be tea, coffee, juice and, if you're lucky we might even be able to rustle up biscuits.' She wrapped her coat tight around again, it's fibres barely shielding her from the Fenland breath that advanced unhindered across the reserve. 'And it's bloody well warmer than out here.' She cupped her reddened hands to her mouth and blew into them. 'I hate bloody nature I do... it's so...'

'What about Spud?'

'Brutal... nature's bloody brutal it is. And lonely, something goes wrong out here, you're on your own, all on your bloody own.'

'What about...?'

'Spud?' said D.I. Jones. 'Bring him along, he's a witness after all.'

2

After Jude walked in on his best friend and his wife having sex on the rug his mother had bought them as a wedding gift, he made a number of lifestyle changes. He divorced his wife, resigned from his job and moved out of London. On a more upbeat note, he decided to return to his first love (career wise), which was tennis. His plan was to become a tennis coach.

Within a couple of weeks of his arrival in Eaststowe he had visited the local tennis club, the college and the park to check out the availability of tennis courts. He had created a business plan and most evenings he sat down in front of his laptop and worked on it. It had all been going so well. Until the body find that is.

The first thing he had done when he found her was to check her pulse. Apart from that he hadn't touched a thing, he knew not to contaminate a crime scene. He had taken photos though; he couldn't help himself. He took them from every angle, her body, her legs, blue from cold, her arms outspread in welcome, her face - a frozen mask.

Two days after the body find, when he and Spud got back from their morning walk, Jude tried to work on his business plan. By 10am he had given up investigating the pricing and availability of tennis courts and had moved himself and his coffee to the sofa where he was stretched out scrolling through the photographs he had taken at the crime scene.

Why am I doing this? It's nothing to do with me.

He sat up and swung his legs down but unknown to him, Spud had crept indoors and spread himself lengthways across the floor alongside the sofa to snooze next to him. His pet yelped awake, nudging over the cup of coffee.

'Sorry mate! So sorry.'

Spud, gazed up at him, eyes doleful, tail thumping in happiness at the attention.

In an effort to make amends, Jude picked up the coffee mug, went to the kitchen and got a pig's ear (for Spud), a cloth (to mop

15

up the spilled coffee) and a twisted closed half-finished packet of chocolate digestive biscuits (for himself). He threw Spud his treat, his pet caught it and headed for the kitchen and out of the back door to the garden again.

Jude mopped up the coffee, went and sat at the dining table and tried again to focus on all things tennis.

Progress was slow but he'd been working for over an hour when the sound of a car made him look up. Out of the window, to his left, through the skeletal branches of a shrub he could see a dark red Volvo estate parked outside number 1. He'd heard from Dexter (his neighbour on the other side at number 3), that the cottage was the second home of a young woman who lived in London and that she was due a visit. Jude watched as the door of the Volvo opened and a young woman got out. She was slender, auburn hair dragged back from her face by a pale green Alice band and she wore a matching green fitted jacket and pale lemon tight fitting jeans. She went around to the passenger side, opened the door, grabbed a wicker pet carrier and headed up her garden path. About halfway up she disappeared from Jude's view, but he heard her keys rattle and a couple of muffled – possibly curse - words before, a few minutes later, she reappeared empty handed. She clicked open the rear door of her Volvo, it was stacked full with boxes and clothes. His neighbour had arrived.

He watched as she pulled out a lidded yellow plastic crate and headed up her garden path again before he returned his attention to his business plan.

He'd gathered information about tennis courts, their locations, prices and booking details. He'd searched the internet for equipment, places to advertise, insurance. He needed to decide on his hours of work and how he was going to market his new venture, and of course, he had to decide on a name, something plain and simple and easy to remember, *Eaststowe Tennis Academy*, *JM Tennis…*

Shouting distracted him. It was a man's voice, coming from outside his house. He looked up; his newly arrived neighbour was standing at the back of her now empty car holding a shallow box of books. An elderly man – the one doing the shouting – was a neighbour from further along the terrace, a Patrick Fox who lived at number 8. The reason Jude knew this was because the old man had stopped him outside the village shop one day, introduced himself and then questioned him for over twenty minutes about the body find. It was on that day that Jude had come to realise for the first time that the village he had moved to was smaller than he first thought.

Mr Fox, wrapped in a dark grey overcoat, stood in front of their newly arrived neighbour and shouted his anger, *'It's people like you...'* *'you have no right...'* His words tumbled out like dirty clothes strung along a washing line. She made no attempt to retaliate or play any part in the old man's melodrama, she just stood and gazed into her box of books. Only when the shouting stopped did she bother to acknowledge him, not with her voice, with her eyes. Hers met his, for a few seconds only before he turned and set pace towards the church.

She watched him go then returned her attention to her Volvo. Balancing the box on her knee, she managed to slam the rear door shut, turned, stared at her cottage for a few seconds and headed up her garden path. Jude kept his eye on her until she disappeared from view. When she did, he returned his attention again to his business plan, but jumped a couple of seconds later as her front door slammed shut.

Jude worked until his stomach rumbled. That was when he checked the time; it was twenty-six minutes past five, time for Spud's walk.

Ten minutes later they were heading out.

'Evening – off for your walkies?'

Jude recognised the voice. It was Dexter at number 3. He was a couple of years younger than Jude, but with his cheerful demeanour, casual clothes, tanned complexion and festival hair he looked four or five years younger. They'd nodded and chatted over the wall out back on several occasions and Jude had heard him playing his guitar, sometimes late into the night, but that was all.

'Yep, off to the Fens. Spud loves it over there,' said Jude. 'And I must admit, so do I.'

'You look so funny sometimes, especially when you're on your bike with Spud running along beside you,' Dexter laughed. 'We're never quite sure who's taking who for their walkies.'

'We?'

'Just a few of us in the village.'

'Well, I'm glad I keep you entertained.' Jude was about to head off but instead stopped. 'My other neighbour arrived earlier today.'

'I spotted her car,' Dexter patted Spud as he spoke. 'I knew she was coming, wasn't sure if it was today or tomorrow.'

'You really have got your finger on the pulse of what's going on around here, haven't you?'

'I do her garden for her; she lets me know when she's gracing us with her presence so I can make sure it's looking good when she gets here.'

'She didn't look too happy…' Jude was about to mention the confrontation with Mr Fox but Dexter got in first.

'Not surprising really, rumour has it, it was her mate you found out on the Fens the other day.'

3

'Welcome to the village, how can I help you?'

Jude had popped into the corner shop at least twice a week since his move to Eaststowe and every time the well-built woman behind the counter greeted him the same way. It was a constant reminder to him – and anybody around – that he was new to the village.

On a previous visit she had asked Jude if he had recovered from the shock of finding a dead body on the Fen. With a straight face he had thanked her for her concern and added that he was absolutely fine because he was used to seeing dead bodies. He managed to wait until he had left the shop before he started to laugh at her shocked reaction.

On this occasion he whizzed around the store, loaded his wire basket with bread, milk, cheese, a tin of tomatoes and a pack of two toilet rolls and returned to the counter.

The shop door buzzed open, bread in hand, the woman behind the counter turned to look, Jude followed her gaze. A man, early forties and a teenage girl with long dark hair entered.

'Do you sell birthday cards?' the man asked.

'Dr Fernsby, good morning,' she turned to her incoming customer. 'Over in the corner, top three shelves.'

'You see,' the doctor turned to the girl. 'They sell them, now you go and pick a card for your friend.'

The girl headed to the end aisle her low-heeled shoes making a rhythmic tap, tap, sound as she crossed the stone floor. Dr Fernsby headed for the chiller cabinets at the back of the shop.

Thinking he was about to be served again, Jude got out his newly purchased wallet to pay. But it was in vain, the woman behind the counter was still focussed on the doctor. Jude spotted Mr Fox in the biscuit aisle; he was standing centimetres away from the custard creams but his eyes were following the doctor too.

Jude remembered he was out of chocolate digestives and headed to the aisle.

'Excuse me,' he said.

Mr Fox stared unsmiling at him for a few seconds, then squeezed up close to the shelves to let him through.

Jude picked up two packs of dark chocolate digestives and got back to the counter at the same time as the teenage girl and the doctor clutching 2 litres of semi skinned milk.

'Dr Fernsby, this way please, over here.' The woman flattened her apron and pointed to an empty space further down the counter. 'I won't have you waiting in the queue.'

The doctor turned his attention to Jude, his expression enquiring, as if asking permission to queue jump. Jude nodded.

'Rum business,' she said as she rang up the doctors semi-skimmed and the birthday card. 'Some folks are calling it karma.'

The doctor did not respond other than to put his hand inside his jacket pocket and pull out a bank card.

'Dr Fernsby, in case you're interested, it was him who found her.' She nodded towards Jude.

Jude now knew the 'her' she was referring to was a woman by the name of Chantal Dubois. He knew this because the details had been published on a local news website the previous day under the headline:

'P.I. Finds Body on Bowmarsh Fen'

A private investigator? Where the hell did they get that from?

The doctor returned his bank card to his inside jacket pocket, picked up his milk and turned to Jude.

'It must have been a shock,' he said. 'Finding her like that.'

'It was,' said Jude. 'But I'm used to it.'

'Yes, the papers said you're a private detective.'

If the doctor noticed Jude redden at his remark, he didn't show it. Jude opened his mouth to correct him.

'I'm not a…'

But the doctor and the girl were heading to the door. It buzzed as she pulled it open and it was only then that the woman behind the counter returned her attention to Jude. But his attention was still with the doctor and he watched as they left the shop and got into their dark blue car.

'Like dark chocolate do you?' she asked when they had gone. 'Not keen on it meself – gives me wind.' She turned the card machine to him.

Jude snapped to present.

'I'm not a Private Investigator,' he said. 'I'm an ex-detective.'

'Isn't that the same bloody thing?' She laughed. 'Once a copper, always a copper.'

'Not me,' he said. 'Not anymore.' He reached inside his jacket pocket, pulled out a leaflet, and placed it down onto the counter. 'In fact, I wondered if you could possibly put this in your window for me?'

She pulled the leaflet to her.

'Mumford Tennis Academy. So you're a tennis person then?'

Jude nodded.

'Two pounds a week,' she said. 'How many weeks do you want?'

'Twelve please, and I'll see how things go.' He offered his bank card again. 'Who were they?'

'That was Dr Fernsby and his eldest daughter, Freya.'

'Were they related to the woman I found?'

'Not exactly,' she paused, returning the card reader to its place snug beside the till. 'They used to be friends with her. Good friends as it happens.' Then, in a matter-of-fact voice she added, 'that is till she almost killed his youngest kiddie.'

4

Jude had always been an early riser and every morning and evening he would take Spud out for his exercise. Sometimes they would both be on foot. They would wander the tracks and venture along winding paths and little used trails but on occasion Jude would take his bike and Spud would lope alongside as they followed the formal sanded lanes. It was something which Jude now realised appeared to amuse his neighbours.

He loved the Fens. The herbal air and the crispness in a Fenland breeze aroused him, not in a sexual way, but in a way that inspired him to live the breadth of his life, not just the length of it. He'd gaze up, stare into the sky and gradually follow it down to the place where it kissed land. On a crystal day he could see the curvature of the earth in the distance. Or he thought he could.

On this particular morning, when Jude and Spud left the house at just after 6:30am, he was on his bike and Spud was loping along beside him open mouthed catching the breeze. Jude was satisfied the crispness in the air and the minimal ground frost promised a kindly weather day. It's true a few clouds were visible, but all were white and fluffy and in no way suggested menace.

They stuck to the formal sanded tracks and Spud stayed with his master even when he slowed down to let other dog walkers pass by. There was always a thank you nod and a giggle when he and Spud set off again.

Forty-five minutes into their jaunt they were slow-moving along a sanded track that crossed the Fen when the clouds darkened and swelled to bursting. It did not take Jude long to realise that on this occasion he had been fooled by the Fenland dawn. His remit was to save himself, and of course Spud. They took shelter under a solitary Oak tree and watched the heavens transform the tranquil reserve to hostile territory in a well-established drama with nature in the starring role.

The storm went on for nearly an hour. By the time the clouds had emptied, the wetlands were exactly that. Air sharpened by the scent of the newly cleansed foliage, branches glistened in the timid light, grasses bent heavy with raindrops, what was a sanded track, now a mudded trail.

Satisfied the brutal force of nature was spent, Jude took several deep breaths and left the shelter of the Oak tree. It was no longer possible to cycle, so with his bike one side and Spud on the other he set off back home.

Invigorated by the soaking, Spud splashed through puddles, rolled in the mud and frolicked in the long grasses. He rescued a felled branch from a muddy puddle and delivered it to Jude, dropping it at his feet for him to throw.

The act of Jude throwing the branch and Spud retrieving it amused them both on their homeward journey.

When they approached the church, Jude called his pet to heel and Spud, muddy, soaked, tired and no longer interested in the branch that had entertained him, returned to his master. He shook himself at the exact moment Jude bent down to pat him.

'Thanks mate,' said Jude. 'Come on, let's get you home.'

As they passed the church gates Jude's mobile phone rang, its 'Tubular Bells' tune interrupting the tranquil scene. He retrieved his phone from his back pocket; he didn't recognise the number.

'Hello'

'Oh, hello...'

He didn't recognise the voice either. It was clearer than a mumble, only slightly louder than a whisper.

'Am I speaking to Mr Mumford please?'

'Speaking.'

'Good morning Mr Mumford, my name is Dr Fernsby.'

'Dr Fernsby.'

'We met briefly the other day, in the corner shop.'

The voice was clearer now.

'Yes, I remember. How on earth did you get my number?'

'I hope you don't mind. I got it from your tennis academy leaflet, the one you put up in the shop window.'

Could this be my first tennis client?

'That's great, is it about tennis lessons? I'm just starting out as a coach.'

Silence.

I guess not.

'Sorry, no it's not. I...I was wondering if we could meet up? I would like to talk with you.'

'You want to meet me? Can I ask what about?'

Silence again, shorter this time, just a couple of seconds.

'It's about Chantal Dubois.'

'What about her?'

'I would rather not discuss it over the phone. Please will you meet with me?'

'Look,' Jude took a deep breath, unsure of what to say.

'Please, a quick chat,' the doctor pleaded. 'That's all I ask; it won't take long.'

'But I've already given my statement to the police.'

Spud recognised the signs, his master with his mobile phone glued to his ear, he sighed and wandered off to investigate the church grounds.

Jude felt the correct and polite reply to the doctor was to say 'no.' After all, there was nothing he was prepared to discuss. He had found Chantal's body, he had spoken to the police, he was a witness, nothing more. But curiosity got the better of him.

'When would suit?'

'I work at the hospital; would you mind meeting me there? I usually have my lunch on one of the benches behind the St. Olaf's building around 2pm.'

'Fine. Is this Thursday okay?'

'That's good. If I am not there, please ask for me at the front desk. Thank you.'

Jude tucked his phone back into his inside pocket and looked around for Spud, but his pet had wandered off.

'Spud!' Jude yelled, then louder, 'SPUD!'

Nothing. Jude's pulse raced as he scanned the lane for his pet; he could feel his heartbeat pulsing in his ears. He rested his bike against the church wall just as a Dachshund with a bright pink collar ran towards him yapping. It was on a long lead; Jude's eyes followed the restraint. At the other end a woman, wrapped up in a woollen scarf and waterproof jacket, was attempting to pull the little Braveheart to her.

'Stop it! Behave now!'

'Excuse me,' said Jude, 'have you seen...?'

'Spud?' She nodded to the church. Spud was standing outside the open doors gazing in. 'I think he's considering his religious options.'

Jude gasped; a slow smile made plain his relief.

'Spud!' he shouted. 'Here!'

Spud was by his side within seconds, gazing up, eager for words of praise but when they were not immediately forthcoming, he headed towards the dachshund. The woman bent down, hand out to entice him towards her.

'Spud, feller, how are you?'

Spud, eager for the attention, bypassed the Dachshund and headed to the welcoming hand. Jude watched and didn't attempt to hide his surprise.

Why is she behaving as if she knows my Spud?

Jude eyed her up. She was in her thirties, dark hair whipped up and tied loosely on top of her head. Clear skin, her face free of make-up. He had never seen her before. Spud was behaving as if he recognised her though, he wagged his tail and greeted her like a long-lost chum. She bent down and patted him gingerly on the only unmuddied part of the top of his head.

'How are you Spuddie boy?'

Spuddie boy? Seriously?

'You are so adorable.' When the greetings and strokes were done, she stood up and grinned. 'You don't recognise me do you?'

'Sorry, have we met before? Clearly Spud seems to think we have.'

'It's me! Fearless, I was there, when you found her.'

'Fearless?' said Jude. 'Of course, your grey eyes… you look different without… well your, you know, your science gear.'

'My forensics,' she laughed. 'Well at least you remembered my eyes, sort of.'

'Sorry,' he reddened. 'But Spud certainly remembers you.'

'No need to apologise,' dimples formed in her cheeks as she smiled approval. 'If it helps, I didn't recognise you either. It was Spud I recognised, he's a very unusual looking dog.' She bent down to greet him some more. 'Spud, how you doing?'

The Dachshund stood and stared at her, betrayal in those dark eyes.

'He is so frigging adorable,' she ruffled Spud's ears.

'I know,' Jude nodded to the Dachshund, 'I think your little one is getting a bit jealous.'

Fearless bent down and stroked her charge.

'And you're adorable too.' She stood up and grinned at Jude. 'He's not mine, I'm walking him for a friend. Aren't I Soz?'

At the mention of his name the little animal jumped up at her, begging to be lifted. She picked him up and once sat cradled in her arms, his confidence returned. He growled. It was a warning to Spud he was not to be messed with.

'Soz?'

'Short for Sausage.'

'Very good,' Jude's expression changed, became serious. 'I hope you don't mind me asking, but is there any news, about Chantal?'

'If by 'any news' you mean have we caught the culprit yet? The answer is no.'

'Culprit? It was definitely a murder then?'

'As you spotted, she had a head injury.'

'Could it have been from a fall?'

Fearless shook her head, a slow movement, her eyes stayed on him.

'Absolutely not. Somebody hit her... and hit her hard.'

'Any ideas as to who it could be?'

'Let's just say, it's early days yet.'

'I read she was involved in a car accident,' said Jude, 'involving a child.'

'She nearly killed poor Nadia Fernsby, left her paralysed. Killed her pony though and injured her mum. I was there after it happened. Really nasty business. Horrific. Trust the papers to drag it all up.'

'Do you think it could have anything to do with her death?'

'Stop fishing, you know I can't tell you that,' she laughed. Soz struggled, eager to free himself from her grasp. She bent down and let him loose and he headed straight for Spud. 'But what I can say is that there is no shortage of suspects. I think they're building quite a list of people to speak to.'

'What? People with a motive?'

'One way or another,' Fearless nodded.

Jude remembered what the lady in the corner shop had said, *'some folks are calling it karma.'*

'You've got your work cut out trying to find her murderer then.'

'Not sure yet if we can call it a murder.'

'But you just said...'

Fearless made eye contact, bit her lip in a moment of uncertainty, unsure whether she should say more.

'What?'

'I've probably said more than I should already, but...'

'Go on.'

27

'You were there the previous evening, weren't you?'

'Sort of, I was at the top of the ridge, walking the path by the river,' Jude nodded. 'Spud was messing about in the trees; I think he may have spotted her. He did bark but I didn't go and investigate what he was barking at.'

'Pity about that.'

Jude's heartbeat quickened. Instinct urged him to distance himself, walk away from her and her words. But years of police training rooted him to the spot and forced him to voice his thoughts.

'What do you mean, exactly?'

Fearless hesitated, when she did speak, she immediately regretted it as within seconds she watched the man in front of her buckle as if he had been hit hard in the stomach.

'She froze to death. She'd only been dead a couple of hours when you found her.'

5

Her frost-bitten hair and eyelashes blended perfectly into the frozen scene. He knelt beside her, reached for her wrist, her pulse a faint rhythmic beat. He cupped her hand in his and blew on it to warm it. Several seconds later she turned her head, opened her eyes and her mouth turned up at the edges in thanks. He whispered words of reassurance, pleaded with her to stay with him, she was going to be okay. Her eyes widened for a second only before her head turned to one side and she greeted death. He shouted at her, tried to reverse her change of state, shake life back into her. But it was Jude who was awake now, heart racing, bed covered in sweat, Spud, sitting on the floor, head cocked to one side, staring, whining his puzzlement at his master's distress.

It was the third night in a row Jude had had that dream.

***

Jude arrived at the hospital at five past two. He spotted the sign for St. Olaf's and followed the recently tarmacked path to the garden at the back.

Dr Fernsby was already there, a lone figure sat on a wooden bench, hunched over, elbows resting on knees, as if being crushed from behind by an invisible force.

'Dr Fernsby?'

The doctor either didn't hear or ignored him so Jude said it again, louder.

'Dr Fernsby?'

This time the doctor turned his head and gave a weak nod to the bench opposite. Jude sat down.

'Thank you for coming.'

'What can I do for you?'

Elbows still rested on knees the doctor lifted his head.

'I... I... need your help.'

'If I can help I will.'

29

'I understand you're a private investigator...'

Jude recalled the short conversation that had taken place in the corner shop.

'Look, sorry,' he said. 'I have no idea why the papers printed that, I'm not a P.I., it's a misunderstanding. You saw my leaflet in the store window, I'm starting up a tennis academy. I moved here to be a tennis coach.'

'But I thought... maybe...' Dr Fernsby didn't try and hide his disappointment. He stooped further forward and covered his face with his hands.

'I did used to work for the police,' said Jude. 'So I guess that's how the rumour got started.' He stood up ready to be on his way, but the sight of this man sitting there, a man whose life had taken such a tragic turn, stopped him. Jude had seen relatives of victims, destroyed by needless, unfathomable acts of cruelty, and in his previous life it had been his goal to fight for them, to help them over the hurdles they faced in an effort to come to terms with their loss and get justice for their loved ones. He sat down again.

'Can I ask what it is you need help with?' He spoke softly, as one might speak to a traumatised child. 'I may know of somebody who can help you.'

The doctor didn't move or say anything, he was enveloped in an invisible cloud of despair.

'Okay,' said Jude. 'Let's just for a minute say that I am a P.I. What is it you were going to ask me to do? Why did you ask me to come here?'

A crumpled cloth appeared; the doctor wiped one eye then the other before he continued his gaze into empty space.

'I was going to ask you to help me.' His words were flat, no emotion, not even anger.

'Help you? But why?'

'You've heard she nearly killed my Nadia?'

'I read about the car accident.'

'She was speeding, not paying attention,' a splinter of anger emerged.

'But I believe it was dealt with by the police.'

'It was,' Dr Fernsby nodded.

Jude thought about offering words of understanding, of sympathy, to the man sitting opposite but he decided to stay silent. How could he even begin to understand what the doctor had been through?

'I'm sorry,' he said. 'But I'm still not sure why you've asked me here.'

Jude's words prompted Dr Fernsby to action. He sat up straight and stared one side and then the other.

'It's the police – they keep asking me questions.'

'That's because you have a motive. You lost so much because of her.'

'They think me, a doctor, could kill someone?' He used the back of his sleeve to wipe away a tear that trickled down his cheek. 'They questioned us, me and also my wife.'

'The police are just doing their job.' Jude breathed the words, not wanting to cause this man any more distress. 'They have to eliminate you from their enquiries. Surely you understand that?'

'I just want… I need this to be over with so that we can get on with what is left of our lives.' The doctor stared at the ground; his head shook from side to side in misunderstanding. 'She had a lot of enemies, a lot.'

'I heard that,' Jude wanted to offer comfort. 'Look at it this way. As you are aware, I found her body, and because I was there, I'm a person of interest. They are treating me, an ex-detective as a suspect.' He watched, waited for a reaction, but there was none. 'Because I was at the scene, they have to eliminate me from their enquiries and obviously I'm not over the moon about it, but I know they are just doing their job so I accept it.'

The doctor lifted his head, stood up and stretched his arms out away from his sides.

'You see me? You see what I am wearing? I am a doctor, I save lives. I don't destroy them.' He sat down, hunched forward, his body crumpled in torment once more. 'I don't want this… my family, we can't take any more. I just need it to stop.'

31

'But it will, just as soon as the police have done their job. They'll gather the evidence,' Jude's gaze stayed with the doctor. 'I'm guessing they will find nothing that will incriminate you?'

'Of course there won't. Yes, that woman ruined my daughter's life. Yes, she ruined all our lives. But I am not a killer. I am a good person, I mend people, no matter who they are, even if… yes, even if they crippled my youngest daughter.'

Sirens. An incoming ambulance, Jude spotted blue flashing lights as it passed. He wanted to offer words of healing, to calm this man and soothe the lacerated emotions laid bare in front of him.

'Once the police have investigated you properly, they won't bother you again.'

Unless you killed her…

The doctor stared unblinking.

'I'm not sorry she's dead.'

'You may not want to say that to the police.'

'I've already told them. You know, so far, I have been questioned for nearly eight hours. Eight hours!' He wiped each eye, one then the other like wiping raindrops from a window.

'As I said they're only doing their jobs.'

'She was a friend.'

'Chantal? I heard.'

'I… I can barely even say her name….' he trailed off. 'My dear wife has had to give up work to take care of Nadia. We have had to move from our beautiful home on the edge of the Manor to a bungalow in the village and Freya, my eldest, she used to be so popular, now she has few friends, she rarely goes out. That woman stole her life, stole all of our lives.'

'I hate to say this, but from the police perspective all of what you have just told me gives you a lot of motive to hurt her.'

'I know, I know,' Dr Fernsby nodded. 'That is why I need your help. The police, they are so blinkered. Will you help me? Help us?'

'To be honest, I'm not exactly sure how I can,' Jude paused. 'But let's just say for a moment I did agree. What exactly would you

32

expect me to do? I used to be a detective, but I have no influence here.'

The doctor looked up and hinted a smile.

'I know who killed her and I would like you to prove it.'

'What? You know who killed her? Have you told the police?'

'Of course I have, but they will not take me seriously.'

'But they have to! They'll investigate all leads and follow the evidence trail.'

'Not in this case.' The doctor knew he had dangled a worm and hooked a fish. 'Would you like to know more?'

Jude nodded.

'She came into money. And let me tell you, if she hadn't, none of this would have happened.'

'I read something about that. Any idea how?'

'She was lucky with some investments.' He swallowed hard before continuing. 'She tried to get us involved, invest our money with that shyster.'

'Shyster? Who are you talking about? '

'The Lord of the Manor of course, Lawson Peterson. He is responsible for this. All of it. He did it, it was him, he killed her.'

Jude stared at the ground; questions emerged that he had no right to ask. The death of Chantal Dubois was nothing to do with him. He was a witness, that was all.

'You know she introduced her brother to him?' said Dr Fensby.

'And that is relevant why?'

'Stefan, her brother, invested most of his money with that man and lost the lot.'

'Look, you really need to tell this to the police.'

'Please, hear me out first.'

'I'm listening.'

'Stefan was one of the most decent people you could ever hope to meet.'

'And?'

'He was a classical pianist, he used to perform at concerts you know. Then he started his IT business, it was very successful. Stefan was one of those people who did well at whatever he set his mind to.'

Jude wanted to ask the doctor to get to the point but he didn't. Instead he watched and listened as the man in front of him transformed to calm as he recollected old times. He talked of his friendship with Chantal and her brother, his previous home on the edge of the Manor, his daughters and their ponies.

'Then Stefan sold his business, invested his money and lost the lot!'

'With Lawson Peterson I take it. Was it a scam?'

'Of course it was.'

'What I mean is, was there any evidence?'

'Chantal and Stefan thought they had evidence; they were always at the police station with information.'

'Did the police investigate?'

'If they did it didn't go anywhere.' Dr Fernsby nodded. 'They were both devastated.' He gave a short laugh, 'then Francine - Stefan's daughter – died.'

'His daughter died?'

'Ovarian cancer. It was why he sold up his business and invested his money in the first place, to help her. He wanted to spend more time with her. But her death, it happened so quickly. It finished him.'

'How awful.'

'He had a mental breakdown, shut himself off from everyone, even Chantal. He stopped eating, he wasn't looking after himself. She used to visit him every day and she'd come back so upset. And then, one day she went around there and he'd gone, disappeared.'

'Disappeared? What? He went off?'

'Some say so,' Dr Fernsby shrugged. 'But others... he didn't take anything you see. He'd had a small pillow made with his daughter's ashes; he didn't even take that. That's why she thought he'd been murdered.'

'Did the police investigate his disappearance?'

'Apparently, but they said they couldn't find any evidence of foul play. I just wonder how hard they looked.'

'Christ.'

The doctor laughed out loud and face flushed he stared unblinking at Jude.

'Christ?' he said. 'There is no Christ.' Uncontrolled tears spilled down his cheeks. 'And then... that woman ran into my daughter and my wife and destroyed our lives as well.' He wiped his face with the back of his sleeve, his chest rising and falling as he fought for breath.

Jude gazed into space and tried to mentally sort through everything he had been told.

'Will you help me?' Dr Fernsby stared at Jude. 'Please?'

'I'm sorry, I still don't see how I can. Besides you need a licence to be a private investigator.' He watched the man in front of him crumple again. 'I really wouldn't worry; the police will soon realise you had nothing to do with it.'

'Huh! That could take months. I need somebody on my side, somebody who knows how they work.'

'But the police aren't your enemy, they're just seeking the truth. Besides, you said yourself you're glad she's dead. Why are you that bothered that they catch her killer?'

'Let me tell you why.' Dr Fernsby's words were slow, deliberate. 'Yes, Chantal was the one who caused the accident and crippled my Nadia, but it was Lawson Peterson who caused it to happen. He caused all of this. It is because of him our lives are ruined. If it wasn't for him, we would still be living in our home. My wife would still be working in the job she loves, my two beautiful daughters would still have their ponies and my Nadia, my beautiful, wonderful Nadia would not be in a wheelchair.'

Jude made mental notes as he listened, it was force of habit, nothing more.

'Lawson Peterson is a crook...' Dr Fernsby raised his voice. 'Stefan and Chantal, they were asking questions, causing him problems and he didn't like it. I think he killed her and yes, I think he killed Stefan too.'

6

The promise of a warm evening beckoned Jude and he decided to work out in his back garden. A couple of days before he'd moved his green plastic table and chairs out of the shed to the paved area outside his kitchen door so that they were ready for use. He grabbed his laptop, phone and notebook and headed out.

He clicked open his business plan and examined it line by line. Tennis courts, contacts, CRB check, it was all coming together. Some of the work was boring, after all, his dream was to coach tennis not fiddle about with a spreadsheet and make business calls about checks, times and prices. But he was realistic enough to know he had to harness his vision before he could follow his path to the tennis courts.

The back gardens of the twelve terrace cottages that formed Willow Walk were each separated by a brick wall about waist height. This meant there was little privacy, neighbours could spot each other and wave, shout across and exchange greetings should they have a mind to. And Jude discovered exactly that after less than twenty minutes.

'I've heard on the grapevine you've been asked to look into my friends murder.'

It was a female voice. He looked up; his newly arrived neighbour at number 1 was sitting on a wrought iron chair just the other side of their dividing wall. Her hair was tied back in a pony-tail, large sunglasses shielded her eyes.

Jude tried to hide his surprise at her question. They had never been introduced, yet she had obviously been listening to gossip about him. He stood up, neared the wall to offer a hand in greeting. But when he got there, he noticed a large spotted cat lay curled asleep on her lap. She wasn't about to move.

She nodded. A simple movement, graced by the sun as it glinted through wisps of her auburn hair.

'Evening,' he said. 'I'm Jude Mumford, but I'm guessing you already know that.'

'Rosebud Paris, and this is Simeon,' she nodded down to the cat. 'A friend mentioned it. This is a village, news, especially bad news, travels fast.'

Jude opened his mouth to say something but stopped himself in time.

Bad news? Why would she consider me being asked to investigate her friend's death to be bad news?

As if reading his thoughts, she said.

'Not that I'm saying what you're doing is bad....' She spoke slower but louder than before.

Is she attempting to backtrack on what she just said?

'In fact it's good, really good news.' She stroked Simeon and he started to purr. 'To be honest I think the police need all the help they can get.' She leaned back, stretched her legs in front, slowly, so as to avoid disturbing her pet.

'Okay,' said Jude. 'Well, no disrespect intended but you heard wrong. I am not investigating your friend's death, although, yes, I was asked to.'

'Of course, you're going to,' she laughed. 'You're an ex-rozzer, you won't be able to help yourself.'

Jude couldn't hide his surprise. Who on earth did this woman think she was? She knew he was an ex-policeman. What else did she know about him?

'You seem to know an awful lot about me,' he said. 'And I don't mean to be rude but why on earth would you make that assumption?'

She smiled, lifted her sunglasses and placed them on top of her head.

'Assuming I'm going to investigate is a bit...' Jude paused, shocked to see the darkened pallor around her half-shut eyes.

'Presumptuous?' she finished his sentence for him. 'You are though aren't you?'

'No I'm not, it's the job of the police.'

'I guess.' She pulled the glasses back down again. 'Pity.'

'Why do you say that?'

'Where do I start.'

'Look, I know there was some friction between your friend and the police.'

'That's putting it mildly.'

She trailed off. Jude watched, waited for her to continue but her silence spoke her thoughts and so he went and sat back at his table and returned to his business plan.

'I suppose you've heard lots of horrible things about her?' she shouted across to him.

'I've heard more bad than good.'

'Sadly some of the bad stuff is true.'

Jude got up, headed to the wall again and listened as his neighbour talked to him of her sorrow.

'She was a dear friend,' she turned to her home, pausing for a few seconds before touring her garden with her eyes. 'She is the reason I decided to move to the village, the reason I bought this cottage in fact.'

'Good friends indeed.'

'She did try to change, she honestly did,' she brushed the back of her hand across her cheek to wipe away a tear. 'I suppose you heard about the accident?'

'I do read the papers,' Jude nodded.

'It was awful, it changed her a lot. After, she wanted to make amends for some of the things she'd done, not just to the Fernsbys, but to other people she'd hurt.'

'Better late than never I suppose.'

'It was too little too late.' Tears spilled down her cheeks. 'A window can sometimes be so dirty it can't be wiped clean.'

'I guess trying to make amends was her way of coping with everything that happened,' Jude spoke quietly, not wanting to distress her further.

'She really changed.' Rosebud nodded. 'She desperately wanted the Fernsbys to forgive her for what she did. It was an accident after all.'

'Well, it was Dr Fernsby who asked me to investigate her death. He really wants to find her kill...' he stopped short, he remembered that she had been attacked, not killed, and that she had frozen to death overnight. 'He really wants to find out who attacked her...and left her there to die.'

It was me. I left her there to die.

'I have to say I'm not surprised,' she stared at him. 'He's so bitter about everything.'

'Can you blame him? He lost so much because of your friend. His youngest daughter will never walk again, his wife had to stop working to care for her, they had to sell their home.'

'I think that was the final straw,' said Rosebud. 'Having to sell their home. He sold it to Lawson Peterson; bastard couldn't wait to get his hands on it.'

'The doctor is very bitter towards Mr Peterson. Seems to think he's the real villain, do you know him?'

Rosebud nodded.

'Let's just say that Lawson might be the Lord of the Manor but you could hardly call him a pillar of the community. He couldn't wait to get Dr Fernsbys house back as part of the estate. Screwed him on the price I think as well. But of course that's how he operates.'

Jude's thoughts worked in solitary silence for a few seconds.

'Dr Fernsby mentioned Chantal had a brother.'

Rosebud shifted her legs, the movement jogged Simeon and he jumped off her lap and stalked, tail high towards the door to the cottage. She turned and watched him go in before returning her attention to Jude.

'Stefan, yes, he lost most of his money in one of Lawsons investment schemes, money which was meant to help his daughter, but then she died.'

'I heard about that, poor man.'

'And then he disappeared.' Her eyes dulled and she turned away for a few seconds. 'It was awful, he was such a dear, kind man.'

'I heard he and Chantal kept going to the police with evidence saying he'd been the victim of a scam.'

'Before his daughter died, yes, they did, they were convinced of it. It never came to anything though. No real proof the police said.' She paused, gasped for breath. 'Chantal called them all sorts of names. Swore they were corrupt.'

'Really?'

Rosebud nodded.

'Lawson threatened to take her to court for slander! The cheek of the man!'

'What about Stefan, do you know anything about his disappearance?'

'No,' she shrugged. 'He literally was there one day and gone the next.'

'Could he have been murdered do you think?'

As soon as he saw her face, he wished he hadn't asked the question. He leaned down and patted Spud to hide his embarrassment.

I've really upset her.

He was about to apologise but she spoke before he could.

'I try to keep an open mind,' she said. 'But it's hard. Certainly, that's the rumour in the village.'

Jude looked at his neighbour, her pale skin, her auburn hair, reminded him of his wife. He cleared his throat, as if it would help clear his mind.

'I got an update from the police the other day,' Rosebud stared at him. 'Whoever attacked Chantal didn't actually kill her,' a tear, then another. 'They just left her there to die. Who could do such a thing?'

Me. I left her there to die.

'I had heard that.'

41

'My poor, dear Chantal, she froze to death. She'd only been dead a few hours when you found her.'

I know.

'It must have been so awful for her laying there, if only you'd got there sooner you might have been able to save her.'

'I'm so sorry, I... I... feel so guilty.'

Did Chantal Dubois see Spud? Did she realise he was there?

Simeon appeared and jumped back onto Rosebud's lap. She waited for him to settle before returning her attention to Jude.

'Sorry, I didn't mean... it was hardly your fault.'

'If only I had found her the night before.'

'Our lives are full of if onlys.' Rosebud shook her head slowly. 'You really mustn't think like that.'

'But,' Jude hesitated. 'We were there, me and Spud, that evening, the evening before.'

Rosebud's pale skin greyed to ash. She lifted her glasses again and green eyes glared at him.

'What do you mean? What are you saying?'

'The previous evening. We were there, Spud, he found her. He barked but I was up walking along the river path. It was just starting to snow again and it was getting dark, so I ignored him.'

'No,' said Rosebud shaking her head. 'No, please tell me you're joking.'

'If I'd taken notice of Spud, maybe I could have...'

Rosebud stood up. Simeon slipped off her lap, fell to the ground like a discarded doll and hissed his fury. But Rosebud did not comfort her pet, her focus, her anger, was directed at Jude.

'So you... you're actually telling me you could have saved her! You bastard! You absolute bastard!'

7

Jude had THAT dream again. He turned and tossed, opened his eyes then closed them tight shut like a child. And like a child he wished that when he opened them again that he would be returned to his previous life. It was not even his life before the body find he wished for. His wish was to be transported back a couple of years, to wake up in his bed in his North London home with his wife by his side.

But when he did open his eyes, he was in the here and now, in a cottage on the edge of the Fens and he was still the central character in his living nightmare.

Ten minutes later he was downstairs sitting at the table in his front room staring out of his window to the Manor House. He stayed unmoving for several minutes then stood up and shook out first his hands and arms, then his legs. He ran his fingers through his uncombed hair. All the while Spud sat beside him, close, alert but unobtrusive, understanding in his own canine way that his master was in crisis and that breakfast would appear in the fullness of time.

Jude headed upstairs and by the time he came back down again nearly an hour later, he was showered, shaved and dressed. But he still hadn't been able to cleanse himself of the memory that plagued his daytime thoughts and his night time terrors.

Why didn't I go and investigate when Spud barked?

He switched on his laptop and watched as it whirred to web-ready. He scanned his emails, a few from concerned London friends, keeping him updated on what was going on at the station, asking why he hadn't been in touch. He replied to some, deleted others. Next, he checked the local news sites, searching for stories about the body find. Nothing. He got up and headed to the kitchen. Spud followed him, sat by his empty food bowl and whined.

'Spud! Sorry, I'm so sorry!'

Spud got fed in seconds, and then Jude started his own breakfast. Within minutes the coffee percolator was bubbling, toast was browning and a jar of Marmite was on the counter waiting to be spread.

43

When he got back to the front room Spud was at the front door, sitting waiting patiently to go for his walk. Jude sat down at the table and turned to him.

'You told me didn't you? If I had listened to you. If I had gone to investigate when you started barking.'

What if she heard you? What if she saw you? What if she thought she was going to be saved?

Jude rubbed his chin as if trying to create an itch that he could satisfy with a scratch.

'If I hadn't ignored you, I would have found her that evening. I… we… could have saved her Spud. She might still be alive.'

Spud cocked his head to one side and whined.

'What did you see boy?'

Spud answered with a single bark, it wasn't a bark to tell his master what he saw, it was a reminder that they should be well on their way on their morning walk. In an attempt to drop a greater hint, he lay down against the front door and stared at his master, dark eyes pleading.

Jude pushed his laptop aside, leant forward and banged his head on the table, once, twice, three times. He stayed still for a couple of minutes before turning his head sideways to his pet. When they made eye contact, Spud approached, jumped up and pawed at him before placing his head on his master's knee.

'Just give me a minute matey,' Jude logged onto a shopping site and ordered a whiteboard, a very large one. When done, he got hold of Spud's head between his hands.

'Well, my friend, we are going to do the right thing here. You and me, we are going to find out who attacked Chantal Dubois.'

8

Out of school, Jude's first career choice had been to become a tennis pro. He played the junior circuit and made the transformation to adult competition with ease. He took pride in the relationship he had with his tennis racket. On a match day, if things were going his way, he and it would become one - as if it were an extension of his arm - and he would smash his way to victory. He was enroute to achieving his goal when a car accident slammed the brakes on his life choice and the resulting shoulder injury ended his career. He lost the game of life 6-0, 6-0, 6-0. Or at least that was how it felt to him at the time.

After the accident, mornings were not a good time for him. Each day, the dawn of his new life shone ever brighter into his eyes and the realisation of his unplanned future blinded him. He would roll over and plead for sleep to take him. On days when his wife did manage to get him out of bed, he became a character playing a part in a play for which he had no script. He was rude and self-indulgent and within weeks he had transformed from a fit and healthy young man into a self-pitying, argumentative pain in the ass.

He selected non pharmaceutical remedies to ease his mental torment, he stayed out late, ate fast food and smoked and drank a lot.

His bender lasted five months and it ended the same way that it had started, the result of a single event. His wife left him. Tennis had been his life but his wife was - in those days - the love of his life. It was not the night he fell out of a cab in a drunken state and kicked open the front door to an empty house that brought him to his senses, in truth, that night he didn't even notice she had gone. It was the following evening when he awoke, dry throated and with an aching head that he realised he was alone.

He accepted he could do nothing to return to his tennis career, but he could do something about his wife's rejection of him, so he shrugged off the shawl of despair and for the first time since his accident turned his gaze from his past to his future. He rejected the stuff that was bad for him and dumped the people who had supplied and encouraged him to indulge in the stuff that was bad for him. Slowly, he won back her love and her trust and although his future was no longer one where he clutched a tennis racket in one hand and a trophy in the other, it was a future with his wife by his side.

It was Zac, his then best friend, who suggested he join the police force. Jude was not a man who lived life working in fractions and he applied the same enthusiasm to his new job as he had to his tennis, as he had to his five-month bender and as he once again applied to his marriage. He was 100% committed to his wife and to his work and he loved both.

Seeking out the bad guys changed over the years and Jude constantly had to adapt to new processes and procedures put in place to ensure compliance with modern crime solving thinking. Many of his colleagues complained, but he embraced the new hoops he needed to jump through with a positive vision.

That was then. His once 'new' life was now another 'old' life as for the second time he had to make drastic changes to ensure his mental wellbeing.

It had taken him several weeks to come to terms with what had taken place between his wife and his best friend in London. For the second time in his life he lost direction, but this time, even though he had no support network, he searched for a solution rather than pick up a spade and dig himself into a pit of despair. When the solution did arrive, it was delivered to him at 3am like an email arriving into an inbox. He had to start afresh again, another new life. And it would have to be away from the people who had betrayed him and away from the places that reminded him of their betrayal. He decided he would sell the house, relocate and become a tennis coach.

He was worried about Spud though; he knew his pet was pining.

'You seem troubled mate,' Jude whispered, *'I'm so sorry. I know you loved her too...'*

Career decided, he just needed to find somewhere outside of London to live. This time the answer to his problem was in the form of a book - one of the few books left in the house after his wife had taken what she wanted. It had belonged to his parents and he had kept it for sentimental reasons because they had gone there on a day trip and got engaged. It was called 'The Village of Eaststowe' and its cover was a black and white photograph of a village fair, swing boats, a helter-skelter, a coconut shy, all from days gone by.

He had always intended to visit the village and so one drizzle damp Wednesday, he put Spud into doggy day-care, caught the train and headed towards the East coast. It was the kick-off, his attempt to recapture and re-assemble his life so that he could once again look forward to getting out of bed in the morning.

He stared out of the window as they sped along. In London the view was of half-finished constructions and desolate buildings. The further they got out of London, the closer they got to nature, blocks of flats, rows of terraced houses, semi-detached homes with gardens, detached homes with fruit trees, garages and rear entrances and as they neared the Fens, farmland and wetlands, Jude took a deep breath; the view nourished his spirit.

With nothing to stop it, trees, bushes, lakes and even wetland puddles moulded to the shape of the wind. He marvelled at the sky, the size of it, its pallet of blues melting into the distance. The low horizon made him feel small, even as a passenger on a train. It was a skyscape not a landscape he was gazing at.

All good so far.

For Jude this journey was a pilgrimage. He had brought his parents' book with him and as the train neared Eaststowe station he took it out of his rucksack. He was looking forward to seeing this village, the place his parents had visited and had a day so perfect they had got engaged.

The train pulled in at eight minutes past eleven. The station was unmanned so, unchallenged, he headed to the street. A yellow cab driver tried to catch his eye. Jude shook his head, hoisted his rucksack onto his back and, book in hand, followed the signpost to the town centre.

The pavement was narrow, and as he made his way, he recognised several landmarks from photographs in his book. A copse, a river, a church, a memorial. He passed a pub, the thatched building appeared the same, but it had been rechristened, what was 'The Glue Pot' was now 'The Cobbler's Children.'

A man with a flat cap, a weathered face, a smile and a small brown dog approached. Jude stood aside to let him pass. A nod, a 'thank-you' and the man was on his way. A couple, pushing a buggy, said 'good morning' and also thanked him, this time for stepping into the road to let them pass, their gurgling dark-haired girl scraping a willow stem along the hedgerow unaware of his gesture.

Jude crossed the road and gazed over a border hedgerow. In the distance, on another rail track, he spotted a steam train chuffing along on its way to the coast and several black and white ponies, their unpulled manes and tails flowing as they galloped away from the steamy intruder.

The village had expanded since the 1970's. A housing estate was built in the 1980s, similar only bigger in the 1990s and the same in the noughties. Each time the villagers' objections were ignored. In the noughties, when planning permission was granted for yet another development a station was added in an attempt to minimise the objections.

After the developers moved out, the hipsters and the townies moved in bringing their wine bars, posh pubs, micro-breweries, bookshops, a leisure centre and an art gallery. Council meetings were forced to include discussions about a noisy cockerel living at Priory Farm, requests for who to contact to pick up horse poo from outside the nursery school and 'Can the Church bells please stop ringing at 9pm?'.

As Jude neared the town centre, he passed by modern houses built on large plots for wealthy incomers who insisted on space for their cars, their children's ponies, their horse boxes, their swimming pools and their tennis courts.

He passed a micro-brewery and went in for lunch. Stained wood flooring and shelves, established plants in matching terracotta pots, a bookcase stashed with literary fiction, a simple smile offered as greeting. He ordered plaice and chips and mushy peas. It was the best he had ever tasted.

Jude returned to work the following Monday and resigned. He mentioned it to a female colleague later that afternoon while they were getting coffee.

'You've resigned? You're moving where? Why?' She had made no attempt to hide her shock. 'Eaststowe? Where the feck is it?'

'Well,' said Jude, 'as to why, although a policy does exist to say that two police officers can have a relationship as long as they do not work in the same department, sadly, there is no such policy to say that officers who work in the same department cannot shag their work colleague's wife. Oh, and Eaststowe is out in the Fens and it's very flat.'

9

From: N. Fernsby

To: Jude Mumford

Subject: The Death of Chantal Dubois

Dear Mr Mumford,

Thank you for meeting with me the other day. I was so pleased when I received your email saying that you have decided to seek the truth about what has happened. Below are some of the people who I think may be able to help you.

Saffron (sorry, I don't know her last name). It was a long while ago but she was very close friends with that woman until they fell out. She is somewhat eccentric but she may be worth talking to. I do not have her contact details (I don't think she 'does' technology!) but she lives towards the edge of the village in the cottage next to the pet cemetery.

Please do speak to Lawson Peterson, but obviously please do not repeat what I told you. If you can get to speak to him, he may give some clues as to what went on, also, his wife Sasha may be able to help. As I mentioned to you, they were close to that woman but they fell out after Stefan lost his money. I think that woman got quite close to their son Charlie as well.

Another person who may be able to help you is Olga Kaine, I know she used to be very close to that woman but they also fell out. It was years ago but she may have some information. She lives somewhere in the village, I'm not sure where, however, if you have problems contacting her let me know and I'll ask my eldest daughter Freya as she is in the year below her daughter Ivy at school.

Of course, if you can contact Stefan (if he is still alive) he may be able to help you. But, as I mentioned, a lot of people (myself included) believe that Lawson Peterson had him killed and that he is buried somewhere on the Fens.

The other people who may be able to help you are your neighbours. Rosebud Paris was very good friends with her as was the gardener, Dexter. He seems to know most people and most

50

things that go on. Please do not misunderstand me, I'm not saying he's a gossip but I think because of his job, he gets to hear things.

Again, thank you, I hope the above is useful to you. Please let me know if you think I can assist you further.

I'll wait to hear from you.

Yours sincerely

Dr Nicholas Fernsby.

Jude made a few notes then got distracted by Dexter as he pulled up outside in his Land Rover. His neighbour often appeared first thing in the morning to load up his open trailer with garden equipment in preparation for his outside day. Dexter was always smiling, always chatty to passers-by. On occasion Jude felt a tinge of envy as his neighbour, whose heart beat to the rhythm of his own drum, pursued his passion in life.

Jude's thoughts turned to the name at the top of the list, Saffron, the woman he had already met out on the Fen that day. He needed to speak to her first. He drained his mug of coffee, placed it onto the table and hit the 'Reply' button, updated the subject line to *Thank you* and hit 'Send.'

Jude searched Google Maps, located the Pet Cemetery and identified Saffron's smallholding which ran alongside a part of it. Next, he wrote a short note to his neighbour.

Hi Dexter, I hear you're a pretty decent gardener and I wondered if you would be able to add me to your list of clients? I don't want to let the terrace down after all.

Jude (No.2)

The fact that Dexter was a gardener and Jude had a garden in dire need of somebody with exactly those skills, was the perfect excuse to make formal contact. Jude didn't know a Daffodil from a Daisy so his line about not wanting to let the terrace down was absolutely true.

He sent the details to the printer and put the note into his back trouser pocket ready to post next door when he took Spud for his evening walk.

Jude and Spud were over the Fens for nearly three hours that evening. It was dark by the time they got back and as he neared his cottage he paused at the gate to listen to Dexter strumming his guitar. The folk tune stirred memories, which in turn stirred dormant emotions of hurt and loss, but as the simple chords penetrated his outer shell and lit a path to his emotions, the melody acted as a mediator and he knew he was at last able to walk as one with his solitude. He was home. He pushed the gate open and it was then he spotted a large package on his doorstep. His newly purchased whiteboard had arrived.

It took him nearly two hours to put it together and it was so big the only place it would fit was along the wall where the flatscreen television hung. That of course meant no television, but he didn't mind. He had plenty to do, - investigating Chantal's death and setting up the Mumford Tennis Academy - he had no time for entertainment any more.

He spent the next two hours mapping his thoughts to his new purchase. He pinned photos across the top, he drew boxes, each with a name and a link to the victim and he dived into Chantal's life and the lives of the people around her. He was well aware of the old saying 'most people are killed by somebody they know, which statistically means you are safer with a stranger' and he wasn't ruling anybody out, not Olga Kaine, not Sasha or Lawson Peterson, not Saffron, not even his neighbours, Rosebud or Dexter. And he wrote underneath each name in red letters 'SUSPECT.'

10

In spite of the chill morning, Spud was out back behaving like an officer of the law, patrolling the boundary wall that divided his and Rosebud's garden ensuring none of the neighbourhood cats – including Simeon - entered his territory.

Jude watched his pet's antics for several minutes before he picked up his first mug of coffee of the day and headed to the front room to start his investigation. He had pondered the ethics of searching the internet for background information on his new neighbours, he was no longer a detective after all. But his curiosity and thirst for the truth was greater than his foibles and within minutes he had opened a door and entered a world of murder, scandal, arguments, land disputes, and disappearing donkeys.

A bark made him jump. Spud was standing in the doorway, a subtle hint to his master that he, Spud, was the next item on the agenda.

Jude had tried twice in the last week to visit Saffron's ramshackle cottage and although on each occasion he had negotiated the pitted driveway and reached the weather splintered front door without tripping over, she had ignored his knocks. He knew she was in because both times he had stepped back and spotted her figure behind the unwashed net curtain in the front room. So, he intended to take more drastic action.

According to Google Maps, Saffron had a considerable size plot and according to Dexter she spent a lot of time out in her back garden. Jude's plan was to try to catch her there.

They set off for their walk a little later than usual, just after 9:30am. They would normally have been back by that time but on this morning they were heading out for more than exercise.

Spud walked in step with Jude, no lagging, no tugging, attentive to his master's every word. They headed to Priory Wood. When they reached the trees, Jude snapped off Spud's lead and his pet stood for a few seconds, before, nose to the ground, he headed off on a scent trail, weaving through trees and bushes as he conducted an investigation all on his own.

'Now stay close,' Jude shouted as they headed along the time-worn track to the monastery ruins.

They passed wooden bridges, stiles, gates and managed hedgerows bordering farmers' fields. But on this morning, when they got to the fields, instead of taking the circular route to return home, Jude veered left and headed in the opposite direction, along a little used public footpath. He knew it was a footpath only from a map he had found on the internet as the wooden post which should have pointed the way was hidden by brambles. He called Spud, and together they headed down the narrow track between a high wooden fence and an overgrown hedgerow and made their way towards the edge of the village.

Eventually the sounds of nature were interrupted by the turbulence of modern-day living as the traffic on a distant 'B' road intruded into the natural world. Jude was nearing the edge of the village. He peered over the unkept hedge and in the distance, he spotted Saffron's smallholding.

They carried on walking until the trail ended at a pot-holed farm road. On the other side of the road a pair of wrought iron gates, locked in the open position, beckoned. It was the pet cemetery.

Jude crossed the road. Just inside the cemetery gates there was a cream painted wooden notice board, behind it a car park, all ten spaces vacant. He ventured through the gates to the notice board and read across the top in large script:

'Eaststowe Pet Cemetery'

'Premises to be used for visitation rights or quiet contemplation only.'

Quiet contemplation. Jude had done a lot of that in recent months, but he could do more. Underneath, behind glass, notices, details of opening times, burial times, who to contact for burial enquiries, who to contact in case of emergency. He recognized the name, Chantal Dubois. Her death had cut short the adventure that was her life, the life she had so desperately wanted to cleanse. But

54

it was too late, self-interest, greed, a dead pony and a crippled child were her legacy.

A map on the notice board showed the main track around the site perimeter and the minor pathways that crisscrossed and divided the land into miniature burial plots. Jude decided to turn right and follow the path by the fence which would eventually return him to where he was via the hedgerow that bordered Saffron's land.

'Wow Spud, this is quite a big place,' but Spud was not within earshot. Jude turned, his pet was sitting just outside the iron gates, eyes on his master, mouth open, tongue lolling to one side.

'Spud, here boy...' Jude knelt down and called to him, arm out, but Spud stayed where he was. Jude stood up, pointed to his feet. 'Here boy,' he shouted it and this time Spud got up and head down, walked through the gates to him.

'Hey boy,' Jude stroked him. 'It's fine mate.'

Trees basked in the welcome rays of the before lunch sun as Jude and Spud – who stayed close to his master - set off. The track was a mix of golden sand and gravel and they scrunched along, faint footfall patterns the only evidence of their visit.

As they walked, Jude set his eye on the view over the perimeter fence to the glistening Fens, a natural world spread as far as the eye could see. He gasped at the beauty of the landscape. But that was not why he had come here. He returned his attention to inside the boundary, to the place where people came to bury their pets.

They passed weathered headstones, elaborate sculptures, marble, bronze, some simple, of carved wood, a sapling with a stone engraving. If a headstone caught Jude's eye, for its gaudiness or its uncomplicated tribute, he would stop and read the inscription, often a few lines of a poem, sometimes a straightforward sentiment.

Most of the animals were cats and dogs but not all;

'Missy – little bunny, will be missed.'

'Wesley – much loved parrot, flying the rainforest in the sky.'

'Mog – beloved tortoise forever in our thoughts.'

'Spud. With me.' Jude called, not wanting his pet to trample the graves. But he need not have worried, Spud stayed at his side.

Forty-eight minutes after they set off, the man-made fence ended and an unkempt red berried hedgerow took over. Jude felt his heartbeat quicken; they had circled and were back at the border of Saffron's land. He stood still, wet his lips.

If I see her, will she talk to me?

He stared over the hedge into her back garden. It was even bigger than he'd imagined, well over an acre. A busy plot, made ready for Spring. Furrows, poles strung together awaiting climbing beans, an established fruit cage, a cluster of fruit trees, pink and white blossom, blooming to life. There were scattered outbuildings and a small paddock. In the distance he could see the back of her grey stone cottage, its door open. But the only sign of life was a white goat, its tethered head in a bucket.

Jude turned off the main track onto a lesser managed mud path running along the back of the plot. It was a more secluded burial place with only a sprinkling of saplings and plaques. He spotted an unseasoned wooden bench partially hidden in a sun spot between bushes. He glanced over the hedge again, still no sign of life so he sat down and faced an elaborate life-size stone carved headstone. It was a Labrador, stood proud on a plinth. Zac.

Spud went over and sniffed around the grave. It was several minutes before he returned, but instead of sitting with his master, he walked past the bench to the hedgerow, jumped up and gazed across Saffron's land.

'Spud, here, with me.'

Spud, jumped down, returned to Jude and with a sigh lay down at his feet, head between his front legs, ears twitching.

The sun sliced through the spindly branches of a silver birch. Jude closed his eyes and breathed deep, in, out, mindful of the serenity in this place of death.

How am I going to contact her?

His question was answered in less than a minute. The silence was brought to an abrupt end by two dogs. Jude could tell it was two dogs because one was a constant yap, yap yap and the other was a mixture of snarling and growling, punctuated with a fit of

56

barking. He recognized the canine 'voices' and so did Spud who, within seconds, was at the hedgerow, paws up on top of it. Barking dogs, especially those two barking dogs, did not scare him. But he did not scare them either, in fact it sent them into even more of a frenzy.

Jude was on his feet in an instant. He had Saffron's attention.

'Spud! Down!'

By the time Jude got to the hedge the Jack Russell was digging a frenzied hole in an effort to tunnel under the hedge. The brown mongrel's attempt to fight Spud involved him jumping in the air non-stop. Although he was a small dog (compared to Spud) he reached the height of the hedge coming level to Spud's face on every occasion. The problem was that although his skills at the high jump were exemplary, he had not mastered the technique of propelling himself forward, so he bounced up and down as if he were on a pogo stick.

Unable to get to them Spud took matters into his own paws and barked, once, twice, before launching into a non-stop bark fest normally reserved for high risk or emergency situations. And it was at that moment Saffron appeared from an outbuilding.

She marched towards them. Jude recognized her immediately. She wore, the same tie-dyed orange and green skirt and anorak, her hair, a single untidy plait hung down her left shoulder, she looked the same as she did on the day of their first meeting, the day that had disrupted Jude's life plan and jolted him into a reality not of his choosing. Two things were different though. Firstly, she did not have binoculars hanging around her neck, and secondly, she carried with her an axe which - when she reached the hedge - she grasped with both hands and pointed at him.

'Oy! What d'you think you're doing?' she shouted. 'You're on private land.'

'Really?' Jude shouted back. 'I understood from the sign at the entrance that we could visit for quiet contemplation.' Jude smiled a greeting then turned to Spud. 'Spud, down boy.' But Spud stayed where he was. 'We meet again. I'm Jude by the way.'

'You again,' she stood square, positioned the axe head down on the ground and rested both hands on its chunky wooden handle. 'Colin! Chris! With me!' She bellowed the words out and first the mongrel then the Jack Russell stopped barking and both walked towards her, showing their reluctance by keeping their heads down. They positioned themselves one either side of her like a pair of pop-eyed gargoyles anxiously awaiting instruction.

Spud, eyes imploring, returned his attention to his master, waiting for the 'Go' word, the one that would give him permission to jump the hedge and let rip at the two terriers on the other side.

'Down,' Jude said. And this time Spud did as he was told.

'You and that… that…' She picked up the axe and waved the thing in front of her as if she were heading into battle. 'What are you doing here? What do you want?'

'We are entitled to walk here.'

'So, you've had your walk. Now bugger off. Go away and leave us alone!'

'That was a bit of fun you had… the last time we met.'

The change was instant, anger turned to amusement as both corners of her mouth turned up in glee.

'Fun for me, not so for you?'

Jude grinned back, relieved at her sudden change of mood.

'When I jumped across the dyke, I didn't realise I wouldn't be able to get back,' adding, by way of explanation. 'I'm new to the area.'

She laughed out loud at that.

'I had to walk all the way back to the bridge to get back over the river.'

Her laughter stopped as suddenly as it had started.

'Well, you learnt something then.' She passed the axe to her right hand and put her left hand into her jacket pocket. Both dogs eyes stayed on her, expectant, tails wagging their excitement. She pulled out a handful of treats and threw a few down in front of each dog, both heads bent to sniff but neither touched what was in front of them. It was only at her whispered command, that first Colin, then Chris darted forward and snaffled up their bounty before returning and sitting down again.

58

As if realizing dog treats were on offer, Spud jumped up and placed his front paws on the top of the hedge again. Saffron stared at him and as she did, she put her hand in her pocket and pulled out more treats. This time she opened her mouth and downed them herself.

'There's no need to be so rude.' Jude watched her crunch up the treats, trying not to think about what it was she was chewing.

'Looking to bury your mutt?' she shouted, waving her axe in the direction of Spud. 'Is that why you're here?'

Jude turned to Spud, contemplating his pet's death was not something he wanted to think about. Not ever.

'Spud,' he said, 'it's alright mate, we'll be out of here soon.'

'Or are you just being nosey?'

'Actually, I came to see you.'

'And you didn't think to come to the front door?'

'Well, I did try. Last week and again the other day. I knocked, several times in fact.'

'I never open the door to strangers.' She scratched her left breast before she put her hand into her jacket pocket and fiddled with whatever was inside. 'So? What do you want?'

'I just wanted to ask you a couple of questions.'

Jude took out a business card from his inside pocket, leant forward and threw it over the hedge. It hung in the air for a micro second then fluttered down onto her soil. A whispered word and Colin ran to it, sniffed it, picked it up, shook his head as if he had a bone between his teeth before returning to his mistress and spitting the soggy remnants at her feet. Task completed he went and sat down again.

'You're the one who found her, aren't you?'

'Word has got round then.'

'I heard…'

Who from?

She turned to go, then paused and caught his eye.

'Did you a favour didn't I? That day,' she shouted.

No, you bloody didn't do me a favour. I'd be at home planning my tennis academy if it weren't for you.

She placed the axe between her legs, holding it upright.

'Lord knows how long she'd have been hidden out there if you hadn't found her.' She got hold of her hair with both hands and started to fiddle with it, unplaiting then re-plaiting it. 'She'd probably have been eaten, carried away by wild animals,' she spoke as if in a dream, her gaze staring at the would-be scene. 'Leaving just a few splintered bones…'

'Well, I did find her and I just wanted to ask you a couple of questions,' said Jude. 'Please.'

She snapped out of her trance and eyed him.

'I heard about the accident – with the pony,' he shouted.

'Firefly… Firefly… Firefly…' she repeated the words to herself.

'I heard she changed after… I heard she wanted to make amends to the people she'd wronged.'

Saffron stared at him for seconds, before, eyes wide, she leant forward, opened her mouth and belly laughed again.

He waited for her to stop. As before, when she did, it was as sudden as when she had started.

'What's so funny? She wanted to be a better person, that's a good thing, isn't it?'

'You think?' Her expression crumpled to a frown; her voice deepened to a growl. She made no attempt to hide her anger. 'Probably wondering who she could screw over next.'

'Not from what I've heard.'

'Let me tell you, you stupid Mr,' she lifted the axe with both hands and pointed it at him. 'Chantal cared for nothing, for no-one, but herself. That land you and your mutt are standing on, the ground beneath your bloody feet.' As she spoke, she banged the axe down into the soil, short sharp jabs, before letting it drop into the mud. Hands free, she stood on tiptoe, lifted and stretched her arms out in an effort to encompass the whole cemetery in a virtual grasp. 'All

60

of it, the pet cemetery, it was all mine. My meadow. Left to me by my mum and my dad.'

Jude gave what he hoped to be an understanding nod but she didn't notice, she was revisiting a trail of memories from a blessed childhood before life events steamrolled her onto a pathway of trauma and mental health failures.

'I was friends with that woman! Friends! We were friends! Good friends – or so I thought. She was a liar; she was horrible to me...'

'Bit harsh.'

'Don't you dare judge me... you've not walked in my shoes.'

Her words prompted Jude to look at her feet and he noticed for the first time she was shoeless, completely barefoot, her feet and ankles covered in dirt.

'Sorry,' he said. 'I didn't mean... can I ask what went wrong?'

'She came into money, that's what went wrong.'

'I heard that.' Jude could see her eyes glisten as they moistened in the light.

'My two donkeys used to graze that land you're standing on. Five years ago, just after she came into all that money, some bastard stole my Sofia and my Marigold! I searched and searched.'

'I'm so sorry to hear that.'

'She even helped me search for them, huh! It was her who stole them!'

'You're sure of that are you?'

'Yes, I bloody am!'

'Did you have any evidence?'

'Evidence?' her eyes narrowed to a pointed stare. 'I know it was her alright.'

'Okay, sorry. So, what did you do?'

'I looked and looked for my girls but I couldn't find them. When I knew they weren't coming back I scattered seeds. I made it a proper wildflower meadow. It was beautiful. Then she made me an offer for it.'

'You sold it her?'

'She knew I was struggling. I had medical bills to pay… I sometimes have to…to…'

Jude nodded in understanding.

'I only sold it to her because she promised she'd keep it as a wildflower meadow, said she wanted to go there to paint. I sold it real cheap too.' She wiped away un-spilled tears with the sleeve of her jacket. 'Next thing she's put in planning permission for a pet cemetery!'

'Did you confront her about it?'

'Course I did! And I objected to the council.'

'What happened?'

'Nothing.'

'I'm guessing your friendship was over?'

She looked to him; her eyes wide in despair.

'Friendship? Who would do that to a friend?'

'But after the accident, I heard she changed, she wanted to make amends.'

'Huh! People like her never change. Not surprised someone killed her.'

'But she wasn't killed. Somebody did attack her but they didn't kill her… she froze to death.'

Because of me. I left her there to die.

'Bloody woman,' she shouted. 'Nothing but trouble when she was alive. Still the bloody same now she's dead.'

'I just want to find out who it was who attacked her.'

Jude recognized a spirit transported to another place by turbulent memories. He watched as she shifted, one foot to the other, she lifted the axe and both hands rested on it again as she rocked slightly from side to side. The motion appeared to comfort

62

her. He waited her return to the present, and when she did it was with a wide grin.

'I'd like that,' she shouted. 'I'd like that a lot. And when you do find out, be sure to let me know straight away. I could do with some good news. Straight away you hear. I'd like that. I'd like that a lot.'

11

The man and the cat were both in the same predicament. Homeless, scratching about for scraps and somewhere to sleep.

A woman sat alone on a bench glancing at the travellers as they passed by, their eyes most often searching the train arrival and departure boards.

In the centre of the forecourt, beside a closed-up cake stand, a battered piano was the woman's real focus of attention and she willed just one commuter to sit down, break the humdrum silence and capture an unheard melody.

A year ago, she would have been sitting on a church pew on a Sunday morning. But a lot can happen in a year.

The man went to the piano and placed his rucksack beside the piano stool. Inside the rucksack, a clue to his identity 'Stefan D.' had – like his memory - faded by nights spent out in the cold and rain. Stefan sat down and within seconds he and the piano united as - glazed eyes staring to space - his fingertips grazed the keys and his soul sang to anyone prepared to listen. The woman was prepared, eyes closed, her body swayed and she gazed into her past and watched her son play Pachelbel's 'Canon in D' as he had so often in life.

When the man and then the piano stilled, the woman took a folded cotton handkerchief from the patch pocket of her coat and wiped away a memory. She opened her eyes, leaned forward and called to him.

'You play so beautifully,' she said. 'Where did you learn?'

The man sat for a moment, he gazed down at his hands still splayed across the keys, hands that minutes earlier had been scrabbling through bins for a leftover breakfast. He turned them over as if seeking the answer to her question amidst the dirt ground into his palms and fingertips. He turned to the woman, as their eyes met so did their pain and their grief.

'I don't know,' he whispered.

12

Eaststowe Manor House was built in the seventeenth century by Ivan Fox, a slave trader. He had decided on that exact spot because it was the only piece of elevated ground around and he wanted to be able to gaze over his land in every direction as far as the eye could see.

The arched and studded front doors of the Manor were so solid that if a team with a battering ram attempted forced entry, they would bounce off it and tumble back down the three well-trod steps that led up to it. In short, the doors were a barrier to the outside world that a villain could rest easy behind and, in truth, over the centuries several had.

Jude had cycled up to the Manor House and he stood on the top step and gazed down the valley. The fields between the Manor and the village still belonged to the big house, and the three horses that grazed the fields were from the Manor's stables. One, a chestnut mare with a white blazed face and four white stockings, was biting the neck of a dark bay pony who just wanted to graze. The pony turned on the larger animal and bucked its resistance. The mare got the hint, strolled to the nearest hedge and started to rub her back-side against it. The third horse, a skewbald, stood head up and stared back at Jude.

The morning dew had left a watery patina on the trees, leaves, hedgerows and fields. Beyond the fields, through the quiet mist, Jude could just see Willow Walk. The terrace of cottages had been erected in the late 19th century on the instructions of Eli Fox - a direct ascendent of Ivan Fox - who had built them to stable his farm workers.

The cottages no longer belonged to the estate; they had been sold off in the noughties and they were now considered prime real estate for the lucky few who could afford to buy one. Jude gazed at number 2, his home. For now anyway.

He turned around and was about to reach for the cast iron horseshoe shaped knocker, but he stopped when he heard the sound of bolts being released from inside. Somebody was there.

Did they know he was on the doorstep? He took a step back as one of the doors was pulled open.

Jude gasped. She was almost as tall as he was, aqua blue eyes, flaxen hair settled in thick waves to her waist, pulled back off her sculpted features by a simple scarlet scarf tied in a bow on top of her head. A pale blue dress with patch pockets, clung to her slender frame. He swallowed hard, he had seen her face before, on the cover of a magazine maybe.

Jude opened his mouth to say something but she got in first.

'Shush…' she held a slender finger to her lips, 'please speak quietly.' She looked back over her shoulder with a nervous smile. 'You're lucky I spotted you from the window, my husband is upstairs working and he mustn't be disturbed.'

'I'm sorry,' Jude whispered. 'I hope I haven't…'

'He gets angry if he's interrupted,' her brow creased and she gave a hesitant smile as she searched his face trying to seek a connection to the stranger on her door-step. 'What can I do for you?'

'I would like to speak with Mr Lawson Peterson. I was told he lives here.' Jude hinted a smile. 'But I'm guessing from what you've just said that may not be possible.'

'He only sees people by appointment. Would you like to make an appointment?'

'Yes please.'

'Does he know you?'

'No.'

'What is it you would like to speak with him about?'

'My name is Jude Mumford…'

'That is not what I asked,' she said. 'I asked you why you would like to speak to my husband.'

Jude felt himself redden.

From within the house a clock started its strike to the eleventh hour. Her smile turned to panic and, like Cinderella escaping at the midnight hour, she stepped back inside and slammed the door shut.

Jude stood staring at the door unsure of what to do. She wouldn't just leave him standing there would she? He turned around, he had cycled to the Manor House and on his arrival, had got off and walked his bike up the gravel driveway, noting a squeak in the wheel for the first time. He had lent his bike against the post and rail fence of the paddock and now the skewbald horse – the one which had locked his gaze earlier - had its head stretched over the top rail and was nibbling the handlebars, examining it in the way a baby might investigate a bunch of keys.

Jude was about to go over and rescue his transport when the front door creaked open again, he turned and their eyes met once more.

'Hello again, sorry,' she said. Slender fingers twiddled around a strand of hair. 'My husband likes his coffee at eleven o'clock sharp.' She stared unsmiling this time. 'Where were we? I know, you were going to tell me why you need to speak with my husband. I hope you're not going to try and sell him something. It would make him very angry.'

'I wanted to talk to him about Chantal Dubois.'

'I see. Are you from the police?'

'No, I'm not.'

'Well, I can tell you now you are wasting your time.' She disengaged, like a loose wire detaching at source. 'He won't see you.'

'I understand he knew her.'

'That is correct,' she nodded. 'But he has already spoken with the police and it is not something he would discuss with anybody else.'

'I see,' said Jude. 'Mrs Peterson, I understand she was also a friend of yours.'

Her eyes misted over; she opened her mouth to say something but was not able to find the words. She blinked back tears, then fanned her face and attempted a weak smile.

'I'm sorry,' she said. 'We can't help you.'

'Please... I really think you may be able to.'

'But who are you? What is your interest in Chantal?'

'I found her body.'

Her face flushed and she looked away.

'It was you…' her eyes focussed on the ground. 'Why on earth do you want to speak to me?'

'I need to speak to people who knew her well, I may be able to help find her attacker.'

She disappeared behind the door for a few seconds before reappearing wrapped in an oversize blue and white wool shawl. She stepped out and pulled the door shut behind her.

Without further discussion, Jude followed her down the steps and around to the left side of the house. She took long strides, gait graceful, like an Arab horse heading out on a frost crisp day. She led him through an open wrought iron gate into a walled kitchen garden. The area had been newly tended, it was a nature haven corrected and proofed to human standard with rows of newly turned soil ready to be sown.

He followed her to a wood-stained pergola in the centre of the lawn, its top covered in withered vines. Underneath, a wooden slatted table, a bench either side and matching wooden chairs, like a throne at either end with their carved backs and broad armrests. She sat down on one of the chairs and nodded Jude to the other.

'Please, take a seat.' Although her words were to him, her gaze was further up the garden on the gate and the pathway they had just trodden.

Jude sat down.

'Do you mind if I take notes?' he said as he reached inside his jacket pocket.

'Actually, I do mind.' She blushed. 'Sorry, I hope that didn't sound rude, it's just that, well, you say you are not from the police?'

Why doesn't she want me to take notes?

He placed his notebook and pencil on the table.

'As I said, I found Chantal's body.'

'I don't think that obligates you in any way.' As she spoke, she hinted a smile. 'To search for her killer I mean.'

'I just thought I might be able to help.'

I failed to save her life, that does obligate me.

'It must have been a bit of shock for you, finding her like that.'

'It was, although to be honest, it was my dog who found her. He alerted me to her body.'

She reached into the pocket of her linen dress, pulled out a cotton handkerchief and patted each eye in turn.

Jude watched, but something else caught his eye, partially hidden by the branches of a plum tree he spotted a fluffy grey cat sitting atop the wall. It stared back at him; it's gaze one of curious calm. Her eyeline followed his.

'Don't mind Blue, he's just being nosey.' She opened her mouth to continue but hesitated, flushed. 'He's got a webcam on his collar; Charlie likes to check out where he's been. But don't worry, I'll get him to remove this footage.'

'Charlie?'

'Charlie is our son. He and Chantal were very close,' she paused, 'before we fell out.'

'It must have been difficult for him, not seeing her anymore.'

Sasha nodded; her voice quietened.

'It was quite odd really. She had a reputation for not liking children but she and Charlie really got on.'

'She didn't like children?'

'I think it was because she used to be a teacher,' she laughed. 'That's probably why. But she was so good with my boy. I guess it's because she didn't treat him like a child. She was always telling me how grown up he is. She gave him French lessons, taught him how to play chess and how to sew. He used to make all of his own clothes; he was brilliant with a sewing machine.'

'Was?'

'It broke, we haven't bothered with a replacement yet.' She pulled her shawl around her. 'We all used to be friends, that was

69

until her brother lost his money, it was through some bad investments. That's when it all went wrong.'

'I heard something about that.'

Sasha nodded and their eyes connected.

'Stefan and Chantal, they both blamed Lawson, said it was all his fault.'

'Was it?'

'Of course not,' she said. 'It was bad luck. But they started to harass him, he had to go to the police more than once. But obviously there was no evidence.'

'So, what happened to your friendship?'

'It ended.'

'That must have been tough.'

'It was, particularly for Charlie, but the things she was saying, they were awful. Then of course he, I mean Stefan, went missing.'

'Any idea what happened to him?'

'Well, if you listen to village gossip, Lawson bumped him off.' She stared to front, wide eyed. 'It's ridiculous of course but it's a village, people talk.'

'So I'm beginning to find out.'

'And then of course she had that terrible accident, I guess you heard about that too?'

Jude nodded.

'That poor little girl. The family used to live in the gate house at the entrance to our estate.'

'I heard your husband bought it from them after the accident.'

'They were desperate to sell and move to a bungalow in the village,' she nodded. 'And he helped them out by buying it.'

Helped them out? That's not what I heard.

'But to be honest I think he had his eyes on it for a long time…' She stopped abruptly, 'I don't mean he wanted it… the accident to happen.'

70

'Of course not.'

'I think he just wanted to bring it back onto the estate, where it belongs.'

'I was told Chantal changed after the accident.'

Sasha nodded, her hair fell forward near covering her face and she pushed it back over her shoulder.

'I heard that too, but of course we were no longer in contact with her by then.'

'So, what was she like before it happened?'

'Well, I don't mean to speak ill of the dead.'

'But?'

I've a feeling you're going to.

'If I'm honest, she was quite a selfish person.'

'In what way?'

'The way she conducted herself and the way she did business.' Sasha, handkerchief still in her hand, dabbed her eyes again. 'I know the signs you see, my husband, he can be a little ruthless sometimes in his business dealings. I think it made her a few enemies.'

'Can you name any of them?'

She let out a short laugh, pulled her hair forward and threaded her fingers through the strands.

'Apart from Lawson you mean?'

She lifted her head and stood up, her gaze on the pathway they had walked down. She tucked the handkerchief into her pocket.

'My husband.'

Jude turned, followed her eyeline. Lawson Peterson was striding towards them, his tan leather shoes glinting in the sunlight. He was about the same age as Jude, mid-thirties, he was tall, about six feet two inches, slender, with neat trimmed dark hair. This was a man who worked out. He wore a perfectly fitting pin striped suit, white shirt and navy tie fastened with a gold pin.

71

'What's going on?' He bellowed as he neared and then eyes on Jude yelled. 'And who the hell are you?'

'This is Mr Mumford,' said Sasha. 'He was just leaving.'

Jude detected panic in her voice.

'So, what's he doing here?' He asked the question first of his wife, second of Jude. 'What the hell are you doing here?'

'He… he's setting up a tennis academy, teaching tennis, and I asked him to come to discuss lessons for Charlie.'

Tennis Academy? I didn't tell her about my tennis academy.

Lawson Peterson flipped his mood as one might toss away a defective tennis ball before a serve. He approached Jude with his hand outstretched, his grin, displaying a perfect set of white teeth.

'So, you're going to teach my boy how to play tennis.'

Jude shook the offered hand.

'I thought I'd book some lessons.' Sasha's eyes pleaded with Jude, willing him to go along with her tale before she returned her smile to her husband. 'He's going to help Charlie, isn't that nice? It was going to be a surprise for you.'

'And I've gone and spoilt it! Sorry love.' He closed in on her, put his arm around her shoulder and pulled her to him. 'Nice one,' he turned to Jude again. 'You get my boy on the tennis circuit and there's money in it for you.'

'I'll do what I can to help him,' said Jude.

'Let me tell you, my lad needs all the help he can get. She…' he glared accusingly at his wife. 'She and that damn Chantal woman had him playing board games and making clothes. Sewing! I ask you; what sort of a hobby is that for a lad? Well, I put a stop to the that nonsense I can tell you.'

'We won't be replacing my son's sewing machine,' said Sasha.

'Too right!' said Lawson. 'Between the two of them they were turning my son into a flaming pansy!'

72

13

Jude decided to clean his bike. It was upside down beside the shed in his back garden and he was kneeling beside it, rubbing his cloth lovingly along each of the front wheel spokes, his eyes focussed on the before and after.

'Bugger!'

It was the voice of his neighbour, not Dexter, it was Rosebud. He turned to look, just in case she was addressing him, but he couldn't see her so he continued cleaning.

'Ouch!' Her voice again.

This time he stopped polishing, stood up and walked over to their boundary wall. She was there, lying flat out in the middle of the lawn, her face pinked up to the shade of the mat she was laying on. Her expression reflected an emotion between displeasure and pain.

'You okay?'

She lifted her head to peer at him.

'Not really.'

'Anything I can do to help?'

'Nope.'

'Okay,' he turned and headed back to his bike, but before he got there her voice stopped him.

'I suppose I should apologise,' she shouted.

Jude stood still for a few seconds then headed back to their boundary. Rosebud was on her feet now, stood tall, she raised her arms out front.

'I'm sorry,' she said.

'Are you talking to me?'

Arms still outstretched she turned her head and looked sideways; their eyes met for seconds.

'I don't see anybody else around,' she lowered her body from her slim waist and lay her hands flat down onto her mat.

73

'Well,' said Jude. 'Thank you, apology accepted. And if you ever feel the need to explain to me exactly what you are apologising for, I'll be all ears.'

She didn't reply so he went back to his bike again. From the wooden trug that held his cleaning gear he picked up a can of polish, shook it, opened it, picked up a fresh cloth and spilled the creamy fluid onto it. The smell hung in the air, it was like perfume to him and returned him to the days when, on the first Monday evening of every month he and his mum and dad would polish their bikes. He knelt down and started on the back wheel.

'I was rude the other day,' Rosebud shouted, interrupting his daydream. 'When you told me you were there.'

He stopped polishing, stood up, chucked the cleaning cloth into the trug and headed to the wall again. She had stopped exercising and she stood and faced him. Their eyes met and there was a mutual engagement of understanding.

'I get it,' he said. 'And believe me, you are not half as sorry as I am. I felt terrible when I found out.'

'I guess.'

'Actually,' he said. 'What I said about investigating your friend's death, I've changed my mind. I am going to now.'

Rosebud grinned.

'I would say I told you so but of course I won't.'

'Glad to hear it,' said Jude. 'So, would you mind if we had a chat sometime? I've got a few questions.'

'Look,' her eyes bore into him. 'Don't get me wrong, I'm pleased you're investigating, but I've said all I'm going to say to the police.'

'Fair enough.' He turned around and headed back to his bike.

'I've done it again, haven't I?'

'No probs. I'm getting used to it,' he shouted.

He continued cleaning and after ten minutes stood up to examine his work.

'Perfect,' he said to himself. He was about to start polishing the handlebars when Rosebud resumed their conversation.

'I suppose you've heard it's the village fair in a couple of weeks?'

'I had heard. I understand it's a big event.'

The estate agent had mentioned the fair when Jude had come to view the cottage but he'd forgotten about it until the previous weekend when he was setting off on his evening walk and had overheard Mr Fox chatting to another neighbour about it. Intrigued by the snippet of conversation he had listened to, he had taken to his phone, searched the internet for details and found out that Eaststowe Fair was one of the oldest fairs in the country and that it took place on the early May bank holiday. It had a range of traditional fairground rides, including a helter skelter, swingboats and a big wheel, a range of craft stalls and there were Morris dancers all afternoon. So when he bumped into Dexter on his way back from his walk he had an inkling of what he was talking about.

'Hey!' A nod, a smile. 'Now my friend, you need to understand the fair. Early May Bank Holiday Monday. It gets opened by the Lord of the Manor at midday. Street party starts at 6PM, barbeque, drinks, bunting, flags, fairy lights, music, the lot. You won't be able to escape it so don't try.'

It was the mention of a barbeque that had caught Jude's attention. He hadn't had one for ages, after all, who would have a barbeque on their own? Only a poor sad loser.

'You must come,' Rosebud shouted over, interrupting the memory.

Still holding his cleaning cloth he headed back to the wall, she was sitting on a chair now, cradling Simeon in her arms. He was purring loudly as if trying to sing himself to sleep with his own lullaby.

'You'll enjoy it,' she said.

Jude spluttered as he held onto a laugh.

'You look and sound like a Bond villain,' he cradled his cleaning cloth in his arms and pretended to stroke it. 'You will come to the street party and you will enjoy it.'

Rosebud loosened her hold, the disgruntled cat jumped down, took a single bound up onto the wall, and fixed his gaze onto Jude.

Jude tried to out stare Simeon for a few seconds only, before flinching and turning to Rosebud.

'Why do I get the impression Simeon is judging me?' he said.

'Because he is,' said Rosebud, that is what cats do, and the exotics are extremely good at it.'

'Okaaay.'

'So you'd best watch yourself,' said Rosebud with a wink. 'Because you are being watched.'

'Thanks for the heads up,' Jude grinned.

'Again,' said Rosebud, 'I'm sorry about what I said, it was all such a shock.'

'I get it,' he said with a nod. 'And about the street party, I've already had my instructions.'

'Dexter?' Rosebud laughed.

Jude nodded.

'No escape, that's what he told me,' he laughed. 'This will be my first ever street party.'

'Well, I now feel duty bound to make sure you enjoy yourself.'

'I shan't be there for long. I'll probably take Spud over the Fens for a marathon walk.'

'Sir, that is unthinkable!'

'Is it?' Jude bit his lip to suppress a grin.

'Of course. The clue is in the title 'Street Party',' said Rosebud with a cheeky grin. 'And you live in the street, so I'm afraid you are going to have to party.'

'I beg to differ.'

'How so?'

'This is Willow Walk, so strictly speaking I live in a Walk.'

'Oh, behave yourself,' Rosebud laughed, she got up and picked up Simeon from where he was now laying on the wall, gaze still locked onto Jude. 'Haven't we got a silly next-door neighbour Simmy.'

Jude stood trying to think of a witty reply but he couldn't. He was grateful that she was relaxed, almost playful, it was so different from their last meeting. He ran his hand through his hair and was about to ask a question but she was gone from view. He neared their wall, she was laying on her mat, in the middle of the lawn gazing skyward.

'Fairy lights were mentioned,' said Jude. 'Are they compulsory?'

'Yep.'

'Bunting?'

'Also compulsory,' she shouted back. 'Do you do it?'

'Come again?'

'Yoga.'

'No.'

But I enjoy watching it.

'You should, keeps you flexible,' she relaxed her pose, lay flat on her mat and turned to him. 'Now, our street party, don't panic about it. All you need to do is bring your table and chair out front.'

'Is that it? What about the food?'

'There'll be plenty, I'm a vegetarian and I always contribute loads, which you're welcome to share. High quality of course, I'm very fussy.'

'I wouldn't want to put you to any trouble.'

'Fear not, you won't.' She stood up, twisted, one arm straight up in the air, the other touching her toe. 'Revolved Triangle Pose,' she shouted. 'Besides it will make up for me being rude to you.'

'Please, forget it.'

Rosebud held her pose for several seconds.

77

'Okay,' she said. 'We need a plan. How about we meet out front at 11:45, we'll go over to the fair. You'll enjoy it, the opening is hilarious. Then back here around five-ish and prepare ourselves for the barbeque.'

'Well...'

'And if that on its own doesn't convince you, I thought about what you're doing - investigating Chantal's death. Of course I'll answer your questions.'

Jude's mouth fell open, he placed his hand on his chest.

'An offer like that, how could I possibly refuse?'

'I was probably a bit hasty before.'

'I can't disagree with that,' said Jude. 'Why the change of heart?'

'Without being rude about our local constabulary, quite frankly, they do need all the help they can get. You might come at things from a different perspective.'

'A different perspective?' Jude laughed. 'What's that meant to mean?'

'Exactly what it says,' Rosebud shrugged. 'Nothing more, nothing less.'

Spud appeared from the cottage. He went up to Jude, whined, sat in front of him dark eyes pleading.

'I think your dog is trying to tell you something,' Rosebud nodded at Spud.

'Spud! You want your walk, don't you mate? Just let me finish this.'

'Hi guy and gal! Have you heard the news?'

Jude and Rosebud both turned to Dexter. He was in his garden waving at them with a garden fork in his hand.

'Hi Dext!' Rosebud shouted over. 'What news?' She leaned towards Jude and hushed her words. 'In case you aren't already aware. Dexter is our top man for all current events.'

'That is a conclusion I was not far from reaching.'

'Well,' said Dexter. 'The police questioned Olga Kaine…'

'Olga Kaine?' Jude recognised the name; it had been in the email he had received from Dr Fernsby.

'Used to be a friend of Chantal,' said Rosebud.

'But they have now released her,' said Dexter.

'Any ideas why they took her in for questioning?' asked Jude.

'I guess it's because they thought she had a motive. They used to be friends,' said Rosebud. 'But they fell out years ago. It can't have been her, not after all this time.'

'You'd be surprised, some people hang onto grudges for years,' said Jude. 'Any idea why they fell out?'

'No, but I know a man who might.' Rosebud shook her head and turned to Dexter, but he was gone from his garden.

14

The following morning started bright and descended to grey clouds and drizzle. Jude was sitting in his front room working on his business plan.

Shouting outside his window distracted him. It was Patrick Fox, he was standing, his hand resting on Jude's front gate having a conversation with Iris Bell, a neat and trim elderly woman who lived next door to Dexter at number 4. Jude knew who she was because he had met her on his second visit to Eaststowe. It was the day he had come to view 2 Willow Walk.

He had arranged to meet the estate agent at midday but had got lost so had turned to his phone for directions.

I must have put in the wrong post code.

He was standing in front of the village haberdashers; scratching his head as a woman in her later years appeared. In spite of the chilled air, she wore a short-sleeved summer dress of lilac stemmed roses and a floppy brimmed straw hat with a miniature bunch of buttercups pinned to the front of the rim above her right eye. She turned to the window display of crochet teddy bears and sheep and without taking her eyes off them addressed Jude.

'Lovely aren't they?'

Jude looked up from his phone, nodded a greeting and glanced at the display.

'Very pretty.'

'Are you lost? Can I help?'

'Could you please tell me where I can find Willow Walk?'

He turned his phone expecting her to point it out to him. But instead she turned her back on him and faced the distant church spire.

'Of course I can,' she said. 'I live there. Follow the road around the bend and you will see the church, as you approach it take the right fork. On the left there is a hill. If you are not already aware, it is the only hill in Eaststowe. At the top of it is Eaststowe Manor House. You can't miss it.' Her voice was loud, but in case Jude didn't hear she included hand signals and finger points like a Girl Scout conducting a lesson in semaphore. 'Once you have feasted your eyes on our beautiful Manor House, you must turn to your right and you will see a terrace of twelve Victorian cottages. That is Willow Walk. Which number are you looking for?'

'Number 2.'

'Number 2. It's been empty for a while. I heard she was trying to find another tenant. The previous owner was murdered you know.'

'Really, the estate agent didn't mention that,' said Jude. He gave a short laugh. 'But I don't suppose he would.'

'Not the owner of the cottage silly, the previous owner of Eaststowe Manor.'

'Oh, I see,' said Jude. 'Anyway, thanks. I'd best be off, I'm a bit late.'

'Good luck…' she had shouted after him as he went off. 'I'm Iris Bell, I live at number 4. Maybe I'll see you again.'

Jude waved a thank-you.

'Maybe I will.'

He followed her instructions, arrived at the church, took the right-hand fork and spotted the Victorian terrace of cottages in front of him. In spite of his lateness he gazed up the hill to Eaststowe Manor, barely visible in the haunting mist. It was a sizeable pile. Between him and the Manor several horses grazed the undulating pasture.

Jude returned his attention to the Victorian Terrace. A black BMW was parked outside the second cottage along and beside it, on the cobbled pavement stood a pin-stripe suit, his attention full on his phone.

'Morning,' said Jude.

The suit vanished his phone, puffed out his chest and with a well-rehearsed smile, offered his hand.

'Sorry I'm late,' Jude said as they shook hands. 'I got a bit lost.'

Get the smile, get the red braces.

The suit gave Jude a run-down of the terrace, explaining how they never came up for sale and only rarely for rent. He soon realised that his client was new to the area so he expanded his repartee of local knowledge. He explained that Eaststowe was a 'fantastic' village full of 'really friendly people,' then he talked about the Manor House, the annual village fair - one of the oldest in the country - which took place in the fields for just one afternoon every May bank holiday. He explained how the village had a King who got crowned every year at the fair and who then threw coins for the local children to pick up. Jude listened as he headed up the garden path and nodded whenever the suit turned around to make sure his client was still there.

The front garden of number 2 was small, a stone path, a weather worn stone circle, a few well established shrubs and a skeletal Buddleia bush. The front door was oak, the top half, two long stained-glass panels, each the picture of a tall stem rose in full bloom, one red, one yellow, facing each other nodding forward as if in greeting. Jude couldn't help but notice the cottages on either side had the same front door.

The suit pushed the front door, a kick and it opened.

'I'll get that fixed,' he said as he stepped back to allow Jude to enter.

Jude stepped inside, it smelt fresh, a hint of lemon. The front room was a good size, freshly painted walls, blank of pictures, original Victorian fireplace, a vase of dried flowers in the grate, a stained wood floor.

He had been in the cottage a couple of minutes only, he didn't know if it was a feeling, an emotion or instinct but he did know that he liked what he saw and he liked how he felt. He could settle in this place. He looked down; he was standing on a coconut bristle doormat which had the word 'Welcome' woven into it.

That will have to go.

'So, tell me about this murder, the one at the Manor House,' he asked as they headed to the kitchen.

82

'Oh,' said the suit. 'You've heard about it then.'

'A woman I met in the village mentioned it.'

'Well, you'll hear the details from somebody so may as well be from me.'

'Go on.'

'It was years ago. The old owner of the Manor, loaded he was. Bit of a villain by all accounts. Well, he was going to move to Spain, but, the day before he was due to go, he was out front, loading the boot of his car and... well... someone took a knife to him.'

Jude was in the kitchen about to turn the key to open the door to the back garden, instead he turned around.

'Really? What happened?'

The suit gave him a withering look.

'It was a murder! He didn't stand a chance. Blade right between the shoulder blades. Bled to death on his own driveway.'

'Did they catch the killer?'

'It was fifteen, sixteen years ago now but I don't think so,' said the estate agent as he unlocked the door to the garden. 'His niece lives there now, with her hubby, another questionable character, so I've heard.'

They went out to the garden. It was long but fairly narrow. There was a lawn, flower borders, a shed and a back gate. Either side, a drystone wall, about waist height, ensured a view across all of the terrace gardens.

Back inside they went upstairs, a large bedroom at the back and a small one at the front next to a bathroom. Jude's first impression was confirmed. This cottage would be the perfect starter home for him and for Spud.

The trouble was he hadn't mentioned Spud to the estate agent and the cottage details said 'no pets.' Jude didn't think of Spud as a pet. Spud was family, in fact, the only family he had left.

'So what do you think?' asked the suit as they walked back down the narrow staircase.

'I've got a dog.'

83

Jude was three steps behind him but he spotted the suit freeze for a few seconds before continuing. At the bottom he turned. The smile was gone, along with – Jude suspected – any chances he had of becoming the new tenant of number 2 Willow Walk.

'He's a very good dog,' Jude said, pleading his case. 'Cleaner than most people I know. Do you think the landlord could be talked into letting me bring him? I'd be willing to pay a bit extra rent.'

The suit coughed, put his hand into his jacket pocket, pulled out a pack of Benson and Hedges, flipped the pack open and selected one.

'Big? Small? Does it bark?' he asked as he fiddled with the cigarette.

'He's quite big,' said Jude. 'And yes, sometimes he barks.'

Jude was not allowed to have any direct contact with the owner of the cottage. The agency managed everything. Emails were composed and swapped, details provided, references taken, guarantees given, a rent increase of £20 a month and Jude signed the contract. It took six weeks and four days. A week after that Jude was handed the keys to their home.

On the day of their move Jude unlatched the front gate and bent down and patted Spud.

Spud wagged his tail and turned and licked his master's cheek.

'Our new home Spud, this is our life now.'

Jude unlocked the front door (it opened without him having to kick it) and stepped inside. Spud bounded in with him and Jude laughed as he watched his pet sniffing his way around the room. Spud investigated the dining table, placed in full light in front of the window, each of the two chairs, the shelves, the sofa, into the kitchen and then upstairs, sniffing each step as he made his way up.

Jude kicked the front door shut, bent down, picked up the 'Welcome' mat and headed to the kitchen. The key was in the back door so he unlocked it and was about to step out but Spud appeared, barged passed him and sniffed his way around his new outdoor space.

84

A winding cobbled brick path wove across the lawn to the shed and the back gate. A back entrance had been essential for those days when they would return from a walk, wet and mud spattered.

Still holding the 'Welcome' mat he headed to the shed, a medium sized wooden structure that had been freshly weather proofed in dark brown stain. He opened the door, it was empty apart from a lawn mower, a few plant pots and a green plastic garden table alongside two matching chairs. He bent down and positioned the 'Welcome' mat just inside the door.

15

The patter of rain played like scales inside Ivy's head, a rhythm enhanced by Fenland gusts rustling through garden trees and bushes enroute to her bedroom, rattling the age weary sash windows in an attempt to gain entry.

It was a few minutes after 8am when she got out of bed, dragged on her fluffy pink oversize dressing gown and went downstairs, her bare feet treading each step as a mime artist, slow, deliberate, not wanting to make a movement that might nudge her chest into a fit of coughing. She stopped as she passed the kitchen door, her mother Olga was stirring a pot of porridge with a wooden spoon.

'Morning,' she said. 'Porridge won't be long.'

'Morning.'

'How are you feeling? I heard you in the night, coughing and wheezing.'

Ivy leant against the door frame letting it support her sagging body.

'I'm okay,' she said.

'You don't look okay,' said her mother. 'Why don't you go back to bed? I'll bring your brekkie up.'

'I said I'm okay. Any juice?'

'In the fridge.'

Ivy yawned, rubbed her eyes, wrapped her dressing gown close and tied it tight. As she trod barefoot across the cold stone floor to the fridge, she woke a little more with each step. She opened the fridge door, it swung towards her and a large pot of plain yoghurt toppled out landing upside down, splat at her feet. A pond of thick white spilled and seeped around her, she cried out, lifted one foot, then the other in an involuntary on-the-spot dance before standing still, in the centre of her puddle.

'I never touched it!' she shouted. 'It just fell.'

'Hey, it's not a problem.'

Ivy left the fridge door open and headed to the sink leaving a trail of white footprints.

'Leave it, I'll clean it up.' Olga went to the sink and took the cloth from her daughter's hand. 'It was my fault; I didn't stack everything right.'

Ivy clung to the side of the sink with both hands and turned to watch as her mother got down on her hands and knees and attempted to mop up the mess.

'Sorry,' said Ivy.

'You go and sit down; I'll be in in a minute. But clean your feet first!'

Ivy grabbed several sheets of kitchen roll from the holder beside the sink, went and sat on one of the two chairs and carefully wiped each foot, softened now from their accidental soaking. Then she stuffed the mushed paper into the swing bin.

'I'll be in the snug,' she said.

The snug was a modest structure; a wooden lean-to built against the original back room of the cottage. It had floor to ceiling windows overlooking the garden and where the original wall of the cottage had been knocked through, a stained-glass window had been installed to ensure there was enough light in the back room. On sunny days as the sun appeared at the back of their little cottage its rays shone through the stained glass and bathed their back room in rainbow colours.

Ivy loved the snug and on this grey shrouded morning, she sat in her designated armchair, lifted her legs up and tucked them under. She picked up the throw to cover herself, rested her head on the wing back and gazed out to the garden. It was a long narrow space with a tidy lawn, a fig tree, a greengage tree, scattered shrubs, dying daffodils and emerging bluebells. The garden was her hobby. It was her favourite outside space, and the snug with its view of it was her favourite inside space.

Ivy had spent most of her previous summer holidays in her garden. When she wasn't tidying up, nurturing, pruning or weeding, she would read. Fantasy novels were her favourite and she would spend hours in deep thought as she slipped into the skin of the characters that inhabited the invented worlds she visited.

On this morning as she sat, dazed and sleepy in her chair, she pulled her phone from her dressing gown pocket to check her social media. Minutes later her mother appeared. Ivy returned her phone to her pocket, uncurled herself and Olga placed the tray onto her lap; a glass of orange juice, a bowl of porridge dusted with cinnamon and a drizzle of maple syrup running through it.

'Ta,' Ivy opened her arms out in a virtual hug before picking up the spoon. She took a couple of mouthfuls then put the spoon down. 'About the mess I made, sorry.'

'It's all sorted now,' said Olga as she turned to leave. 'Give me a shout when you're done.'

But there was no shout and so half an hour later Olga reappeared.

'How you doing?'

'I'm done,' Ivy nodded to the tray which she had placed on her mother's armchair.

'Can I get you anything else?'

Ivy shook her head.

'Mum…'

'What?'

'You know the woman that was found dead…'

'Chantal? What about her?'

'She wasn't a very nice person, was she?'

'What makes you say that?'

'They're saying stuff.'

'Who's saying stuff?'

'Kids at school.'

Olga picked up the tray, put it on the floor and sat down. Her armchair was the place where she relaxed, where she would sit and think or read, or – on this occasion – where she would listen.

'Well, I must say, the gossips have been busy. What are they saying?'

'Really horrible things.'

'What exactly?'

'And they're saying you used to know her.'

Ivy picked up a cushion, hugged it for comfort and stared out to her garden. The door on her curiosity was ajar and her creative mind invented a random range of scenarios built on gossip and speculation. Sometimes her mother was a hero and Chantal a villain, other times her mother was the villain and Chantal her victim.

'You, okay?' Olga asked.

'Freya said you rowed...'

'Freya Fernsby? What? What did she say exactly?'

'Only that she heard you used to know Chantal really well and that the two of you had a really bad row.'

'Why on earth would she say that! Did she say where she heard it from?'

Ivy shook her head. Her mother's plain faced expression told her nothing.

'I've already spoken to the police about Chantal.' Olga spoke slowly, quietly. 'I guess they called me in because they'd already heard the gossip. Quite frankly love, this is the last thing we need.'

'But why? Didn't you tell them the truth?'

'Of course I told the truth... but...'

'But?'

'Okay, I may not have told them absolutely everything. But what I did tell them was the absolute truth.'

Ivy giggled.

'It's not funny love. Believe me, we do not need the police sniffing around.'

'Sorry.' She coughed then looked at her mother. 'Mum.'

'Yes?'

'It... it wasn't you was it?'

'What wasn't me?'

89

'You… you didn't hurt her did you?'

Olga winced like she had been struck a physical blow. She stood up, shock reflected in her darkened eyes, voiced through her words.

'What! How dare you! Why would you think that?'

'I don't. But it's what they're saying at school.'

'Who? That Freya Fernsby? Well, you tell her to come and tell her tales to me in future. And you can also tell her I'm going to be paying that know all doctor father of hers a visit as well.'

'But it's not just her, it's everyone, they're all saying it.'

Olga stood silent, she wanted to explain to her daughter, tell her about her past, but she didn't want to hurt her child.

'Right,' she said. 'I'll tell you this much. Yes, years ago Chantal and I were good friends and yes, we did row. But no, I did not kill her,' she lowered her voice. 'But believe me I've bloody well wanted to, on more than one occasion.'

16

J ude's mother had once said to him, *'you must listen to nature and then you will learn to love it.'* Her advice had grown faint to his ears during his heady years in North London but in the solitude of his new life he heard her voice once more and each day as he trod the Fenland trails, her words became louder and clearer until he understood their meaning.

His transformation first manifested itself as a self-satisfied smile as he strolled the lonely tracks, but over time his heart would beat with the excitement of watching a group of Fenland ponies gallop to catch the wind and his soul would pain him when he spotted hare coursers or rubbish littering the land. He was no longer a mere observer of nature he was a participant.

Jude and Spud had been out on the Fens for a couple of hours. They had long since left the track, weaving through trees unhurriedly trying to find a managed pathway that they could follow home. Jude's lungs filled with the purified breeze that rustled through the branches delivering a spiced bouquet of its route. His skin tingled as those same trees and the wildlife that called them home played their melody of the natural world.

But on this morning they had a problem. They were completely lost. It was all Spud's fault. They had been on a public footpath walking around a farmer's field when he had spotted a rabbit, he veered off the footpath like a skier heading off-piste and taken a route across the field weaving this way and that around invisible bending poles. Spud rarely chased an animal or ignored a command from Jude, but on this occasion he did both. He chased the breeze ignoring Jude's shouts which got captured by a gust and sent off to the next village. Even after the rabbit had long found its safe haven, Spud continued his rowdy conduct, adopting puppy-like behaviour and enabling his rarely emerging inner imp. Jude tramped across the fields after his pet, shouting him to heel, but Spud ignored him. And then he disappeared from view.

'Spud! Here!'

Jude's pulses started to race as he frantically gazed through the bushes and trees for a sighting of his pet. Nothing. His attention turned to the open countryside. A distant muntjac headed for the long grasses, three black and white ponies stood still, heads up, staring at him. Friend or foe? At this moment, with Spud missing, it was all just background.

Spud's flighty excursion only ended when Jude spotted his tail as he disappeared behind a bush heading into a scrubby copse. That was when Jude's tightened lips relaxed into a slow smile of relief. He shook his head and taking long strides set off into the trees. It took several minutes but eventually he managed to head Spud off.

The second Spud saw Jude in front of him, he turned his back on his life as a runaway and returned to his role as a domestic pet and Jude's best friend. Exhilarated, disheveled and tired, he walked up to his master with his head down. He sat down then lay down at Jude's feet and rolled over, doleful eyes staring up. Total submission.

'Spud, you bad boy.'

After a scolding they continued their walk, they snaked around bushes, stepped over brambles and bobbed beneath low branches. As they headed deeper into the woods, tree density blocked out light and shadows appeared on the track in front of them. Still, they traipsed through the undergrowth until a lack of sunlight left damp hanging in the air and it was local creatures, not humans, who whittled out the tracks and the trails they trod.

Eventually they reached a stream. Jude watched the trickle of water as it carved its way over the cobbles enroute to the river. Spud stood, head up, gazing to the other side, hackles raised, threatening a growl. Jude went and stood behind the ivy bound trunk of an aged oak tree and followed Spud's eyeline. Together they stared across the water to a sunlit glade.

'Spud,' Jude put his finger to his lips and beckoned. 'Shhhhhh. To me.'

Spud lowered his head, walked over, sat down and let out a sigh. He knew this game; they were in hiding.

The glade was a human structure made by taking a chainsaw to a large number of aged trees and, as they lay dead, rested in their own sawdust like slain animals, their trunks were winched and repositioned into a pre-designed circle, a patch of land which now -

due to their felling – was well placed for the rays of the sun. The destruction and construction had taken place several years previously, its purpose to build an outdoor nature stage where schoolchildren could come and learn about how to protect their environment.

Over the years nature had forgiven the human correction forced upon it and the circle of logs and the space within it had become a habitat for moss, brambles and ivy. Once the sunlit stage returned to nature, the insects and forest creatures moved back in.

From his position behind the oak tree, Jude could see a young woman sitting on one of the logs, she wore a powder blue boiled wool jacket and colour matched bobble hat. Long dark hair hung down her back swaying this way and that as she alternated between staring down at her phone and shouting to somebody who Jude could not see.

He wished he could spot who she was talking to, or at least hear what she was saying. He stood still for a couple of minutes unsure what to do. A rabbit scuttled out from under a bush, it turned and ran off, disappearing in seconds. Spud sat up, looked at Jude and then at the path the rabbit had taken.

'Spud, stay!' Jude whispered.

Spud sighed, lay down and closed his eyes against further temptation.

Jude didn't want to just step out from behind the tree in case he scared the woman. Neither did he want to walk away, just in case she was on her own, having some sort of personal crisis. Downstream he spotted a couple of stepping stones. He could cross the stream, send Spud ahead - hopefully she was not afraid of dogs – and then he could make a noise by calling Spud as he neared. That way she would be alerted to the fact that he was there. He could then pass her by with a *good morning, how are you today?'*

He was about to step out when a movement in the bushes near to her stopped him. Spud lifted his head and let out a low growl. Jude put his finger to his lips.

'Shhhh!'

A few seconds later a lad in a purple quilted jacket appeared zipping up his olive-green trousers before brushing them down. He took a handkerchief from his jacket pocket, wiped his hands then sat on the log next to the young woman and placed his arm around her shoulder. She responded by resting her head on his. Jude sighed; she was obviously okay. The boy leant forward and they kissed. Jude watched for seconds then turned away. He stepped out from behind the tree, decided to head back the way he had come and search again for the track to take them home.

'Here Spud.'

Spud stood up and barked.

The boy and girl jumped, they both got to their feet and turned to where Spud was standing. The girl let out a scream.

'Look!' she shouted, pointing at him. 'That dog!'

Jude could see their faces now. He did not recognize the boy but he had seen the girl before, in the corner shop with her father. It was Freya Fernsby.

17

The frost was starting to melt into her straggled hair, he bent down, saw her catch her breath. He lifted her wrist, a pulse, it was faint but there was a beat. She turned her head and eyes still closed smiled at him.

A sound startled Jude awake. He opened his eyes, flinched, Spud was sitting next to the bed, staring, his head cocked to one side. He whined a morning greeting.

Jude sat up, relieved to be awake before he got to the next stage of his dream.

'Spud! How long have you been sitting there?'

Spud whined, lifted a paw and placed it on the bed.

Jude picked up his phone, it was eight minutes past seven. He wasn't surprised it was so late, he'd had a restless night.

'Spud,' said Jude. 'Here boy.' He patted the bedclothes and with a single bound Spud was on him. Jude put his arms around him and a man/dog play fight started. It lasted a couple of minutes, until Spud ended it by jumping off the bed and heading to the door. He stood in the doorway, half in, half out of the room his eyes on his master.

'Yeah, I get it matey. No time to stay in bed. It's time to eat and walkies.'

After they'd had their breakfast Jude sat at the dining room table and gazed out of the window. As soon as he heard Dexter's front door open, he snapped on Spud's lead. By the time he opened his own front door Dexter was at his garden gate.

'Dexter,' he shouted. 'Have you got a minute?'

Dexter turned to Jude and grinned.

'I was going to drop in later, I've got news.'

'More news?' said Jude. 'I'm listening. But first off, can I just ask you about Olga Kaine? I'd like to know more about her.

'Chantal and Olga were friends but they fell out big time. It was years ago though.'

'That appears to be a theme in Chantal's life, falling out with friends,' said Jude. 'Do you know her well? Olga, I mean?'

'Nobody knows Olga, or that daughter of hers.' Dexter laughed. 'Not properly. They keep themselves to themselves.'

'I'd like to speak to her, any idea how I can get in contact?'

'I suggest you go to the pet cemetery. They buried their dog there a year or so back. They go there two or three times a week.'

'Any idea what time?'

'Usually after school's out, four, four-thirty I think.'

'Any idea where their dog's buried?'

'Far left as you walk in, the path that runs alongside Saffron's smallholding. They were devastated when he died, put up a massive memorial they did. No expense spared.'

'Zac!'

'You've seen it!' Dexter laughed. 'You going to try and catch them there? Good luck with that – that pair are seriously weird.'

18

Jude had a late lunch and when done he set up the ironing board in the kitchen and pressed his green round neck jumper and a pair of navy trousers. Spud stretched out on the sofa, his head on the arm, and watched.

An hour later they headed out. Spud was on best behaviour. He walked beside Jude, sat kerb-side and waited for permission before crossing the road. He even ignored Iris Bell's chocolate cocker spaniel as it yapped at him when they crossed paths at the church.

Once out on the Fen, Spud yelped and tugged at his lead eager to be granted his freedom. Jude unclipped him and Spud headed off.

With all of the detours Spud went on, it took them nearly an hour to walk to the pet cemetery. At one point Jude wondered if he had done the right thing by bringing him. When they at last reached the gates, Jude bent down and got hold of Spud's head between his hands.

'It's gonna be alright mate.'

Spud licked his face.

The gates were still set in the locked open position, but a tarpaulin had been placed over the notice board. There was no letter of explanation. Jude clipped Spud's lead on and together they headed along the centre path before veering onto a narrow track.

They wandered, exploring the threadlike pathways, until they eventually ended up on the path leading to Zac's grave. As Jude approached the bend, he could see through the thinning branches of a shrub, Zac's statue and the wooden bench. Two women were sitting there, both well wrapped up in spite of the early evening sun.

They wore matching green parkas with zip fronts and fake fur collars, denim jeans and walking boots. The older woman wore a brown fur lined trapper hat, its ear flaps down, while the younger had on a woolly hat with a fluffy white bobble. He was in the right place at the right time.

The younger woman spotted him first and nudged the other. As Jude neared, both faces stared his way. He stopped a short distance from them.

'Afternoon,' he nodded a greeting.

Olga pointed to Spud.

'Being a bit cruel, aren't you?' she said. 'Bringing that here, you do realise dogs can smell death?'

'Thank you. He's been here before and he's fine.' He bent down and ruffled Spud's head. 'Aren't you mate?'

'Do you realise you're on private land?'

'It says - or I should say - it used to say, that you can come here for quiet contemplation,' said Jude. 'Before they covered up the notice board.'

'Is that what you're doing here? Visiting for quiet contemplation?'

It was the older woman doing all of the talking. Jude nodded then smiled at Ivy but she looked away.

'I have come here because it's peaceful,' said Jude.

Olga pushed her hands deep into her pockets and stretched out her legs.

'It was until you came along.'

'It's full of dead animals,' said Ivy. 'That's why it's peaceful.'

'Chantal never used to mind people walking through,' said Olga. 'Not sure about the new owners though, I guess we'll all find out at some point.'

'I understand she's dead, the owner I mean. I'm Jude Mumford by the way.' He stepped forward and offered a hand but neither of the women moved so he stepped back again. 'I've recently moved to the village.'

'Your mutt! Olga stood up and shouted. 'Stop him!'

Jude turned around, Spud was sniffing around Zac's grave and he lifted his leg against it. Jude was powerless to stop him.

Ivy glared at him, bent down and turned her attention to a straw bag leaning against the leg of the bench. She took out a glass bottle, carefully flipped the lid and gulped down the contents, eyes still on them.

'Do you visit here often?' Jude asked the question of Olga. He already knew the answer of course, but it was his way of trying to engage her in conversation.

'We come to visit our friend,' she nodded to Zac's statue. 'The one your mutt just pissed on.'

'Sorry about that,' said Jude. 'Dogs will be dogs. If he does anything bad, I'll pick it up,' he reached into his back pocket and pulled out his poo bags.

Spud saw the bags and took it as a hint because he squatted and crapped next to Zac's grave.

'I'm so sorry,' said Jude, his face flushed. 'I will pick it up.'

'You'd better,' Olga turned her face from them. As far as she was concerned Jude and Spud were cancelled.

Jude cleared his throat and pretended the previous five minutes had not happened. He tried to think of something to say that would not antagonize either of the women. He scratched his head.

'Actually,' he said, 'my being here is no coincidence, I wanted to speak to you.'

'Speak to us?' said Ivy. 'Why?'

Her mother glared at her.

'I wanted to ask you about Chantal Dubois.'

'I've already been questioned by the police,' said Olga. 'And I've said all I'm going to say.'

'Here is my card,' Jude pulled one of his tennis cards out of his back trouser pocket stepped forward and offered it to her.

Ivy leaned forward, snatched it from him and examined it.

'It says here you're a tennis coach!' she said. 'Mum, when I'm better can I have tennis lessons?'

99

'No,' Olga turned to Jude. 'Who told you we would be here? I guess it was Saffron? She told you, didn't she?'

'No, it wasn't Saffron,' said Jude, 'it was a neighbour, he told me you come here around this time a couple of days a week.'

Olga stared at him blank faced while Ivy tucked the card into the side of her straw bag.

'Okay,' said Jude. 'Let me explain, I'm an ex-detective.'

'For God's sake!' said Olga. 'You're just another nosey flaming parker.'

'No I'm not, but I was the one who found her body, and…'

'It was you!' Olga let out a short laugh. 'You're that Private Dick. I read about you in the paper. As I said, a nosey parker.'

'I'm not a private detective.'

Spud, guessing they were going to be a while, sighed and lay down, not in his usual position with his head between his front legs, but down flat, on his side, as if feigning death.

'Won't be long mate. I promise,' Jude whispered.

'Look, you're even boring your mutt to near death,' said Olga. 'Now why don't you just clear off.'

But Jude was not going to let a little thing like a bad attitude turn him away.

'I was told that you fell out with her, Chantal I mean.'

'Not you as well!' Olga laughed. 'It's gossip. We fell out years ago!'

'Some people do hold a grudge for years.'

'Excuse me?'

'I'm just saying that some people don't forget and they brood on things over the years. Can I ask why you fell out?'

Olga stood up.

'You can ask but I shan't tell you, because none of it is any of your business.'

'In theory of course you are right,' he said. 'But…'

100

'Don't even try to disagree with my mum,' said Ivy, shaking her head from side to side.

Olga turned to her daughter.

'Ivy, go off for a walk, I'll catch you up in a bit.'

'No! Why should I?'

'Because you need exercise.'

'If I need exercise, why can't I have tennis lessons?'

'Just go. I need to speak to Mr Nosey Parker here in private.'

'Secrets! Always flaming secrets! What's so secret I can't hear, that's what I want to know.'

Jude tried to hide his surprise at how quickly Ivy's aggression surfaced, like warm milk in a pan, suddenly boiling over.

Olga turned to her daughter, her voice calm.

'I don't know yet,' she said. 'That's what I'm going to find out.'

'Stop it!' Ivy stood up and turned on her mother. 'I'm an adult. Your treating me like I'm a child!' She stomped off down the track.

Olga watched Ivy go and Jude watched Olga.

'None of this is any of my business but you're prepared to talk to me anyway?' he said.

'I guess you're not going to go away any time soon and I don't want Ivy upset. She's been upset enough as it is.'

'What do you mean?'

'The kids at school, making wild accusations.'

'Sorry, it wasn't my intention to upset you, or Ivy.'

'So, what is it you want?'

'I just wandered what happened all of those years ago, why you fell out with Chantal.'

'We used to be friends,' she turned to Jude with sad eyes. 'But let's just say I didn't like the way she treated people.'

'I see,' said Jude. 'I heard she was a shrewd business woman.'

'Huh! It was nothing to do with business.'

'Can you tell me what it was to do with?'

'Chantal cared only for herself. She was a self-centred egoist who didn't care one bit about the people around her.'

'Any actual specifics, any details?'

'That's all you're getting.' Her attention turned to Spud as he got up and sniffed around the statue again. 'Look. I've had enough of this. Now pick that up!' she pointed to Spud's toilet break. 'And go away and leave us alone!' She stood up and headed off along the track following the path that Ivy had taken.

Jude watched her go convinced she was emerging as a character from the shadows, but he had no idea what part she played or whether she had anything to do with Chantal's death.

She apparently had motive, something had happened all of those years ago, something serious enough for her to be the subject of village gossip and for the police to question her. He got out his phone and turned to the internet to answer his questions. Like a lab rat he pressed keys in order to be rewarded with snippets of information. And the information highway did not disappoint. It returned results from all of its corners, like notes being passed around a classroom. He sifted through and discovered more about the German woman who had lived in France before arriving in England some fourteen years previously. It was then that he contacted a colleague in France for help.

A whine from Spud returned him to the present.

'Sorry mate, sorry, here, let's go for a wander.' He got up and turned his attention to Zac's grave to pick up the mess. 'Come on Spud.' Clutching the poo bag, he turned onto the track going the opposite way that Ivy and Olga had gone. 'Let's have a quick wander then we'll head back.'

They followed the track which ran alongside the hedgerow bordering Saffron's land. To their right, more headstones, a bronze sculpture of a Siamese cat 'Tonks' with a single word 'Missed,' a wooden cross with 'Teddy' carved into it giving no clue as to what lay beneath. Other headstones, words of trust, of friendship, expressions of devotion. The more inscriptions Jude read the more emotional he started to feel as he suppressed thoughts of one day losing Spud.

He paused, smothered his thoughts and stared over the hedge. In the distance he could see Saffron's cottage, the back door open. She was nearby, leading her braying goat towards a dilapidated wood-store. She tethered it, placed a small wooden stool beside it, sat down and attempted to milk it. But the goat didn't want to be milked and vocalised its objections loudly. It tugged at its tether and attempted to eat her jacket. After a couple of minutes, she stood up, wagged her finger at it, picked up her axe and shook it towards the animal. Then she got hold of a lump of wood, placed it on a block and split it in one.

'Come on Spud, let's get out of here,' Jude turned and headed back up the track hoping Olga and Ivy would be long gone. A bark stopped him, he turned around; he couldn't see Spud. He called him; Spud barked again. Twice this time. Jude walked back around the bend. He spotted Spud, standing further down the track in front of a well grown holly bush.

'What's up mate?'

Spud barked again. He was gazing at the ground, Jude followed his eyeline, there was something - barely visible – beneath the branches of holly. Spud whined and pawed the ground, as if trying to tell him something.

Jude went and knelt beside his pet, pushed the branches of holly aside and spotted a withered bunch of flowers tied in garden string; it was beside a tiny weathered headstone.

This has been here for years.

Wishing to be friends is quick work,

But friendship is a slow ripening fruit.

Aristotle

19

The annual fair was an important day in the village calendar and every year Eaststowe Parish Council and the majority of villagers discussed the weather forecast knowing full well that the only thing they could do was pray for sunshine but erect marquees just in case.

Most villagers prayed in silence, an unconscious act of hope, but the churchgoers of Eaststowe took it one step further and for three weeks before the event, voiced their requests on a Sunday morning, giving the type of weather required and the exact date.

On the Bank holiday Monday, it was clear the villagers' requests had been granted. At dawn's early light, Willow Walk was a street wrapped in colour. Red, blue, green, purple and yellow bunting fluttered from the guttering and the lamp-posts.

The residents had Dexter to thank for the adornments. He had spent most of the previous evening at the top of his ladder, pinning the bunting in place along the guttering of several of the cottages, his customers assuming the skills required to hang the little flags to be a logical extension to his job description as a gardener. But he gained a new customer so he was pleased. He had also strung up the fairy lights between the old-fashioned street lamp posts, where they would store up enough solar energy ready to pop open later in the evening when the sun and the fair goers disappeared over the horizon leaving the residents of Willow Walk to party.

Cottages Numbers 4, 6, and 8 Willow Walk had opted out of having bunting pinned along their guttering. Instead, Iris Bell at number 4 had erected a rotary clothes line in the middle of her front garden and draped hers around it making it look like a bunting tree. The couple at number 6 had chosen to drape their little flags along the ironwork fence at the front of their property, while Patrick Fox at number 8 did not have bunting, he had erected a flagpole in his front garden and the Union flag hung there, limp as a drunk on a wet Wednesday night.

It was a verbal understanding in Willow Walk that all flags and bunting and any other evidence of the party would be removed by sun-down the following day. This was required to ensure the matter would not be discussed in the next Parish Council meeting.

Only one cottage was bunting and flag free. Number 2.

Jude got woken up by Spud on that morning. His pet had been snoring peacefully on the other side of the bed but at just after 6:30am he lifted his head, ears up, and let out a low growl. He jumped off the bed, went to the door and stood, head cocked to one side. He stared out for a couple of seconds before heading off down the stairs. A single bark woke Jude up.

'Spud? You okay?'

'Woof.'

Jude got up and put on his dressing gown. He reached the top of the stairs as Spud was walking up the steps towards him, a bunting flag clamped between his teeth like a pony bit, the rest of the little flags trailing either side like reins. When Spud got to the top step, he dropped the flag he was holding at Jude's feet and stared up at his master. Jude snorted a laugh.

'Looks like somebody's dropping us a hint mate.'

Spud whined, turned around and went back down the stairs. At the bottom he sat and waited, the sprite in his eyes imploring Jude to join him. Jude made his way down picking up and folding the little triangles into a neat pile. He placed them on the dining room table and headed to the kitchen. He opened the back door and Spud bounded out to the garden and chased off a black and white cat that had been asleep by the shed.

Jude watched him for a few seconds and sighed. He did not expect to enjoy the day, in truth he was finding it a little overwhelming. He was not a fan of crowds, and he was not a fan of fairs, but he tried to think about the positives. Rosebud had said she would answer his questions and he may even be able to network and find a few tennis clients.

Jude got dressed and after breakfast flipped open his laptop to read the newspapers, but the neatly stacked flags kept catching his eye. He sighed, picked them up, opened his front door and stepped out into the day of celebration. At the front gate he turned and stared up at the guttering of his cottage.

'You took the hint then.'

108

Jude recognised Dexter's voice. His neighbour was carrying a weather worn wooden table, he placed it down next to their adjoining wall and grinned.

'I take it this was your doing?' Jude held out the bunting.

'Not me,' Dexter shook his head.

'My doing.' It was Rosebud's voice. She was standing in her garden, carefully positioning a white table cloth. 'I thought you might need a gentle nudge.'

'Gentle?' Jude laughed.

'Believe me, from Rosie, that is gentle,' Dexter winked at Rosebud as he spoke before turning up his excitement levels and gazing at one and then the other. 'Guess what! I've got important news about the case.'

'Go on,' said Jude.

'Well, they questioned Olga.'

'That's not news,' said Jude with a grin. 'That's history.'

'Ungrateful! Well hear this. They are now questioning Lawson Peterson again! You heard it here first!'

'I knew it!' Rosebud yelled over. 'I knew he was involved!'

'They're questioning him again?' Jude spoke in a gentler tone, almost to himself. 'They must have discovered some new evidence.'

Why would Lawson Peterson attack Chantal? What would be his motive? Sure, Chantal had been seen pestering him, but to somebody like Lawson who had few friends and a lifetime's list of people he had upset that would mean nothing.

But Chantal was not murdered, she froze to death.

Surely if somebody like Lawson Peterson had wanted her dead, he would have made sure he had killed her?

Lawson Peterson didn't strike Jude as somebody who only did half a job.

Maybe they had rowed and he thought she was going to get up and walk away?

109

Maybe that was his plan, he did attack her and knew she wouldn't be able to walk away. He knew she would freeze to death. Lawson Peterson was a clever man.

As each question surfaced, Jude filed it away.

'Are you okay?' asked Dexter.

'Sure,' Jude returned his attention to his chatty neighbour.

'You don't look it,' said Dexter, 'you look completely gobsmacked. Surely it can't be that much of a surprise. He's a nasty piece of work.'

'How did you find out?'

'I was up there, early yesterday morning, working in their kitchen garden when the police arrived and picked him up. It all got a bit aggressive.'

'Why doesn't that surprise me. How bad was it?'

'The Lord of the Manor did not go quietly. He was yelling about police corruption and all sorts.'

'I thought he had mates in the police?' Rosebud yelled over.

'That's what Chantal kept banging on about,' Dexter shrugged. 'It was one of her bugbears. But whether it's true or not, who knows?' He turned to Rosebud. 'Rosie, you going to be dressing up?'

'Of course.' She turned and winked at Jude. 'And I hope you're going to dress up later.'

'Hold on, nobody said anything about dressing up.'

'All part of the tradition,' she said. 'As is the street party.'

'In truth, the party was a later tradition,' Dexter interrupted. 'Started in Victorian times by the then Lord of the Manor. He decided that each year he would lay on a feast for his servants and farm workers, to say thank you to them.'

'Sounds like a good guy,' said Jude.

'Yep,' Dexter shouted over. 'He was certainly classier than some of his descendants anyway.'

Curiosity got the better of Jude and he opened his mouth to ask more but Rosebud got in first.

'The street party starts at around 6pm, and of course, there's the barbeque.'

'And as per usual I'm head chef,' Dexter shouted. 'I tell you, we're all gonna be stuffed by tonight.'

'I'd best get my table through then,' Jude grinned, returned his attention to the flags he was carrying, and looked along the row of front gardens seeking inspiration.

'Wouldn't do to be a party pooper,' Dexter nodded at the bunting.

'In all honesty I think I probably am, what you just said.' Jude stepped out of his front garden and onto the pavement before adding, 'a bit of a party pooper.' He approached the railings. 'I think I'll just hang them along here.'

Rosebud nodded approval.

Jude draped the flags along the length of the railings of his front garden, being careful to adjust each hang point to ensure each little arc was a perfectly aligned Bezier curve. When done, he stood back to admire his handywork.

'Perfect, and minimum attachment intervention needed.'

'Very good,' Rosebud laughed.

Jude gave a short bow.

'See you later,' Rosebud grinned and with a child-like wave turned to go indoors. At her front door she kicked up her back leg, it was a flippant action from a woman confident enough to know Jude would be watching. He was. And so was Dexter.

At 11:45 Jude answered a knock on his front door. It was Rosebud.

'You ready?'

'Wow!' he looked her up and down. 'You look great!'

'You like?' She twirled around, one arm in the air. The full skirt of her 1950s flower dress billowed out around her until she came to

111

a stop facing him. She beamed; her perfect white teeth framed within scarlet lips.

'You look beautiful.'

'Why thank you,' her breathless smile lay open her joy at his compliment.

'Sorry, I… I mean you look very in keeping with the era.'

'No need to apologise,' her smile transformed to a mischievous grin. 'Most of the villagers, especially the children, who get dressed up go as poor people in sack-cloths and ragged clothing. I prefer to go as a lady.' She twirled again, halting in front of Jude once more, a vixen in action. 'You should dress up, get into the spirit of the day.'

'Maybe next year,' Jude swallowed hard. 'Do you mind if I follow you over? I've got a couple of things I need to do.'

'I do mind. You must come now. It opens at 12:00, I did tell you.'

'I remember, but…'

'No buts. They crown the King at midday!'

'Crown the King?'

'You've not been paying attention, have you?'

'I thought I had.'

'Eaststowe has a King, had one for years. And every year at the opening of the fair he gets crowned, and to show his gratitude he throws coins to the kids. It's a tradition.'

'Blimey,' said Jude. 'Actually, I think the estate agent mentioned something about it when I viewed the place. I wasn't really listening to be honest.'

Some traditions are really over-rated.

'It's all completely mad but quite good fun. Come on, you don't want to miss it.'

'Clearly it's something I need to see.' Jude turned around and shouted 'Spud! Here!'

Spud was with him in seconds and together the three of them headed across the road to the field, transformed now from a country meadow with grazing horses, to a 1950s village fairground, complete with suitably attired fairgoers. There were no neon lights, no loud music, but there were swing-boats, a Helter-Skelter, a coconut shy, all from a time long ago.

As Jude passed through the gate into the field, he was transported back to that time before he was born, and he watched two people in this field, on this day, as they talked about getting married. His parents. They had visited and they had bought the book that had guided him here, 'The Village of Eaststowe.'

They stopped several feet from a makeshift stage, on it a throne, painted gold, it's seat plush red velvet and, on a side table a gold crown.

'So, who's the King?' asked Jude.

Rosebud frowned.

'Take a guess.'

'I have absolutely no idea.'

'Okay, a clue. A shouty little man who hates people like myself.'

Jude recalled the day he saw Rosebud for the first time and he watched her being shouted out by his neighbour at number 8.

'Not Patrick Fox?'

'Gave it away, didn't I?'

'How on earth did he become King? Who voted him in?'

'I don't know exactly, but I know a man who does!' She turned and shouted. 'Hey Dext! Over here!'

Dexter appeared, he wore a badly fitting brown suit with worn leather patches at the elbows, topped off with a matching flat cap. He neared and with a flourish bowed to Rosebud.

'May I compliment you on your outfit my Lady, you look divine,' he took hold of her hand and kissed it before returning to Dexter the gardener of 3 Willow Walk. 'Christ Rosie you look hot!'

113

'Why thank you kind sir,' Rosebud curtsied, '1950s manners, I love it.' She winked at Jude. 'You see what I was saying? He's come as a poor labourer.'

'Excuse me,' Dexter feigned hurt. 'I'll have you know young lady that I come from a long line of local labourers, my family…'

'Yeah, yeah, we get it Dext, enough now.' She lifted her arms to encompass their surroundings. 'We have a first-time visitor, an explanation please.'

'Indeed, I can see I'm needed here,' he grinned, 'to try to explain away the madness that is taking place in front of our very eyes.'

'That would be appreciated,' said Jude.

'What you are about to see, put out of your mind forever,' his seriousness lasted a few seconds only. 'Or at least until it happens all over again next year, cos it'll save me having to go through the whole flaming lot again.'

'Oh stop waffling Dext' Rosebud laughed. 'And get on with it.'

'I shall begin,' Dexter turned to Jude. 'Have you ever heard the expression, who died and made you King?'

'Of course.'

'Well, in Eaststowe that is exactly what happened. This fair has been going since the 13th century and in the 17th century the then Lord of the Manor, Lord Titus Aquinas Fox, a direct descendant of Eli Fox, he's the one who built the pile up there,' he turned and pointed to the Manor, 'well, he decided to make himself the King of Eaststowe and the title has been handed down ever since.'

'So the Fox family used to live in the Manor?' said Jude.

'Well deduced detective,' Dexter nodded. 'They lived there for centuries apparently.'

'Wow! What happened?'

'If you mean why is Patrick Fox not resident up there,' Dexter put on his pretend sad face, 'well, according to local legend, the descendants of the kindly and socially aware Lord Titus spawned a succession of wrong uns, and - long story short - Patrick's grandfather was a gambler and lost the lot, the Manor, their fortune, everything.'

'That explains a great deal,' said Rosebud.

'Does it?' said Jude.

'Course, it explains why the old man is so delusional, bitter and twisted.'

'But shouldn't Lawson Peterson be the King?' said Jude. 'After all he lives in the Manor.'

'Aha! Not according to Patrick's old man, who insisted on keeping the title of King as he said it belonged to him and his descendants, not to the Manor itself.' Dexter grinned at them. 'And I guess the people who bought the Manor didn't give a monkeys.' He sighed. 'So I guess we're stuck with him until he pops off. The Lord of the Manor does get to open the fair though,' he hinted amusement. 'But not today obvs. because he is currently assisting our local coppers with their enquiries.'

'So who's going to open it?' asked Rosebud.

'Mrs Peterson I guess,' Dexter shrugged. 'But who knows?'

'So what happens when old Fox dies?' asked Jude, his eyes on the preparations taking place on the stage.

'First we have a party,' said Dexter. 'And then, well, here's the thing, the title gets handed down from father to son and Daddy Fox doesn't have a little boy fox cub.'

'Oh dear,' said Rosebud with a grin, 'now that is a shame.'

'But he does have a foxy little vixen.'

'Does he?' Rosebud didn't attempt to hide her surprise.

'Indeed he does.'

'He's actually a father?' said Rosebud. 'To a daughter?'

'In name only.'

'Poor kid.'

'They're estranged, have been for years. Nice lass too, bit up herself sometimes but we all have our funny little ways.' He paused and turned to Rosebud. 'Don't we?'

115

Rosebud pinked up and turned away.

Jude didn't tune into the subtle undertones of the exchange that had taken place between his two neighbours. He was still aghast by the eccentricity of what was taking place around him and so it was he who broke the awkward silence that followed.

'Okay,' he said. 'So when Patrick dies will that be the end of it?'

'Your guess is as good as mine,' Dexter shrugged. 'I guess nowadays they'd be prepared to have a Queen of Eaststowe, but to be honest, I doubt she'd want the job.'

'You know who she is then?' said Jude.

'Yep. You do too.'

The sound of a handbell, like one that would announce the end of playtime in an olden day children's playground, interrupted their chatter and they turned their attention to the stage.

A large woman dressed as a town crier in a red and gold braded jacket with a black triangle hat was standing on the stage. She stilled the bell and raised her voice.

'Hear ye! Hear ye! Thank you good people for being here on this glorious sunshine day! I would like you all to welcome our King.'

The crowd and Dexter cheered their approval. Jude and Rosebud did not.

'Come on,' Dexter turned to his neighbours. 'Join in the fun.'

Overly dressed in the garb of a pantomime King and head held high, Patrick Fox paced slowly onto the stage, headed to his throne and sat down. Once seated he nodded to his subjects. Iris Bell appeared, she crossed to the table and picked up the crown.

'By the power invested in me,' she shouted as she slow stepped towards the King in waiting, 'I hereby crown you, our King. King of Eaststowe,' she positioned the crown on his head, stood back a pace and bobbed a curtsey, before turning and bobbing one to the crowd.

The enthusiasm of the cheering onlookers was equally matched by an excitement of small children as they materialised from every direction and swarmed the front of the stage. Many were

116

dressed in tattered shorts and shirts, a flat cap setting off their street urchin outfits in an effort to recreate an age of poverty long since passed. And each child played their part, grabbing at the coins that the newly crowned King of Eaststowe chucked out to them.

When the last child picked up the last coin Sasha Peterson appeared on the stage and declared the fair to be open.

Half an hour later Dexter had dissolved into the crowd. Inspired by the olde worlde atmosphere, Jude and Rosebud wandered from ride to ride, nostalgia jogging memories as they took it in turns to swap stories of their growing up experiences and they both agreed that – like the old-fashioned fairground rides – life had been a lot simpler in the olden days.

Spud dutifully followed the two of them and sat down beside Jude whenever they stopped to admire a ride, or relate a childhood tale. It was during one such conversation that he let out a bark, interrupting them.

Jude turned to his pet.

'You alright boy?'

Spud barked again and at that moment Jude spotted Dr Fernsby and a woman a couple of feet away.

'Dr Fernsby,' he yelled over, then louder, 'Dr Fernsby.'

The doctor turned around.

'I'm glad you're here,' said Jude. 'Apologies, I've honestly been meaning to contact you, to give you an update.'

'Update?' It was the woman who spoke.

'An update on my investigation.'

'Investigation?' The woman raised her eyebrows.

'Mr Mumford,' the doctor reddened. 'Oh you don't have to worry about that now, call me in a couple of days.'

'What investigation?' asked the woman.

'Mr Mumford, this is my wife.' The doctor cleared his throat and turned to her. 'I'll explain later dear. Mr Mumford has moved to the village to become a tennis coach. Do you think Freya would like lessons?'

117

'What investigation?'

'I'll contact you in a couple of days,' the doctor nodded to Jude. 'Great weather for the fair don't you think? Please excuse us, we need to go and find Freya and Nadia.'

Jude watched the doctor and his wife as they made an awkward getaway.

'What was that all about?' asked Rosebud.

'No idea whatsoever,' Jude shrugged. 'Fancy a drink?'

'Yes please,' it was a female voice, not Rosebud's. Jude spun around and turned on a smile, it was Fearless.

'Hi there, good to see you. How are you?'

'Good thanks. Yourself?'

'I'm doing okay thanks. Any news?'

Fearless laughed.

'If you mean about Chantal, you know I can't tell you.'

'Sorry, can't blame a guy for trying though, can you?' He looked around her. 'Are you on your own?'

'I'm meeting with a friend a bit later.'

'We were just off to the beer tent. Would you like to join us?'

'Hi, I'm Rosebud Paris,' she smiled at Fearless. 'And you are?'

'Sorry, my bad manners,' said Jude. 'Rosebud this is Fearless, she works in the forensics lab. Fearless, this is Rosebud. Rosebud is a writer.'

The two women, nodded to each other.

'Fearless? Please tell me that's your real name,' Rosebud grinned, 'I love it.'

'I'm afraid not,' said Fearless. 'It's what my colleagues, and now indeed most people call me. My real name is Fatema.'

'Well I shall call you Fearless,' said Rosebud. 'So you're investigating Chantal's death?'

'I am indeed.'

118

'How are things going?'

'As I said, I really can't discuss it.'

'Oh well that's told me.'

'Rosebud was a close friend of Chantal's,' said Jude by way of explanation.

'I see,' said Fearless. 'I'm sorry for your loss. It must have been a shock.'

'It was,' Rosebud turned to Jude. 'So how is your investigation going?'

'You're investigating her death?' Fearless turned to Jude. 'Now why doesn't that surprise me.'

They arrived at the beer tent.

'Look, over there, a free table.' Eager to change the subject Jude pointed to a table in the corner.

'Great, what are you having?' Rosebud headed to the bar. 'I'll get the drinks in.'

Several minutes later the three of them were settled, each with a drink in front of them. Spud lay under the table and closed his eyes.

'That is good,' said Rosebud having taken a deep sup of locally made cider. 'Do you ever drink?' She nodded to Jude's glass of soda water and lime.

'I do, only when I'm in the mood though.'

'So what gets you in the mood?' Fearless asked.

'Excuse me?'

'What makes you want to have a drink?' Fearless laughed. 'Is it stressful situations? Is it dependent on the time of day?'

As if she were part of a relay, Rosebud grabbed the baton and took over the conversation.

'Do you drink to relax, or does it depend on who you are with?'

Jude laughed and shook his head.

'I've never really thought about it. I do have to be enjoying myself though.'

'What! You're not enjoying yourself now?' Fearless feigned shock and with a wink returned the baton to Rosebud. She accepted it willingly.

'Here you are with two beautiful women, at the heart of village life and you have the nerve to say you're not enjoying the experience.'

Jude didn't attempt to defend himself; he knew when he was defeated. Mentally he chucked the shovel away and stepped back from the virtual hole he had dug himself.

He picked up his pint glass and stared at Rosebud and then at Fearless as he drunk from it trying not to laugh at their obvious disappointment that their teasing was going no further.

'Well this is fun,' he said as he placed his glass back on the table and looked around the crowded marquee.

People were greeting each other, hugging, kissing, laughing, friends, families and neighbours enjoying the day. Dexter was in the thick of it all, wandering around as a host might at a party. He was indeed popular.

When noise levels allowed, Jude, Rosebud and Fearless made polite conversation. When the laughter got too loud, they paused and drank and smiled at each other.

'Now,' said Rosebud, during a quiet moment. She turned to Jude. 'Come on, the investigation, give us a hint as to how it's going.'

'It's going okay,' he said, taking a sip of his drink. 'I'm beginning to build up a picture.'

'I'm not sure I want to listen to this,' said Fearless.

'But he's doing nothing wrong!' Rosebud turned to Jude. 'You're just digging about a bit, aren't you? Let's face it the police need all the help they can get.'

'I couldn't possibly comment,' said Fearless.

Out of the corner of his eye, Jude spotted a lone figure sitting in the opposite corner, her only companions a bottle of red wine and a half empty glass. It was Sasha Peterson.

'I hate to be rude but would you ladies please excuse me a sec?' He stood up. 'I won't be long.'

'I'm not going anywhere,' Rosebud whispered.

'Neither am I,' said Fearless. 'I've texted my friend and she's meeting me here around 4ish.'

'Spud stay,' Jude got up and looked at his pet. Spud opened his eyes, lifted his head and watched as his master headed off to where Sasha was sitting.

'Mind if I join you?'

'It's a free country.'

'You okay?'

'I'm good.'

'Any news?'

'If you want gossip about my husband, you're wasting your time.'

'I'm not interested in gossip,' he said. 'I just wondered how you are doing?'

'I'm here aren't I?'

'They'll have to release him or charge him soon.'

'He'll be home by tonight.'

'You're sure of that are you?'

'Oh yes.' Sasha picked up her wine glass. 'His lawyer's with him. He'll bring my husband back to me.' She placed the glass between her lips and drained it.

Jude puzzled at her words, she didn't seem very happy about her husband returning, she appeared more resigned to it. He suspected the bottle on the table may not have been her first.

'They'll just want to know where he was when Chantal was attacked.'

'He was with me,' she said. 'I've already told them that.'

Jude spotted Freya Fernsby by the entrance.

'Sorry,' he said. 'You see that young girl by the entrance, you don't happen to know the boy with her do you?'

Sasha followed his gaze and as if a light had been switched on in a darkened room, her eyes lit up.

'That's my darling son Charlie,' she giggled before returning her attention to Jude. 'You must meet him; you are going to have to give him tennis lessons.'

'Am I?'

'You are,' she nodded. 'If you don't, my husband will know that I lied to him the other day and he will put two and two together, come up with sixty-nine and think that we're sleeping together. I can't have that and believe me you don't want that.' She giggled again. 'I'm afraid you have no choice in the matter.' She poured the last of the wine, lifted her glass and attempted a serious instruction. 'Now, you are going to have to be patient with my darling boy. He's not actually at all interested in playing tennis.' Another giggle, 'or any other sport for that matter. But I've explained it to him and he's fine with it.'

'To be honest I'm not sure teaching somebody who doesn't actually want to play tennis is a good idea.'

'Trust me, it's a good idea. Charlie loves his father and he knows it will please him. Can we start say, in three weeks? I'll call you to arrange a time.'

'If you're sure…'

My first actual booking.

'I am. Besides, it will cheer Lawson up when he gets…'

Her son's voice interrupted her.

'Mum!'

Sasha and Jude watched Charlie as he pushed through the throng of people and made his way towards them.

'Mum! It's dad! He's here! They've released him.' He hissed the words as if attempting to ensure they reached only his mother's

122

ears. But the news had penetrated the crowd and a path opened up in front of him like waves parting across a sea. He was now the focus of attention and the locals followed him with their ears, their eyes and their tongues.

Within seconds the owner of the ground they all stood on appeared at the entrance. His presence shushed the crowd to silence. He spotted his wife and son and made his way towards them.

'Told you,' Sasha whispered to Jude before turning to face her husband.

'Lawson, darling, you're here… are you okay? Isn't it a lovely day for the fair?'

'There you are!' he shouted at her before he turned to Jude. 'You again!'

'We were talking about tennis lessons for Charlie,' said Sasha. 'He's so looking forward to them.'

'Course yeah,' said Lawson, backtracking on his anger. 'Well you'll have to chat some other time.' He turned to his wife. 'Come on, I need you at home.'

The path to the entrance was still clear, Lawson nodded to Jude by way of farewell and headed out, followed by his wife, followed by their son.

At the marquee entrance Lawson stopped and gazed up the hill towards his Manor House for several seconds before turning to face the ocean of eyes keeping watch on him.

'Right you lot,' he shouted. 'I'm telling you now, I had nothing to do with Chantal's death,' his words silenced the hum of whispers. 'And I'll sue any bugger who suggests otherwise. You hear me!' He grabbed his wife's hand and pulled her to him. 'Come on love, I need a shower… and I could murder a flaming drink.'

20

Rosebud was in her front garden putting the finishing touches to her table. At the centre, were three bottles of Dom Perignon, three flute glasses, a jug of iced water and a couple of bowls of nuts.

Next door Jude was sitting in his garden chair, clasping a can of beer, his feet resting on their dividing wall.

'How is this going to work?' he asked as he eyed Rosebud's rather full table and then compared it to his own empty plastic one.

'Well, we normally just share everything,' she said. 'But don't worry as it's your first time you don't have to contribute.' She nodded to her table. 'Feeling thirsty or peckish?'

'I am a bit,' he took a swig from his beer can, 'but I'll hold fire, save my hunger for the barbeque. It's been ages.'

'Shouldn't be too long, Dexter's on the case.'

As if the subject of food had been transmitted along the terrace of cottages, Dexter appeared at the garden gate carrying a plate in each hand.

'Anybody hungry?'

'Starving,' said Jude.

'What he said,' said Rosebud.

'Well,' Dexter lifted the smaller of the two plates, 'that there is all your veggie food cooked by my own fair hands,' he grinned at Rosebud. 'On a separate grill, using separate utensils of course.'

'Thanks Dext, it looks brill.'

'Brill? Brill? Is that all the thanks I get for my efforts?' He placed both plates onto the table and stretched out his arm. 'Madam, I think my expert culinary skills deserve a quick snog.'

Rosebud leant forward and, giggling like a teenager, grasped his hand. He pulled her up and she fell into his arms. The kiss lasted a few seconds only. As their lips joined, Jude reddened and bent down to talk to Spud who was half asleep under the table. By the time he returned to a usual seating position, Rosebud was rested back giggling in her deckchair again. She turned to Jude and laughed.

'I hope we didn't embarrass you.'

'He's an ex-copper, he doesn't get embarrassed,' said Dexter. 'I bet he's seen it all.'

'Are you two,' Jude hesitated for a few seconds, pointed to Rosebud then Dexter, 'together? A thing?'

'Of course not!' Rosebud shrunk back in pretend shock. 'We're just friends.'

'Good friends,' said Dexter with a wink to her. 'That was just a bit of fun.' He nodded to the larger of the two plates he had placed on the table. It was piled high with cooked meats, 'that one there is for those of us who need dead animal flesh to survive.'

'Do you have to?' said Rosebud.

'Apologies dear lady,' Dexter gave a short bow. 'That was meant to be a bit of fun also, but upon reflection it was an insensitive comment. Now where shall we eat?'

'I thought we were eating out here?' said Jude.

'I mean,' said Dexter, 'at which table. It seems a bit anti-social if we each stay in our own garden.'

'I would say we could eat in my garden,' said Rosebud 'But Spud would have to stay put. He'd upset Simeon.'

'What do you usually do?' Jude asked. 'What did you do last year?'

Rosebud recalled the joyous event that had taken place the previous year for a split second only before agonising memories of recent events resurfaced, she paled and turned away.

'Sorry,' said Jude, 'I'm sorry...'

'It's okay,' she stood up, forced a smile, pulled out a tissue from her pocket, and turned and went indoors.

'Numpty,' said Dexter.

'I didn't think.'

125

'Clearly,' said Dexter. 'I know what, how about we all come to you? You've got the largest table so it makes sense.'

Jude agreed and so between them they moved chairs, grabbed Rosebud's table cloth, champagne and snacks and set the table. Dexter even went and got a jam jar from his cottage and picked a small bunch of bright orange California Poppy's and pink Salvias from his back garden and placed them at the centre.

When Rosebud appeared again carrying a large salad bowl, the table was dressed and waiting for diners. Dexter stood at Jude's open garden gate with a tea towel over his arm and a smile.

'Will Madam kindly step this way?'

A couple of minutes later the three of them were sitting around the table enjoying their food. They drank champagne as they ate and as their tongues loosened they started to chat about themselves. Rosebud spoke about her home in North London, Dexter talked about his time away travelling while Jude successfully managed to change the subject.

'That was great meeting up with Fearless today,' he said looking at Rosebud. 'You two really seemed to hit it off.'

'She's a very interesting lady,' said Rosebud. 'Cutting up and examining bodies though. Yuk, all that blood!' She picked up her phone and looked at the time. 'Excuse me a sec.'

She got up and went back to her cottage.

'Was it something I said?' Jude looked at Dexter and shrugged. 'Again.'

'Not this time,' Dexter grinned. 'Nope, it's time for dessert.' He stood up, cleared the dirty plates and brushed the table cloth clean. When Rosebud returned to Jude's garden a couple of minutes later she carried a tray with a freshly baked plate of scones and three pots, butter, jam and cream.

'They smell good,' said Jude nodding at the scones.

'Oh they are,' said Dexter. 'Rosie's freshly baked scones are bloody fab.'

'Why thank you,' she nodded at Dexter then turned to Jude, 'Are you a butter, cream, jam person or a butter, jam, cream person?'

'I have absolutely no idea,' Jude laughed.

'I've always thought it was a load of bollocks too,' she said. 'I normally do one of each - both taste the same to me.'

'So, are you going to enlighten us?' Jude grinned at Dexter.

'I'd love to mate, but you'll have to tell me what you're on about.'

'Who is old Fox's daughter?'

'You said we knew who she was,' said Rosebud. 'Come on, spill the beans.'

'Okay, okay,' Dexter's eyes glinted mischief. 'Keep it to yourselves though, she don't like it spread around.'

'Come on Dext, who you talking about?'

'Promise you'll keep it to yourselves?'

'Will do,' said Jude.

'I promise,' Rosebud ran her finger and thumb zip like along her lips to confirm her silence.

'It's none other than our very own Detective Inspector Jones.'

Neither Jude nor Rosebud attempted to hide their shock. Jude's was the silent form, his facial expression speaking his feelings. Rosebud's shock took the form of a verbal assault, questioning how 'that old bastard' could have fathered somebody who seemed relatively normal (Dexter grinned when she said that), an upstanding citizen and an officer of the law at that. Dexter did point out that it was probably because she had moved away from Eaststowe and him at the age of five.

Knees up Mother Brown blared over the sound system, and in an effort to comply with the instructions in the song, a group of perfectly choreographed teenagers and young children were chucking up their knees as if they were in a music hall dance off, before transforming their routine to a formulated version of 'Step in Time' from the film Mary Poppins.

A squeal from the sound system made Dexter wince.

'Bloody hell, that's my sound system,' he said. 'Best go before they knacker it. Save me some scones Rosie.'

'Rosie?' said Jude when Dexter was out of earshot. 'Do you mind being called that?'

Rosebud reddened and nodded.

'I do!' she said. 'He just does it to annoy me, I think. I call him Dext in return, trouble is, I think he likes it.'

'Probably,' Jude grinned.

'So, let's get it over with.'

'Pardon?'

'Ask me anything,' Rosebud sat back, eyes closed, legs stretched out enjoying the evening sun. 'I said I'd answer your questions, remember?'

'Of course I remember,' Jude opened his mouth and was just about to ask his first question but Rosebud stood up suddenly.

'Hang on a sec.' She picked up a full bottle of champagne, wedged it between her knees and popped it open, the fizz gushed everywhere.

'Yaaay,' she shouted as the cork headed off to the street.

Two women standing in front of Jude's gate turned to her.

'Show-off,' shouted the younger of the two, a skinny lass with pink and blue hair.

'Blimey! You have really upset them,' Jude whispered to Rosebud. He expected her to snipe back, or to sit with a self-conscious look of hurt. There was neither. 'Well, I must say, you've taken that well.'

Rosebud refilled her glass, poured another and handed it to Jude.

'The way I see life is that you can take things well or you can take things badly,' she laughed. 'And if a person I really do not care for makes a rude comment about me why on earth would I let it bother me?'

'How very mature of you.'

'Cheers. Let's get pissed.'

They chinked glasses.

Spud was still half asleep under the table and Jude heard him let out a heavy sigh. He leant down, patted his pet's head and slipped him a segment of scone. It was gone in a mouthful.

'I saw that.'

'It was just a small piece. So, are you going to let me into the secret of why some of the villagers don't like you?'

'Aha! Is this anything to do with the case? Or are you just being nosey?'

'Depends on your answer.'

'How very honest of you,' she giggled. 'Well, I bought this house just over six years ago.'

'You've been here a while then.'

'Sort of.'

'Sort of?'

'As I suppose you've already gathered, I don't actually live here all the time.'

'Okay, so It's your second home – but surely there must be loads of people who have second homes here?'

'There are. But according to some villagers we put up house prices and price locals out of the market.'

'Aha!' Jude cleared his throat. 'Do you think they've got a point?'

'Maybe,' she lifted her glass to her eyeline and gazed into the bubbles.

'You'd think they'd be quite excited having a successful writer in the village.' Jude spoke just as Rosebud was about to sip her champagne, she spluttered and burst out laughing.

'You think?'

'You could open fetes maybe, give something back.'

'Oh yes! I can see the local headlines, Rosebud Paris, author of....'

But her sentence was drowned out by the sound system blasting out that a conga line was forming. They both turned their attention to the street where their neighbours were forming a disorderly line. There was much hilarity, laughter and drunken shouting as a ragged conga set off enroute to the church, hollering, singing, arms waving, legs kicking, all completely out of synch with the music and with each other.

'Not tempted to join in?' said Jude.

'You must be joking! You?'

'Me?' Jude shook his head. 'No thanks. I'm not a conga person, not my idea of fun at all.'

Jude had only ever once in his life been involved in a conga. It was at his wedding reception; he and his new wife were about to leave to jet off to their Seychelles honeymoon when they were grabbed and folded into the bosom of their guests' conga line-up. It was only now, upon reflection, that he recalled the details. He was behind his wife and she was behind Zac, his best man, clinging to his waist.

'You know, some people in this village actually think I'm weird,' Rosebud feigned shock. 'Moi? Weird? I ask you.'

Jude wiped the conga image from his mind. It wasn't easy, not helped in the least because Rosebud, with her auburn hair and wide smile, struck an uncanny likeness to the woman he had once been wed to.

'Weird? You don't strike me as being particularly odd,' before adding with a grin, 'well, maybe just a little, but in a good way…'

'Thank you,' she giggled. 'I'll take that as a compliment.'

'It's a village. Small communities work with an alternative mindset.'

'Get you with your personality study,' she burst out laughing but it was short lived. She leant forward, placed her champagne flute onto the table and in a second, humour deserted her again. 'And then of course there's the whole Chantal thing.'

'She wasn't very popular, was she?'

'Some would say with good reason.'

'There's quite a lot on the web, a car accident, a couple of donkeys went missing. Are you going to fill me in?'

130

She shook her head.

'No. It was extremely unpleasant and it was all years ago so it can't have anything to do with her death.'

'Are you certain of that?'

'I'm absolutely sure,' Rosebud nodded.

'Okay,' said Jude. 'Here's a question for you. I don't suppose you've got any idea who inherits her estate?'

'What? Do you think that might be a motive?'

'Could well be, money is a great motivator to kill...'

But she wasn't killed, she was attacked, and it was me who left her to die.

'... I mean, to hurt somebody. Any ideas?'

'Well Stefan of course, that's if he's still alive.'

'Did Chantal think he was?'

'At one point she seemed convinced Lawson had killed him,' she said. 'But in spite of that she never stopped looking for him. I do know she made a new Will though.'

'Did she indeed? Any idea what was in it?'

'All she said was that if Stefan turned up alive, he got everything and if he didn't, she'd made alternative arrangements. She didn't say what they were.'

'I see,' he paused for a few seconds. 'Do you mind if I ask how you and Chantal met?'

'It was at a conference,' she said. 'Nearly twenty years ago now.'

'You've known her a while then.'

'I was just a kid,' she smiled and fluttered her eyelashes.

'Of course,' this time it was Jude who grinned.

'And, well, we kept in touch over the years. Christmas cards that sort of thing. We met up again about eight years ago after my writing career really took off and long story short, I came to visit her here one day and fell in love with the place.'

131

'It's a beautiful village.'

'So, when I was on the look-out for investment property outside of London,' she paused, 'it seemed like the obvious place.'

'I'm guessing your cottage has gone up in value since you bought it?'

'Now you're just being bloody nosey!'

'Sorry, yes, I suppose I am,' Jude reddened. 'Can't help myself sometimes.'

'If you must know, my investments have nearly doubled in value so all good.' She lowered her eyes, and looked thoughtful for a few seconds. 'The only downer really is that I didn't realise when I moved here just how much Chantal was disliked in the village.'

'Would it have made a difference if you had known?'

'Probably not,' she shrugged.

'Any idea how Chantal landed up here?'

'Originally she moved here to be closer to her brother, she got a job as a teacher at the local school.' She sat silent for a short while. 'By the way, don't expect any sleep later, there's going to be singing and dancing for half the night.'

'Oh dear. Not my idea of fun, but at least it's only once a year.'

Relaxed from the alcohol, Rosebud sat back and shut her eyes. Jude mirrored her movement reclining in his chair and stretching his legs out.

'So, what is your idea of fun then?' Rosebud asked.

'I'm not sure anymore,' Jude thought for a moment, his voice a whisper against the backdrop of shrieks and laughter. 'Spending time at home, going out walking over the Fens with Spud, I suppose.'

'Anything else? There must be something.'

'I listen to music, watch films, the usual stuff. You?'

'Apart from writing? Well, yoga, oh, and I do jigsaws, I've been doing a lot lately.'

132

'Snap!' said Jude. 'Sorry, I know that's a card game. I love a jigsaw. We used to do them when I was a kid.'

'Have you got any? I've got loads. Maybe we could do swaps?'

'Sounds good,' he said. He picked up his champagne glass and drained it. 'So what other hobbies do you have? You look like a fun-time girl to me.'

'Fun-time girl?' she placed her hand on her heart and feigned shock. 'Mr Mumford, are you chatting me up by any chance?'

'Would that be a problem?'

She tried to lean forward out of her laid-back deckchair but didn't quite make it, she giggled, took a deep breath and then tried again. She managed it this time and placed her empty glass on the table. Their eyes met; her laughter stilled.

'Look, sorry,' she reddened. 'I've had way too much to drink.'

The silence that followed spoke louder than the laughter from the street and told Jude all he needed to know. He cleared his throat.

'Okay,' he said after a couple of minutes. 'Back to Chantal, I heard she came into money?'

'She did. It wasn't a huge sum but I was amazed at how quickly she spent it. I know she didn't pay that much for the land she bought from Saffron.'

'I heard that. I also heard she promised Saffron she'd keep it as a wildflower meadow.'

'She was sorry she lied,' Rosebud stared at the ground. 'But I think she looked upon it as a means to an end. I mean, if she had paid what the land was actually worth, she would never have been able to afford to build the pet cemetery.'

'Don't defend her. She befriended a vulnerable person so that she could take advantage of her.'

'She didn't, it wasn't like that!'

The sun whispered its' goodnight to the residents of Willow Walk and as it did Rosebud and Jude sat silent, each pursuing their own thoughts, pondering the twists and swerves of their conversation.

'Well I'm glad I got that sorted.' It was Dexter walking up the path with an unopened bottle of cider. 'Missed me?'

Dexter was oblivious to the fact that he was not on Rosebud's or Jude's radar so he continued his one-sided conversation.

'I've just been giving two young would-be DJ's lessons on how not to bugger up my sound system,' he placed his bottle of cider onto the table and poured himself a glass of champagne. 'And it's bloody hard work I can tell you.' After a couple of gulps he realised he was being ignored and turned to Rosebud.

'Please tell me you haven't asked him yet.'

Rosebud returned his gaze but said nothing.

'Oh man! You've asked him haven't you?' he spoke louder this time. 'We agreed! We said we'd ask him together.'

'Relax,' said Rosebud. 'I haven't asked him.'

'Asked me?' said Jude. 'Asked me what?'

'Good,' Dexter sat down. 'Now is as good a time as any.' He turned to Jude. 'Right…'

Jude's phone pinged; he reached for it from his back pocket. A new email from his colleague in France. It told him one thing he already knew; Olga Kaine had lived in France for several years, and it told him something he did not know; there was no record of an Olga Kaine ever having been married or giving birth to a baby.

Dexter coughed loudly but Jude's full attention was on his phone.

'Bloody blimey,' Dexter shouted. 'Dude! Wakey bloody wakey.'

Jude looked up; two pairs of eyes stared unblinking at him.

'Sorry, just checking my emails.' He put his phone back into his pocket. 'So what is it you wanted to ask me?'

'Well,' said Dexter, 'I… sorry, I mean we,' he pointed at Rosebud and then at himself. 'Well, we've been thinking…'

'And talking,' said Rosebud. 'And we had a great idea, you're going to love it.'

'Am I?' said Jude, 'you're sure about that are you?'

'Absolutely,' said Dexter.

'Why do I think I'm not going to like the sound of this?'

'Relax mate,' said Dexter. 'Seriously, it's a great idea. Just keep an open mind.'

'Come on then, don't keep me in suspense, out with it.'

'Well,' Dexter spoke slowly, chose his words carefully, 'You know how you are looking into Chantal's death?'

Suspicious now, Jude nodded, pondering eyes seeking out what the two of them were up to.

I let her die. I owe her.

'We, I mean me and Rosebud, we can help you investigate. We can be like your assistants.'

'Brilliant isn't it?' said Rosebud. 'We knew you'd love it.'

The three neighbours took it in turns to look at each other. During the exchange Rosebud and Dexter grinned at each other and then at Jude while Jude for his part didn't smile, or grin or look even the slightest bit happy at the suggestion.

'Oh no, sorry, that would never work,' he shook his head.

'But we'd make a great team,' said Rosebud. 'And let's face it I do have a vested interest.'

'As do I,' said Dexter.

'Do you?' said Jude.

'Course I do, these people, the ones you're investigating, they're my people, my tribe, I know them.'

'And?'

'He'd be like our Indian guide,' said Rosebud. 'Our wisened sage.'

'Exactly that,' said Dexter. 'Every sleuth needs a sage, somebody who knows the people, the lie of the land. I grew up here,

I know who to trust and who to be wary of. I can stop you getting into trouble, I can…'

'I'm sorry, it's out of the question,' said Jude. 'I have to do this on my own.'

I owe Chantal Dubois.

He watched as their faces, which, only minutes ago had been brimming with hope and positivity, flattened in defeat.

'Well in that case I withdraw my services,' said Dexter. 'Completely.' He picked up the champagne bottle and refilled Rosebud's glass, then opened his bottle of cider, picked it up and pointed it at Rosebud. 'And so does she.'

'Confirmed,' said Rosebud, nodding her agreement. 'I will no longer be available to answer any of your questions.'

'Now don't be like that,' Jude looked one to the other.

'Mate,' said Dexter. 'You are not a team player. So go play on your own.'

Jude reddened and unsure of what to say, stood up.

'Excuse me, I need the loo,' he said and disappeared indoors.

A few seconds after Jude disappeared into his cottage, Simeon appeared on Rosebud's dividing wall.

'Simmy, here my darling,' Rosebud patted her lap.

Simeon jumped down onto the ground, went to jump onto his mistress's lap but spotted Spud still asleep under the table. He veered away, bolted towards Jude's cottage and disappeared through the front door.

'SIMEON!' Rosebud shouted so loudly, several people in the street turned around and stared. She stood up but swayed slightly and put her hand on the table to steady herself.

'You stay put,' Dexter jumped up and followed Simeon. 'I'll go get him.'

After a few seconds Simeon had not reappeared, neither had Dexter. After a minute or so the shouting started. Dexter's voice, then Jude's, then Dexter's, then both at once. Dexter reappeared first, he stood, filling the doorway, Jude was just behind him.

'We're bloody suspects!' Dexter shouted to Rosebud.

'What?' Rosebud stared at Dexter, at Jude and then back to Dexter. 'What are you talking about?'

'No wonder he doesn't want us helping him! We're on his bloody whiteboard thing - as suspects!'

Rosebud turned to Jude, her usually pale face turned ashen grey.

'He's got everything written down...'

'It's my whiteboard,' said Jude. 'It's where I dump all of the information I gather.'

'You, me, we're on it! We're suspects! It's there written down in big red letters!'

Rosebud stood up, stared at Jude, shook her head and weaving slightly headed for his front door.

Dexter stood aside to let her pass but Jude stood his ground just inside the door, barring her way.

'Don't,' he said, 'please don't.'

'Mate, move before I make you,' said Dexter.

Jude sighed and stepped aside.

Rosebud was in the cottage for nearly five minutes. When she reappeared in the doorway she stared at Jude.

'How could you?' she said, her eyes brimming with tears. 'So that's why you don't want us to help you.'

'Let me explain...'

'I... I can't believe it. You actually think I could have killed my dear, dear friend.'

Without another word, she headed for the front gate and back to her own home.

21

The woman waited again for Stefan at the station. She yearned to hear the piano sing out Pachelbel's 'Canon in D' once more so that she could be transported back to a happier time, a happier place. She was there the following Sunday morning and the Sunday morning after that. Each time she waited nearly two hours before making her way to the cemetery to place flowers on her son's grave.

On the third Sunday morning, instead of going to the station, she packed a carrier bag with food - bread, biscuits, tins of beans and fruit - and went in search of him.

She eventually found him, crashed out in the corner of an alleyway. She waited for him to wake up but when he did stir, he didn't recognise her, or remember the piano, or the conversation they had had.

She tried to get help for him, but he turned it down, even walking out of an overnight shelter because it was 'too noisy.'

But she was persistent. And every week she went and sought him out, a bag of food in one hand and often a jacket or blanket or a pair of trainers in the other. Most times he would be asleep when she found him, hidden from view under a railway arch or similar. He looked, as ever, scruffy, unkempt, but more peaceful in sleep than he ever looked during waking hours.

She would never wake him. She had been told by the homeless shelter that people who live on the streets often sleep in the day because it was safer for them, so she would place her gifts beside him then back away and return home to what was left of her family.

22

'Blimey, it's you,' Dexter looked shocked to see Jude standing on his doorstep. 'What do you want?'

'I've come to say sorry,' said Jude. 'For the whole suspect thing.'

'Mate, it's not me you need to be apologizing to,' Dexter put his hands into the top pockets of his jeans, as if he were a naughty schoolboy, 'If I were you, I'd be knocking on Rosie's front door and groveling an apology to her. Not just yet though. She'll probably lump you one.'

Head down, Jude nodded

'Okay.'

'Bloody blimey, you're unbelievable. How could you? Me and Rosebud, suspects! What the hell were you thinking?'

'How was I to know you were going to go inside my bloody house?'

'Mate, I went to rescue Simeon.'

'You read my personal mood board. You had no right.'

'Oh, pull your finger out of your backside. Course we've got a right to know if you think we're killers. You bloody arse!'

'I'm sorry, but 'suspect' it's just a word, I don't actually think you or Rosebud for that matter actually killed her.'

Neither of them killed her, it was me, I let her die.

'Mate,' said Dexter. 'Trust me, I'm now okay on this.' His face broke a smile. 'Me mates think it's hilarious.'

'You've told your mates?'

'Course, they think I'm well hard.'

'I write everything down,' said Jude, 'and okay I added the word suspect against yours and Rosebud's names, but that was ages ago…'

'Me, I sort of get that. But Rosie? Suggesting she killed her closest friend? It's bloody ridiculous. She wouldn't hurt a living thing. I do her garden so believe me I know.'

'If it helps, I've updated my whiteboard, rubbed it out, the word I mean.'

'That's a start. Now mate, if you want to right this, I suggest that in a couple of weeks – when she's calmed a bit - you go round there, knock on her front door, get down on your knees and grovel an apology.'

23

Jude was at home updating his tennis spreadsheet. He had had several enquiries and had three clients booked in for the following week. One of them was Charlie Peterson and as Sasha had made it clear to him that her son was only taking lessons to appease his bullying father, Jude was not looking forward to it.

He was so engrossed in his spreadsheet, he did not notice a dark blue Nissan hatchback pull up outside his cottage, or the man that got out of it. It was the sound of his front gate clicking open that alerted him. He recognised the man walking up his path and he opened the front door just as Dr Fernsby arrived on the doorstep.

The doctor reddened and stepped back.

'I'm sorry to disturb you,' he said.

'No problem,' Jude opened the door wide. 'Please come in.'

The doctor didn't move other than to lower his eyes.

'Apologies,' said Jude, 'I've been meaning to get in touch to give you an update. You were on my list of things to do.'

Dr Fernsby lifted his head and made eye contact for the first time.

'No, no,' he shook his head, rubbed his nose with his hand then moved around to his ear, tugging at the lobe. 'I don't want, I… don't need an update.'

'Okaaay,' Jude stretched the word out, he was puzzled now. The doctor appeared nervous, he didn't want to come in and he didn't want an update. 'So what can I do for you?'

Dr Fernsby's eyes wandered around the front garden. When he did speak, his words were mumbled.

'I need to stop this,' he said. 'All of it. I need to stop it now.'

'In what way?'

'I need to accept what's happened and move on.'

141

'That sounds like a plan,' said Jude. He wasn't sure if he was being listened to so he spoke louder. 'If it helps, I think you're doing the right thing. For yourself and for your family.'

'Thank you.' The doctor made eye contact again and gave a polite nod. He didn't move though.

'Is there anything else?'

'I need you to stop your investigation. Now.'

'May I ask why?'

'You were right. I didn't do it and as you said the police have now realised that. I just need to put it all behind me.'

'Not to worry,' said Jude. 'Of course I shan't bother you with any future updates.'

'But I need you to stop,' said the doctor. 'Please.'

Jude stepped forward, when he spoke he surprised himself at how loud his voice was. His anger was not directed fully at the doctor. It was at the characters with their hush hush backgrounds and their mysterious motives and their furtive secrets. But of course, Dr Fernsby was not to know that.

'Rest assured I will not bother you with any updates,' he said. 'But also rest assured that I will not stop my investigation. I will find out who attacked Chantal and I will make sure that whoever it was is brought to justice.'

24

Jude didn't wait two weeks to go and apologise to Rosebud. He waited one week. He didn't go and knock on her front door either. He waited until the sun was setting on an early summer evening, a time when he knew his neighbour would be out in her back garden.

Rosebud was on her blue and white sunbed in the middle of the lawn. She had on oversized shades so Jude could not see if she were awake or asleep. Simeon was laying on her middle and Jude could see her hand on his back as it stroked him gently, so he took a chance.

He had on his table a newly purchased bottle of Dom Perignon. Clutching it and a couple of tumblers he went and stood by their wall. He coughed, waited several seconds, nothing. He coughed again, louder this time. Still nothing.

'Rosebud,' he spoke quietly. 'Are you awake?'

'Get lost.'

'I'll take that as a yes,' he said. 'I come in peace.'

'When I open my eyes, I expect to see a white flag then.'

'I've got better than that,' he lifted the champagne bottle and clinked together the tumblers. 'Much better.'

Rosebud turned and lifted her glasses.

'As peace offerings go, that's not bad.'

'Look, I'm sorry. Can we talk? I just want to explain.'

'You've got until that bottle runs dry,' she said.

The bottle and tumblers were balanced on top of the wall and Jude and Rosebud pulled up their chairs either side. Jude poured the champagne and explained to her about his mood board, how he liked to be open minded and look at every option and how he had learned to look at a case from every angle.

The alcohol softened them both. She teased him about drinking, he didn't try to defend himself and when the champagne ran dry Jude leapt the wall into her garden and they sat around her patio table with a second bottle from her fridge.

It wasn't the warm evening or the red hues of the setting sun or Rosebud forgiving him, it was a combination of all three of those things combined with the several glasses of champagne that he downed, that prompted Jude to change his mind.

'Look, if you want to give me a hand to try to find out what happened to Chantal, you can.'

Rosebud jumped up, screamed with joy and opened her arms, Jude pushed himself up, let out a quiet shriek of pretend joy and the two of them hugged it out.

'Dexter too?' Rosebud shouted. 'You know he couldn't have hurt her, don't you?'

Jude nodded.

'Dexter too.'

'He's going to be such a help. He knows all about everyone. Hang on, I'll text him.'

Forty-five minutes later the sun had disappeared and the two of them were still out there, halfway through their third bottle.

'Right, now we're a team,' she winked at him. 'I need to understand you better. I want to be clear in my own mind that you could not have attacked my friend.'

Jude sighed but held his smile.

Do me a favour…

'I'm listening.'

'Who are you?'

'Pardon?' Jude spurted a short drunken laugh.

'I want to know who you are. I mean who you really are.'

'Blimey,' Jude laughed. 'I've no idea, but I'll tell you what, when I find out you'll be the first to know!'

'Good answer!' she laughed. 'Let's start with,' she picked up the bottle of Dom Perignon and emptied the last of the champagne into his glass, 'why are you here?'

144

'To apologise,' said Jude. 'I was wrong to suggest you were a suspect and I'm here to beg your forgiveness.'

'I don't mean sitting here silly.' The shadows patchworked across her face and hair, but her eyes glistened. 'I mean really here, in Eaststowe? You don't come across as a country boy to me. I reckon you're more of a townie.' She picked up her glass, held it to her lips, stared to space for a few seconds, before draining it and returning it to the table.

Jude stayed silent, trying to formulate an answer.

'I needed a change of direction in life,' he said. 'And, well, I decided on here. My parents came here years ago, in fact they got engaged here, on the day of the fair apparently. When I realised I needed to turn a corner in life, I thought I'd pay the place a visit and I fell in love with it.'

'Same as me then.'

'Yep. So, as my assistant, can you tell me about your friend? I would like to know who she really was.'

Jude could see the change as the woman sitting opposite transferred her gaze from the present to the past.

'I'll tell you something,' she paused and after a few seconds added, 'Chantal… in spite of everything she did and what happened, deep down, she was a good person, honestly she was.'

'You were her friend,' said Jude. 'So you would say that.'

When she did speak again, her voice was flat, reciting a fact as she understood it.

'She changed when her niece died,' she said without moving. 'And again, when her brother disappeared. She was frantic, they were so close. And then, after she had the accident, well, she became a totally different person.'

'I heard.'

'I think she thought she was being punished for some of the things she'd done,' said Rosebud. 'And, well, she did a lot of soul searching, she really wanted to make amends, right her wrongs.'

'Tragic events can change a person, and she certainly sounds as if she had her fair share, and over such a short period of time too.'

'She was genuinely sorry for the way she'd behaved.'

'She said that to you, did she?'

'Not in so many words, but she did start to talk about karma.' She bent forward loosened her hair from its pony tail and shook it out. Auburn strands tumbled across her face and she combed her fingers through them before sitting up. Her eyes moistened again and she wiped away a tear.

'She pleaded guilty after the accident; she didn't try and wriggle out of it.'

'Ahoy there!' It was Dexter in his garden.

'Over here, we're on my patio,' Rosebud shouted back.

Clutching a bottle of cider, Dexter was over his and Rosebud's walls and with them in seconds. He turned to Jude.

'Respect mate.' He opened the bottle and placed it on the table. 'I knew you'd come right in the end.'

'Took his time but he got there,' said Rosebud.

'Now, we need a team name,' Dexter looked at Jude. 'I know! I know! How about Team Mumford?'

Dexter grinned at Rosebud who beamed her approval. He then turned his gaze to Jude, who, thanks to the several glasses of champagne he had downed, nodded his approval and agreed it was a great name.

25

Two days later and Jude still had a headache from the champagne. A marathon walk over the Fens had helped, but he swore to himself he would never touch the stuff again. He sat gazing out of his front window. Dexter was outside securing garden tools to the roof of his Land Rover. It reminded him that his neighbour was due round later that afternoon to tidy the garden.

He sighed a breath of envy at the obvious pleasure Dexter got from his work. One day, when the Mumford Tennis Academy was up and running, he hoped he would get as much satisfaction and give as much pleasure to his neighbours and to the community he now lived in.

After lunch Jude moved his laptop outside to his back garden. It was a quiet place with few distractions other than birdsong and he quickly settled down to work. Just before 3pm, a thump made him look up. A garden rake had landed on his lawn, thump, a spade, thump, a garden fork, thump, a canvas bag. Then Dexter arrived the same way flying over the wall wearing a bright blue t-shirt and khaki shorts and landing a perfect ten between two lavender bushes.

'Greetings boss,' he shouted over to Jude, lifting his arm in salute. 'Anything in particular you want doing?'

'No, no, you carry on, do whatever it is you need to,' said Jude waving him to get on with it. 'You are after all the expert.'

And that is what Dexter did.

Nearly two hours later a cough interrupted Jude. Dexter was standing in the middle of the lawn arms outspread.

'What do you think?' he shouted.

Jude hardly recognized his garden, it was tidier, more colourful, newly planted Verbena Bonariensis, fresh trimmed Salvias, newly cut grass, he breathed deeply, inhaling the scent.

'Brill.,' he said. 'Thanks. I'm no longer letting the side down.'

147

'Very important that,' said Dexter. 'Not letting the side down. People in this terrace like out back to look good.'

'So I've heard.'

'They frown at untidy gardens,' Dexter gave a short laugh. 'At least that's what I tell my customers.'

'Cup of tea? Coffee maybe?'

'No thanks. A glass of water would be great though.'

Jude got a jug of iced water and two tumblers from the kitchen. Spud followed him in and then back out again expecting a treat. But on this occasion, there was none.

By the time Jude got back, Dexter was chucking his tools and bag back over the wall into his own garden. When done, he sat in the middle of the lawn.

'There you go,' Jude handed him the tumbler and sat down next to him. 'So do you mind if I ask, how long have you been playing guitar?'

Dexter's expression changed to one of concern.

'It doesn't annoy you does it?'

'No, no, not at all,' Jude tried to reassure his neighbour. 'I was listening to you the other night. You play really well.'

'Be a bit sad if I couldn't knock out a tune. I've been playing for yonks. Do you play?'

Jude shook his head.

'Playing an instrument has always been a total mystery to me.'

Spud sighed and headed off to the bush beside the shed where he had hidden a half-eaten bone.

'It's really not hard, it's like anything, you just have to practice.' Dexter leant over and picked up the tumbler. 'How's our investigation going? Any updates?'

'Bit slow.'

Dexter stretched his legs out in front of him at angles, placed the tumbler between them and chuckled.

148

'So now we are officially your assistants we should catch up on a regular basis.'

'I suppose so,' Jude laughed.

'We must talk to each other, keep each other informed. You should try it sometime.'

'Thanks for that.'

'Now don't be like that boss. I'm excited. You do realise this is the most exciting thing to happen to me since…'

'Since when?'

'Since forever…'

'What about Rosebud?'

'Oh, it won't be the most exciting thing that's happened to her. But she's all for it, course she is. They were good mates.'

'I know.'

'So where do we start? You now have access to my extensive knowledge base. Use me, ask me whatever you like. My mind is at your disposal.'

'Okay,' Jude smiled at his over enthusiastic neighbour. 'You've lived around here a while, haven't you?'

'All my life.'

'So, you must know Saffron then, the woman in the cottage by the pet cemetery?'

'Course, we were at school together,' he picked up the tumbler and drained it.

'Really?' Jude hesitated. 'So, was she as weird then as she is now?'

'She wasn't weird at all, the opposite in fact. She was perfectly normal, a great kid.'

'Was she?'

'And she had loads of friends. A few wrong-uns, as you would expect, attracted by the money.'

'Woah!' said Jude. 'Attracted by the money?'

149

'Her parents were loaded,' said Dexter. 'Loads of the lads were after her, in truth I think she enjoyed the attention.'

'Any names?'

'Lawson for one, he was always asking her out. He was an arsehole even in those days, they were mates I think, but that was all.'

'What about her parents?'

'They owned all the land around the cottage she's living in, and a few of the cottages dotted around. A couple in this terrace in fact. Numbers 8 and 12 I think.' Dexter chuckled, placed his tumbler down beside him, lay down and stretched out flat. 'Next question boss.'

'I'd just like to understand her,' said Jude, 'I met her, she threatened me with a flaming axe.'

Dexter laughed.

'It didn't seem funny at the time,' said Jude. 'Do you think she could have attacked Chantal?'

Dexter sat up, rested back on his elbows.

'God knows she had good reason to after everything that Chantal did to her,' he said. 'But rest easy, she didn't hurt Chantal.'

'So, what happened?'

'Any more water?' Dexter picked up his tumbler and offered it to Jude for a refill. 'There was a scandal.'

'I heard there was a scandal but everyone is being very tight lipped about the details.'

Dexter put his hand up in front of his eyes to shield them from the sun.

'Look, I doubt it has anything to do with Chantal's death but as I am now officially your assistant, I'll give you the facts, the ones I know at least.'

'Go on.'

'Well, way back, when Saffron turned seventeen, she ran off to France.'

'Did she?'

'With her French teacher no less,' said Dexter nodding. 'Apparently they had been, shall we say, 'very close' for at least a couple of years.'

'Blimey! What happened to him?'

Dexter grinned and shook his head.

'For an ex-detective you're not very bright sometimes are you?'

Rude

'Think about it. Who do you know that was French and that worked as a teacher,' said Dexter, 'you've got the information, I saw it on your board mate,' he said in an effort to nudge Jude to unite two facts and come up with an obvious conclusion. 'Come on detective, wakey, wakey.'

Jude's eyes widened; his mouth fell open as he recollected what Rosebud had told him.

She moved here to be closer to her brother. She got a job as a teacher.

'Not Chantal?'

'Well done detective!' said Dexter nodding his head. 'She was Saffron's French teacher. It was a huge scandal at the time. Huge. You can imagine, absolute horror in the village! I would however say it was only a few of them, led by our dear neighbour Patrick Fox of course. For him it was a double whammy! French teacher runs off with pupil, shock, horror AND bloody blimey they're lesbians! He was an ardent churchgoer at the time and he wound up those few people daft enough to listen to him, good and proper. Sadly, two of those people were Saffron's parents.' Dexter's eyes were on Jude now, seeking his reaction. 'Nobody really mentions it nowadays, out of respect for Saffy.'

'So, what happened?'

'I was away travelling around Asia some of the time so I'm not exactly sure.' Dexter drained his glass. 'Her parents were of course devastated by the whole thing. They were big in the church and I think they felt ashamed by it all. To be honest I think their plan was to move away, somebody did mention the coast. They sold off some of their land, and most of their property.'

'Did they move away?'

Dexter shook his head.

'Unfortunately not. Her father died suddenly.'

'Did Saffron come back?'

Dexter shook his head again, a slow movement, all the time his eyes on Jude.

'To be honest, I'm not even sure if her mother told her. That's how much she'd been wound up by the old goat Fox. That old man really poisoned her with his toxic judgements and homophobic rants.'

'So, when did she come back?'

'A couple of years later, after her mother died.'

'I see.'

'It was so sad, she died of the big C. But as her health deteriorated, she mellowed and she managed to see Patrick Fox for the toxic piece of crap that he was. Trouble is by that time most of her money had gone.'

'What? How?'

'Are you sure you used to be a detective?'

Excuse me?

'As I told you at the fair, Patrick's grandfather lost them the Manor House. Now here's the thing, after Saffy's father died our dear neighbour Patrick Fox started to take a great deal of interest in her mum.'

'Did he indeed?'

'He was on his own, his own wife had buggered off back to Wales with his daughter years before, and, well, the point I am trying to make is, that before his 'relationship' – and I use the term loosely - with Saffy's mum, Patrick was living in a flat on Orchard Road and had a job with the council. After his 'relationship' he'd packed in his job and bought number 8, the cottage he still lives in. I'll leave you to draw your own conclusions from that, detective.'

152

Jude gasped. He visualised his whiteboard, the new connections he could make.

'Fortunately, Mr Hill, the family solicitor eventually intervened,' said Dexter. 'I think he threatened Patrick, said he'd go to the police if he contacted her again, but it was way too late if you ask me. The only good thing to come out of it was that Mr Hill reached out to Saffron. Her mother really wanted to make amends, wanted to see her only child again before she... you know... croaked.'

'Did Saffron come over? Did they make up?'

Dexter shook his head.

'Sadly no, they never got the chance. She died.' He snapped his fingers. 'In her sleep, just like that. Saffy came back for her funeral though, Mr Hill contacted her. I think he'd been given instructions to look out for her.' Dexter lay back, closed his eyes and soaked in the sunshine. 'You see how much help I am. Bet you're pleased I'm your assistant.'

Jude waited for Dexter to continue his story but he just lay absorbing the sun.

'So, what happened next?' he asked eventually.

'Depends who you ask,' said Dexter without even opening his eyes. 'So we're defo Team Mumford then, our name?'

'Apparently so,' said Jude. 'Come on, tell me what happened next.'

'It's a fact, gossip, rumour, mash-up, nobody, apart from Saffy of course, knows exactly what went on.'

'Drink?' said Jude standing up. 'I mean a proper drink, beer?'

'Got any cider?' asked Dexter still without moving.

'Nope. I've got a bottle of red wine though.'

'That'll do.'

A couple of minutes later Jude was back sat on the grass, with a newly opened bottle of red.

'Anyone would think you were trying to get me drunk,' said Dexter. He took a sip. 'That's good, still prefer cider though.'

153

'I'll remember,' said Jude. 'What happened, after Saffron's mum died?'

'Well, Saffy came back for her mum's funeral, and...' Dexter shrugged, 'a lot of her friends turned up to support her.'

'Any idea who?'

'Most of her mates from school,' he paused, picked up the glass and took another sip. 'I guess they wanted to pay their respects. And all I know is that a few of them went out afterwards, a sort of wake I suppose, and...'

'Yes?'

'Saffy went back to France two days later without saying a word to anybody.'

'Any idea what happened?'

'Nope,' said Dexter holding out his glass for more wine. 'And nobody heard from her or anything, until the following year she turned up again, properly this time. Apparently, it was to sort out what was left of her mother's estate. I guess Mr Hill had been in touch with her.'

'And Chantal, did she come back with her?' said Jude.

'Of course, they were still together then and guess what...'

'Go on,' Jude picked up the bottle of wine, leant over and refilled Dexter's glass. Dexter lifted his head and nodded appreciation.

'According to a couple of very reliable sources, they had a baby with them.'

'Seriously?'

'I cannot confirm or deny that of course as I was halfway up the Himalaya's at the time.' He took a sip from his glass of wine, 'but then they split up.'

'Any idea who broke off with who?'

Dexter shook his head.

'Whom!' he said. 'Nope.'

'Any idea why?'

154

'Nope, but Saffy was in a right state, fortunately Mr Hill and a few family friends helped sort her out. Rumour has it she tried to top herself.'

Jude gasped, then breathed in slowly, taking in the scent of his prettied-up garden while trying to assimilate what he was being told. He was slowly building up a picture of Saffron and her struggles and he was definitely closer to understanding her behaviour.

'And that is the extent of my knowledge on the subject.' Dexter sat up. 'Blimey it's hot.' He got hold of his t-shirt and stretched up, lifting it over his head revealing an evenly tanned torso, no fat, just muscle, honed on a daily basis doing the job he loved. He lay flat out on the grass again, his t-shirt splatted next to him like a can of spilled blue paint.

Jude leant over and refilled his glass.

'You don't have to you know,' Dexter laughed and lifted his hand across his face to shelter his eyes from the sun.

'What?'

'You're trying to get me drunk, and you really don't have to. I've told you, now we're a team, my knowledge base is at your disposal. Most of it anyway. Go on, ask me another question. Anything you like.'

'Olga Kaine, do you have her address?'

'I told you how to contact her, she goes to the pet cemetery every couple of days with that somewhat sinister daughter of hers.'

'I need to speak to her on her own.'

'Behind the village store, Blacksmith's Yard, number 3.' He drained his glass. 'Oooh! And I've just thought of another little snippet you might like.'

'You really are a mine of information aren't you?'

'Course. Saffy's mother used to own the cottage Olga and Ivy live in, and guess what, Saffy still owns it.' His phone rang, he sat up and reached into the pocket of his shorts.

'Sorry,' he said. 'Important client, I could be a while.' He turned his attention back to the phone. 'Hi mate, bear with me, I'll call you back in five.' He grabbed his t-shirt, stood up and brushed himself off.

'I'll see myself out.'

He took a run up to the wall, placed his right hand on the top layer of stone and vaulted over.

Jude heard a crash and his neighbour disappeared as he landed in a heap on the other side.

'Aaargh!'

26

'You again!'

'I just want a quick chat.'

'Seriously? What is it in piss off and leave us alone that is unclear to you?'

It had been over three weeks since Jude had met Olga and Ivy in the cemetery and since that day Jude had visited her cottage on two occasions. The first time there had been no reply when he rang the bell and the second time – the previous afternoon – Olga had opened the door and told him to piss off before slamming it shut in his face.

But Jude decided to try again. He stood back from the doorstep, ignored her anger and spoke in a loud but calm voice.

'Well,' he said. 'I could piss off as you suggest. Or, there is one other option of course.' The door had not slammed shut so he was feeling hopeful. 'I could go and talk to Saffron.'

The door started to open, it was slow, a few centimetres only. But it was a gap.

'I know she's involved in all this,' he said. 'Whatever 'this' is.'

Olga stepped into the opening, feet square, chin high, eyes blazing.

'I just want to talk to you without Ivy around,' said Jude.

Olga gave a single nod.

'At the cemetery,' she said. 'In a couple of hours.'

'Thanks.'

An hour and a half later, Jude was sitting on the bench opposite Zac's memorial staring at the sculpture of an animal, who, he suspected, had been the only true friend of the two lonely women.

Olga arrived twenty minutes after he did. In spite of a sky clear of clouds and the near sweltering heat, she wore her parka and her deerstalker hat with the ear flaps pinned up. On a cold day she would have blended unnoticed in a crowd, but on this day, she struck a lonely figure out of touch with herself and her surroundings. He stood up to let her sit down, but she chose not to, instead she leant against the statue of her pet and rested her head against his leg.

'So, what is it you want?' She pushed her hands deep into her jacket pockets. The breeze rustled through the treetops, the sound unsettled her and she stared along the track.

'I've been on the internet.'

'Vile bloody internet,' she spat the words out.

'Why do you think it's vile?'

'Because the combination of stupid people being able to write crap for other stupid people to believe was never going to benefit anybody.'

'That's a very generalised statement. Are you talking about anything specific?'

'That Fernsby girl…'

'Is she still causing you problems?'

'I went to see her father, he pretended to be horrified when I told him his oldest had been spreading rumours about me.'

'Has it helped?'

'It's too late, she put it all over her social media. It's out there now.'

Standing there resting against the statue of her dead friend Olga struck a lonely figure.

'May I say in defence of the internet,' said Jude, 'spreading lies is a spiteful thing to do. But there is also a lot of good out there.'

'I'll take your word on that.'

'You can find out all sorts of things. Access to death records, access to birth records.'

They sat in silence for a short while, brown eyes stared dolefully at him, pleading him to stop. He didn't, but he did whisper his words as if trying to make them easier for her to hear.

158

'I know that you are not Ivy's mother,' he said.

She lowered her head, waited a couple of minutes before lifting it to engage with him once more.

She sat down beside him.

'I suggest you quantify exactly what you mean by the word mother.'

Their discussion on the topic of what constitutes a mother went on for several minutes. Like a tennis ball bouncing backwards and forwards over a virtual net, each said their piece and positioned themselves as they waited the batting back.

'Okay. Let me be blunt,' said Jude. 'Yes, you may have brought Ivy up, but you did not give birth to her. Is that clear enough for you?'

The silence lasted a few seconds but to Jude it seemed longer. When Olga did speak again, her voice resonated anger.

'Excuse me, but I fail to see what my relationship with my daughter has got to do with you, or any of this for that matter.'

'To be honest,' said Jude, 'at the moment, neither do I.'

'At least we agree on something.'

'So how about I take what I've learned to the police to see if they can make anything of it?'

Olga glared at him; her anger unleashed now.

'You wouldn't dare!' she shouted. 'You'd have to explain how you got it for a start!'

Good point.

'Go on!' she shouted. 'Go tell them I didn't give birth to Ivy. If you think they're going to give a damn you're dafter than you look.'

Thanks for that.

Jude was stunned by her lack of fear. He knew things about this woman, things that were wrong, and she didn't care if he took his knowledge to the police. She was right about one thing though; he wouldn't go to them because he didn't want to have to explain where he'd got his information from.

159

'Was Chantal her mother? Is that why you fell out?'

Olga laughed out loud.

'Seriously? You're not much of a detective if that's the best you can come up with.'

When Olga spoke again, she was calmer, more composed.

'Ivy's adoption was private. A private arrangement between friends. We were abroad.'

'I know,' said Jude. 'France'

Olga stared into her lap, her eyes moistened, a tear glanced her cheek and she wiped it away with the palm of her hand.

'So nobody knew?' said Jude. 'About your private arrangement.'

'A few people did.'

'The mother?' Jude asked.

Olga laughed.

'Good Lord, give me strength, of course she did. You think I kidnapped a baby?'

'No, I don't think that,' said Jude. 'I would just like to know who she is.'

'Detective, detective, I don't mean to be rude,' she laughed, 'if you were that clever, you'd already know.' She zipped up her jacket, cocooning herself into it.

'Can't you just tell me?'

'But why? It's nothing to do with you.'

Jude decided on a new tactic.

'I'd like to know who she is because I'd like to know where she is.' He caught her eye and turned his gaze to the unmanaged track. He got up and headed along it hoping she would follow. He breathed a sigh of relief when he heard the rustle of her coat brushing against the bushes behind him.

When he reached the holly bush, he turned and waited. She stopped a short distance away. He heard a gasp, a near silent sob.

160

Her eyes moistened, a tear spilled, she pulled a handkerchief from her pocket to wipe it away.

Jude knelt and cleared the branches so the headstone could be seen. He dipped into his pocket and got out his glasses case, snapped it open and put them on. He rubbed at the headstone, clearing the weathered moss. Then he stood up and watched as Olga crumbled.

She knows who is buried here.

She knelt down, kissed two of her fingers and touched the stone.

'In truth,' she said, 'I always knew this day would come.'

'It says here RIP,' Jude took his phone out of his pocket and snapped a photograph. 'Now, I'll tell you what I think. I think there's a body buried under this headstone and I don't think it's somebody's pet. Is it Ivy's mother?'

For a few seconds Olga didn't move, barely took a breath. Eventually, she sat back on her knees, her eyes swollen with tears.

'What do you know?' she said.

If that's the way you want to play it.

'Okay, how about I'll tell you and you fill in the gaps...'

She nodded, her short sharp nod.

'I know that Chantal was a teacher at the local school, I know that she was in a relationship with Saffron, and I also know that they ran off to France together when she was seventeen.' He paused; he could hear Olga sob quietly. He waited patiently for her to gather her thoughts.

When she spoke, the previously self-assured woman was broken.

'When Saffron ran off to France, her parents were devastated,' she said. 'It was a such a scandal in the village. The school committee were mortified. A female French teacher running off with a final year student, girl at that. In those days, well, people round here can be a bit narrow minded now but years ago...'

'But wasn't Chantal committing a criminal offence?'

'Saffron was nearly eighteen when she left, and the school well, they just wanted to shut it down, pretend it never happened.' She paused, looked up at him. 'But none of it has anything to do with what happened to Chantal.'

'With respect, you don't know that and neither do I.' Jude paused and stared down at her. 'But I do intend to get to the bottom of all this.'

'But why? It was so long ago.' She flinched, gave a low moan, defeated. She sat down on the grass, her eyes on the headstone. 'Saffron and Chantal were so happy in France. They were a lovely couple, so well matched, in spite of their age difference.' She leant forward and stroked the stone. 'They'd been there about two years when Saffron had to come back for her mother's funeral.'

'I heard about that,' Jude nodded as he spoke.

'That was when it happened.'

'It?'

Olga nodded. Not a short sharp nod, this time it was slow, thoughtful, the word 'it' triggering a time-worn memory.

'It was only when she got back to France that she realised she was pregnant.'

'I'm guessing that was difficult to explain away.'

'Chantal was furious. They split up for a short while.' She wiped a tear away with the back of her sleeve. 'Until Saffron told her what had happened...'

Jude could see the pain of the woman in front of him. Her tears were unstoppable, her whole body trembled. He didn't prompt her to continue, instead he waited patiently to hear the what, the how and the why. But only when she was ready.

'You okay?'

'Saffron had been raped, it happened when she came back to bury her mother. It was after the funeral I think. She had twins in France, two days before Christmas.'

'Twins?'

162

'I... I helped with the birth. I was their neighbour you see. I was a vet in those days and used to take care of their animals. We became friends.'

'But what actually happened?'

Olga stared up at him; the pain clearly visible.

'Please, stop your investigation,' she said. 'Just leave it be.'

'I'm sorry,' he said. 'But I can't do that.' He stood silent, waiting for a response, but there was none.

Olga lifted herself onto her knees, paused and slowly stood up. Jude offered his hand to help but she waved it away. She turned and walked back along the track. Jude opened his mouth to say something then shut it again and followed her in silence. When she got to the bench, she sat down one side. Jude paused, she nodded, granting him permission to sit beside her.

Olga sighed, her expression one of resignation, lost hope, knowing she was now a passenger in a car that he was driving.

'I didn't like Chantal but I didn't hurt her, honestly.'

'That's as maybe, but something went on and I intend to find out what.'

As if joining Olga in her misery, speckled clouds cast shadows through the trees, a draft whistled along the track, brushing the bushes and branches either side.

'The death of her father, then her mother, the rape…, having twins…, it was all too much for Saffron.'

'We all have our breaking point,' said Jude, and after a pause he asked. 'Are you going to tell me who it is buried under the holly bush?'

'Holly.'

'Holly! Of course, the other twin! It's Ivy's sister, isn't it?'

Olga nodded.

'But what happened to her?'

'The truth is, I don't know. After Saffron gave birth, Chantal was no help whatsoever. To be fair, she did sort of try, but she just didn't want kids you see. She didn't like them,' she crossed her legs

163

and rocked gently back and forth before turning to him. 'I think being a teacher put her off.'

'It happens.'

'Saffron wanted to keep her babies but Chantal, well she wanted nothing to do with them.'

'Did Saffron tell her she'd been raped?'

'Not straight away,' she smeared tears away, one eye, the other, then blew her nose and stuffed the handkerchief into her pocket. 'She went mad when Saffron did tell her.'

'Did they go to the police?'

Olga shook her head.

'After she found out, Chantal agreed to keeping one baby.'

'What? She wanted to split them up?'

Olga nodded.

'It was Chantal who asked me to care for Ivy.' Her expression softened. 'She said Saffron would be able to cope with one.' She sat silent for a few seconds. 'I was overjoyed. I love children and to be honest I'd given up hope of having one of my own. It seemed like a dream come true for me,' she paused before turning and making eye contact. 'At the time.'

'So what went wrong?'

'Saffron had to come back to the UK again, to sort out her mother's estate. She reckoned it would take three or four months so Chantal and Holly came back with her. Saffron was so fragile, she shouldn't have come back at all really, but I don't think she had a choice.'

'And?'

'A few days after they came back Chantal phoned me one night and ordered me to come over to help because they weren't coping. Not with Holly, not with anything.'

'So that's why you came here.'

She nodded and the tears started again. This time they were uncontrolled and she made no effort to wipe them away.

'Not straight away, I had to sort out a passport, for Ivy.'

'How?'

'It wasn't difficult, I knew someone.' She turned her face to him and shrugged. 'And by the time I got here Holly was dead and buried. Saffron was in a hell of a state and Chantal wasn't coping either.'

'Any idea how Holly died?'

'Chantal said it was a cot death.'

'Did you believe her? Could she have killed her?'

Olga shook her head slowly and firmly.

'Yes, I did believe her. It's true Chantal was a hard-nosed business woman and okay, she did not like kids. But she couldn't kill somebody. It just wasn't her; she was devastated when she hit that little girl and her pony.'

'What about Saffron? Could she have hurt Holly?'

Again, Olga shook her head.

'Saffron was, and still is one of the sweetest people you will ever meet.'

'She threatened me with an axe.'

'Trust me, she's harmless.'

'So, people keep telling me.'

'And that's it really.'

'Hardly. Weren't the police involved when the baby died?'

Olga shook her head.

'Chantal and Saffron had only been in the country a week or so when it happened. They were under everybody's radar.'

'What happened next, when you got here?'

'As I said, by the time I got here Holly was dead. It was Chantal who buried her and she planted the holly bush, this was just a field in those days, it belonged to Saffron.'

'I've heard all about that,' said Jude. 'She used to graze her donkey's here.'

165

'Yes, that was later. Anyway, next thing I knew, Saffron was in the hospital, she'd try to kill herself.'

'Christ.'

'She was admitted to a private hospital, Mr Hill, her solicitor arranged it.'

'What about you? What did you do?'

'I was going to go back to France. It wouldn't have bothered Chantal at all and Saffron was in no position to stop me.'

'Why didn't you?'

Olga hesitated before answering.

'A few days before I was due to go, Mr Hill came to see me and handed me a tenancy agreement for the cottage.'

'I'm guessing that was a bit of a shock?'

'It was a complete shock.'

'So Mr Hill arranged everything?'

Olga nodded.

'I guess between Chantal and Saffron he somehow found out what had happened.'

'And so you decided to stay?'

Olga nodded.

'The original plan was that when Saffron came out of hospital, she'd have some contact with Ivy.'

'You didn't mind that?'

'Of course not, she was her mother,' she let out a quiet sob. 'But of course, that never happened.'

'Any idea why not?'

'Saffron was in the hospital for nearly two years. By the time she came out she'd wiped all the memories of Chantal and of her babies from her life. And of the rape I guess.'

'That poor woman.'

'Chantal was devasted, she left the village.'

166

'I did hear that she left for a while.'

'Only for a few years though, bloody well came back again and caused more trouble. Mr Hill was dead by then and so Chantal managed to wheedle her way back into Saffron's life.'

'What? They lived together again?'

'Good God no, nothing like that, besides by that time Chantal had a new best friend.'

'Did she?'

'That writer woman who lives on Willow Walk.'

'Rosebud?'

Olga nodded.

'That's her.'

I knew they were friends but Rosebud… a lesbian?

Jude's mouth fell open, he felt his heart race and struggled to catch his breath.

'What? They were together?'

How could I have got it so wrong?

Olga nodded.

'That's what I heard,' she tilted her head to one side, narrowed her eyes and stared at him. 'And that's everything I know. Now please just stop this.'

'Not quite everything,' Jude tried to put all thoughts of Rosebud to the back of his mind. 'Do you know who it was raped Saffron? Who Ivy's father is?'

Olga froze, her previous deflated demeanour now challenged by a fear that burned a crease into her face, her only movement involuntary tears that spilled again.

'She told Chantal it was a stranger.'

'You know who it was don't you?'

Olga nodded.

'She made me swear I'd never tell.'

167

'Who was it? Somebody she knew?'

She nodded again, vigorously this time.

'It was that bastard Lawson Peterson.'

'Lawson Peterson?' Jude didn't try to hide his surprise. 'And Saffron didn't tell Chantal it was him?'

'God no. Chantal would have gone mad.'

'Does Ivy know he's her father?'

'She does now!'

They both turned, Ivy stepped out from behind Zac's statue.

'Liar!' she stared at Olga, her face bleeding anger. 'You liar! You told me my daddy was dead!'

27

Jude was sitting at the table on his patio listening to the rhythmic hum of Dexter's lawnmower. He could just see his neighbour wandering shirtless up and down his patch of grass in uniform lines. A female voice made him turn around.

'Evening.'

It was Rosebud, she was stood by her wall with a jigsaw box, holding it so that the picture on the front faced him.

'Hi,' said Jude.

'Pressie for you,' she offered it to him. 'Just to prove that I've forgiven you, for the whole suspect thing.'

Jude neared, gave an uncertain half smile and took the box from her.

'A jigsaw, how nice.'

Rosebud cringed.

'Nice? Nice? I've just given you the mother of all jigsaws and you describe it as nice.'

'Sorry,' Jude laughed. 'Thanks.'

The picture on the box was of a living room, it was decorated for Christmas, a pale green sofa with a Stuart tartan throw draped over the back, a pine dresser with barley twist edging, a copper vase and several small books in a line along the shelves. There was a brick fireplace with an open fire blazing and beside it a dark red vase with an arrangement of winter stems, and along the wall a string of fairy lights. A large brown dog sat in front of ornate French doors gazing out onto a mosaic patio and the winter woodland scene beyond.

'That's great,' said Jude. 'Lots going on.'

Rosebud's mobile chimed out, its 'ripples' ringtone adding another instrument to the melody of the evening.

'Sorry,' she said. 'I've got to take this.' She nodded at the box. 'Let me know if you get stuck.'

169

Phone glued to her ear, Rosebud scurried indoors and the evening sounds returned to nature as – at the same time - Dexter turned off his lawnmower. The quiet didn't last long.

'Oy! Jude!' It was Dexter.

Jude turned around; his neighbour was holding a rake skyward in a wave.

'Beautiful evening.' He dropped the rake, approached their boundary wall and was over in an instant.

'Now, about Team Mumford, I think we should hold regular meetings,' he nodded towards Rosebud's cottage. 'Was it something I said?'

'Probably something you did,' said Jude. 'Fancy a drink? I've got cider.'

'Mate, I thought you'd never ask.'

Jude laughed and turned to head inside but Rosebud appeared her side of the wall.

'Drink?' Jude shouted over to her.

'Team Mumford, our first meeting.' Dexter waved at her. 'Come on Rosie.'

Rosebud stared at Dexter and then at Jude, her expression a gaunt shadow, so different to the cheery woman who had - only minutes earlier - handed him the jigsaw.

'Rosie,' said Dexter, 'what's wrong?'

She opened her mouth to speak but no words came out. When they did her reply did not answer the question she was asked.

'Don't call me that! I hate being called that.'

'Got your attention though, didn't I?'

Rosebud nodded and as she did, tears spilled over onto her cheeks. She quickly wiped them away with the back of her hand.

'They've found Stefan.'

'But that's a good thing, right?' said Jude.

Dexter gave him a withering look.

'Mate,' he said pointing to Rosebud, 'they're not bloody tears of joy.'

'He's dead,' she let out a sob.

'Oh no!' said Jude, 'I'm so sorry, any idea what happened?'

'Christ,' said Dexter. 'Can I do anything?'

'Thanks Dext, but no,' she shook her head. 'I'm fine, honestly. It's just a bit of a shock.'

'I'm so sorry,' said Dexter. 'Let me know if you change your mind.'

'I will,' Rosebud nodded.

'Make sure you do,' he said. 'Promise?'

Rosebud lifted her head slightly and nodded.

Jude watched his neighbours, envious at the moment of tenderness taking place between them. Dexter's concern for Rosebud was touching, as was her appreciation of it.

'Just give me a call if you need me,' Dexter said. 'Anytime.'

'Thanks.'

'Do you need to talk? Would you like to come over?' asked Jude.

'I'd appreciate that,' Rosebud nodded, 'I could do with a bit of company.'

Five minutes later the three members of Team Mumford were laying stretched flat out like snow angels in the middle of Jude's lawn, each with a tin of cider within finger touching distance.

'Any details?' asked Dext, 'Do they know how he died?'

Rosebud shook her head.

'He was living rough,' she said. 'Near York.'

'Could he have been murdered?' asked Jude.

'Bloody blimey,' said Dexter. 'The thought of another murder and that's woken you up.'

'Not by the sound of it,' Rosebud shook her head. 'There appears to be little doubt he died of natural causes.'

171

They stayed silent until Rosebud was ready to talk. When she did she spoke of Stefan, his life and his love of classical music while Dexter and Jude listened.

'In truth, it's not a total surprise,' she said. 'But it all seems so unfair.' She sat up, picked up her cider and sipped and spoke and sipped and spoke until in the distance a siren, and then another trailed through the village. It was only when the emergency services distanced themselves from Willow Walk that Rosebud was able to continue her reminiscences, but even then it was only for a few seconds before another siren and then another passed by. That was the one that got their full attention.

'What is going on?' Jude sat up and turned to the back of his cottage as if it might provide a clue.

Dexter's phone rang, he answered, he listened, he said a few words but neither Jude nor Rosebud could hear what because there were more sirens. They watched him though as his expression transformed to shock. He ended the call as the sirens faded to silence. For a few seconds he held his phone in front of him and stared at it in disbelief.

'What? What's happened?' asked Jude.

'Something's gone on up at the Manor,' said Dexter. 'Something serious by the sound of it.'

28

An hour later the locals were gathered in pockets around the village. Gossips sharpened their tongues speculating on events that were none of their business, rumours were exchanged as if they were a marketing commodity, 'I'll swap you a spiteful scandal for some malicious hearsay.'

'I heard it was a shooting.'

'There were two ambulances, it must be pretty bloody.'

'I always thought he had shifty eyes.'

It was distant, but from his upstairs bedroom window Jude gazed up the hill to the Manor at the four police cars, van and two ambulances parked on the sweeping drive.

He went downstairs, Spud had brought the bone he'd been gnawing near the shed into the front room and he lay in the middle of the rug asleep with it in front of his nose, inhaling the aroma as if enjoying a meal in his doggy dreamworld. On any other day Jude would have scolded his pet for daring to do such a thing, but on this day, at this time, he let it go and headed outside to his shed.

Five minutes later he was cycling to the Manor. He was spotted by the villagers as he peddled along, often they heard him before they saw him - he had forgotten to oil the squeak in his back wheel and it had got worse.

One or two locals nodded as he passed and when that happened, he politely mirrored their greeting and continued his journey. As he turned into the lane leading to Eaststowe Manor, he could see a police car in the road partially blocking the entrance. He got off his bike and walked towards it, the squeaky wheel interrupting the silence.

A young policeman was standing by the car. Jude wheeled his bike towards him.

'You wanna get that fixed,' the policeman nodded to the bike.

'Hi,' said Jude. 'I know, I'll get out the WD40 when I get home. What's going on?'

'There's been an incident.'

'I gathered that. What sort of an incident?'

'I'm sorry I can't discuss that sir.'

A van arrived and pulled up alongside the police car. The policeman went over to speak to the driver. Jude spotted Fearless in the passenger seat.

'Fearless,' he shouted to her. She turned and smiled in recognition. The van was about to pull around the police car to head up the drive but she asked the driver to hold on.

'Jude? What on earth are you doing here?'

'I heard something had happened. I just wondered what was going on?'

'There's been an incident.'

'So people keep telling me. Any details? You're here so I'm guessing it's violent?'

Fearless nudged the driver to continue their journey.

'You got that right,' she said as the van drove off. 'Be good to catch up some time,' she yelled out of the window as the van headed up the drive.

The policeman approached arm outstretched as if to sweep him away.

'I'm sorry sir, but I'm going to have to ask you to leave.'

'Any clues?' said Jude. 'I do have an interest.'

'Do you indeed? Might I ask what? Are you in any way related to the victim?'

'Victim? Tell me who's been hurt and I'll tell you.'

The young policemen reddened in frustration.

'Nice try sir.'

'Look, I'm an ex-detective, I've been investigating the death of Chantal Dubois.'

'Oh that's you is it! I've heard all about you from my colleagues. How you're trying to help out us yokels.'

174

'That is absolutely not true,' said Jude. 'Please, who is it that's hurt? Surely you can tell me that?'

'It's the house owner, sir.'

'What! Sasha!'

'Not her sir. Him.'

'Lawson Peterson?'

'I probably shouldn't really say sir,' said the constable. 'But being as though you were one of us so to speak. I think he was stabbed.'

'Is he okay?'

'I'm not party to that information sir.'

'What about, Sasha and their son Charlie, are they okay?'

'Mrs Peterson is helping the police with their enquiries,' he said. 'As is her son.'

29

'I'd like to see D.I. Jones please.' Jude nodded a greeting to the bored looking constable behind the desk.

'She's out I'm afraid. Can somebody else help you?'

'I'll wait.'

Three and a half hours later he was in interview room 2 sitting opposite D.I. Jones.

'What can I do for you?'

A knock on the door and a mug of coffee and a sandwich appeared and were placed in front of her.

'I'm on lunch,' she said. 'You'll need to be quick. What is it you want?'

'It's about Sasha Peterson.'

'What about her?'

'I understand you're still questioning her about her husband's murder.'

'And that is your business how exactly?'

'I agree it's not my business, but I just wanted to say something.'

'Go on, out with it.'

'She did not kill her husband.'

'You are stating that as fact, are you?'

'I am,' Jude nodded.

D.I. Jones took a bite out of her sandwich. She chewed slowly, eyes on Jude.

'Where's your evidence?'

'Well…'

'Or are you just giving us village people the benefit of your experience. Helping us out like.'

'Not exactly.'

'Come on then, tell me why you think that Mrs Peterson didn't kill her husband.'

'Because her son Charlie found the body.'

D.I. Jones placed the mug onto the table and stared at Jude.

'Please will you explain to me how you know that the boy found his father's body. That information has not been made public.'

Jude reddened. The previous evening he had bumped into Fearless outside the village shop and she had let slip in conversation that it was Charlie who had found the body of his father. But he wasn't about to reveal his source.

'I heard somebody talking… in the village.'

It's sort of true.

'I see. And how does that exonerate Mrs Peterson exactly?'

'No mother in her right mind would kill her husband and let her child find the body… she'd have to be a proper nutter.'

'And so you are telling me that as far as you are concerned Mrs Peterson is definitely not a 'proper nutter,' your words not mine.'

'I just can't see her…'

'Mr Mumford, can I please ask what your relationship with Mrs Peterson is?'

'I've only met her a couple of times, but I do know she loves her son, and Charlie loved his father. If she killed her husband, I can't believe she'd let Charlie find his body.'

'I disagree Mr Mumford. Let's face it, if she did kill him, I can't think of a better way to deflect suspicion from herself.'

30

'Morning!'

It was Dexter, cheery as always, greeting Jude as he returned with Spud from their early morning walk. They had taken a short route around the church as Jude had a list of things to do.

'Morning,' Jude shouted back.

Dexter had been about to get into his Land Rover, but instead he slammed the door shut and approached Jude, leaning down to pat Spud.

'Hi matey, how you doing?' He stood up. 'Good walk?'

'Fantastic as always,' Jude nodded.

'How are things going, with our investigation?'

'Haha! Shall I just send you a weekly newsletter?'

'You could, but I'd rather we had a regular meeting, that way you could talk to us, me and Rosebud, keep us up to date with what's going on.'

'Sorry, sorry, I will,' said Jude. 'I'm just not used to working with other people.'

'Mate. You were a detective; you must have worked in a team then.'

'I know, I did,' Jude nodded. 'But this, I'm not a detective any more. It's different.'

'Well, I'm new to this investigation lark,' Dexter paused. 'And you need to understand this is my new hobby. It's fun.'

'Fun? Seriously?'

'Fair enough,' Dexter held his hands up. 'Maybe fun is not quite the right word. It's exciting though isn't it?'

'Again, I'd say it was a poor choice of words on your part.'

'Point taken,' said Dexter. 'I'm sure the excitement will soon wear off.'

'I hope so,' Jude grinned.

It was laundry day so back indoors Jude packed the washing machine with bed linen. He was having chicken for tea so he took a frozen chicken out of the freezer and placed it on a tray to defrost. Next, he filled Spud's bowl with biscuits, knelt down in front of him and squidged his pet's head between his hands.

'Right matey, I'm going out. I'll leave the back door open so you can go into the garden, you can watch Rosebud doing her yoga but try not to drool at her. I may be a couple of hours and when I get back, we'll go for a marathon hike over the Fens.'

Spud licked his masters face, wriggled free and headed for his biscuit bowl.

Half an hour later dressed in washed out jeans and a white short sleaved t-shirt Jude was on the doorstep of Olga's cottage. He knocked twice, no response. He knocked again and stepped back. Upstairs he spotted a curtain twitch. He was about to step forward to knock again when he heard somebody inside. A bolt was undone, then another before the door opened a crack and Ivy's head appeared. She stared, the sullen gaze of a spoilt child.

'Is your mother in?'

She shook her head.

'About the other day,' said Jude. 'I'm sorry... what you heard.'

Sullen eyes stared at him, she shrugged.

'And now... your dad.'

'She told me he was dead, now he is.'

Jude stood wanting to contribute something positive, make this young girl realise he had only been trying to help.

'I need to speak with your mother, when will she be back?'

'Don't know,' she turned away and started to shut the door.

Jude stepped forward, put his arm out to stop the door being closed and accidentally pushed it open. She stood, sullen, skimpy t-shirt and shorts hanging from her bony frame.

'Will she be long?'

She shrugged, an action that carried with it an air of indifference.

179

'Do you mind if I wait for her?'

'Yes.'

'I really need to speak to her.'

'You'll have to come back when she's here then.'

'Or I could go to the police and talk to them.'

The threat of the police had not frightened her mother but it did frighten Ivy. She stared at him wide eyed for a few seconds before fully opening the door. He stepped into the rundown cottage and jumped as the door slammed shut behind him. He followed her into the back room.

A combination of instinct and habit took over and Jude observed his surroundings with a detective's eye. A scratched table, a bookshelf, books, trinkets, all coated in a film of dust.

'Drink?' said Ivy.

'A cup of coffee would be great,' he said. 'Black, no sugar,' he shouted after her as she left the room.

He went over to the stained-glass window and stared through to the snug. The worn armchairs adding to his view that Ivy and her mother were not very well off. The door to the garden was open and he peered out to what was obviously a well-loved space.

A loud thump on the ceiling interrupted his thoughts, he looked up for a few seconds before he returned his gaze to the stained glass, the only splash of colour in the room. He smiled at his rainbow reflection. A movement behind him caught his eye and he spotted Ivy, he turned around. She clutched a glass of water, sipped it then placed it onto the table.

'Kettle's boiling,' she said.

'Is there somebody else in the house?' asked Jude.

'Why you asking?'

'I just heard a thump; it came from upstairs.'

'Oh, it's probably the cat knocked the vase over,' she bit her bottom lip.

'Any idea where your mother's gone?'

180

'Didn't tell me,' she said. 'Not sure I'd have believed her if she had.'

Although she was physically in the room with him, her voice, like her eyes, was distant.

'About the other day…,' said Jude.

'I said forget about it.'

'Did you really have no idea that you were adopted?'

'Nope,' she said turning around. 'I'll go check the kettle.'

Jude watched her go then turned to the garden again, a bush of purple buddleia was budding to flower, he watched the distant butterfly's air dancing around the tiny buds. They fluttered off and his gaze returned to his reflection in the stained glass. He spotted a tuft of unruly hair at the front and tried to flatten it with spit and the palm of his hand. A separate movement caught his eye, he returned to the here and now and saw Ivy's reflection as she re-entered the room. Her unusually slow pace kept his attention. As she closed in on him, she slowly raised both arms and it was at that moment Jude saw she was holding a large carving knife.

He spun round at the exact moment she slashed at him. It sliced through his left arm and he yelled as blood spurted out covering him and spraying her. The sight and feel of her victim's blood energized Ivy. Her eyes narrowed and her mouth hinted a smug satisfaction.

Jude was taller, stronger and cleverer than his attacker and without the knife and element of surprise she would have been no match for him. It was not the first time he had fought for his life but it was the first time he'd been bloodied by a girl who was fast closing in on him. Blood loss weakened him and he clamped his right hand against the cut in an effort to stem the flow. He knocked over furniture and ornaments as he attempted to dodge the blade as she thrust and slashed, screaming her frustration at her near misses as she made him dance to her murderous tune of death.

Jude backed his way to the door, out to the hallway, he turned towards the front door but spotted it was bolted so he headed for the stairs. At the top there were three doors, all closed. He headed for the room directly above where the attack started, pushed the door open, ran inside and slammed it shut. He fell against the door his dead weight keeping Ivy from pushing it open. She screamed her anger.

He felt even weaker now, he'd lost a lot of blood. He scanned the room and that was when he spotted her. A gagged and bruised Olga gaffer taped to a chair, struggling to free herself.

'Christ,' he whispered. 'Hold on,' the words were to himself as well as to Olga. 'Hold on…'

A bang and the door rattled as Ivy in her frustration sank the knife into it. But it was oak so it merely shed a few splinters. Jude's eyes met Olga's, he pulled his phone out of his pocket and hit the emergency call button as – drenched in his own blood - he slowly slid down to the floor.

'Help, police… I need the police….and an ambulance…'

31

What happened at 3 Blacksmiths Yard gave the village gossips even more to cling on to. Like a game of Chinese whispers, the tale of the attack was embroidered with a different colour thread each time it was retold, until a detailed tapestry emerged telling an intricate story of violence, blood-shed and killing, very little of which matched what actually went on.

What did happen after the attack was a mystery to Jude as well. He had lost a lot of blood and didn't come round until the following evening when he opened his eyes and saw grey pools and a dimpled smile watching over him.

'You're awake at last.'

He recognized the voice, it was Fearless.

'Hi,' he said, aware how weak he sounded. He wanted to say more but his throat was so dry he couldn't.

'How you doing?'

'Okay,' Jude struggled to sit up then spotted his heavily bandaged arm, and fell back.

'Would you like a drink of water?' Fearless nodded to the water jug on his bedside table.

'Please,' he whispered.

She filled a glass, leant over, placed her hand behind his head, lifted him gently and held the drink to his lips.

'Thanks.'

'You had us all worried for a while there.'

'Us?'

'Rosebud, Dexter, everyone here.'

'I'm okay.'

'I'm glad to hear it.'

'But is it bad that I can't feel my arm?'

'Don't worry,' she gave a short laugh. 'You will, when the painkillers wear off. You lost a lot of blood.'

'I.. I remember… I thought I was going to die.'

Jude returned to the moment when, one minute he was spitting and patting down his hair in the reflection of a stained-glass window and the next he was fighting a fearless teenager with a knife and a will to kill. He winced.

'You okay?'

'Sure.'

'D.I. Jones is going to need to speak to you. She's going to want to know everything that you can remember. Let me know when you're ready to speak to her.'

He returned to the previous day. It had started as any other. He had put the laundry in the washing machine fully expecting to hang it out on the line later in the day. He had taken a chicken out of the freezer, fully expecting to cook it for his tea. He had told Spud that he would be a couple of hours and that when he got back they would go for a marathon walk over the Fens.

'Spud!' He struggled to get up forgetting he was in no fit state to seek out his pet. His attempt at shouting tightened his throat.

'Relax,' said Fearless. 'Rosebud and Dexter are taking care of him. They said not to worry about anything, in fact, Dexter asked me to give you this note.

Jude rested again. He felt too groggy to even open the envelope, let alone read what was inside so he whispered to her to read it to him.

Fearless smiled and ripped open the envelope.

Mate,

Heard what happened, real bummer. But I did tell you that chick was seriously weird, didn't I? I would come and see you but I'm allergic to hospitals - they bring me out in hives. Don't take it personally mate. Rosie wanted to come along; she even

184

bought some grapes (in a bottle) but I persuaded her to wait till you got home as I think she might find it a bit depressing.

Between us we're taking care of Spud. I really think he likes us (prefers me though), he's one very clever mutt. I think I might have to get a dog.

They reckon you're going to be out in a couple of days so see you then.

Dexter.

P.S. If you see Nurse Isabella she'll give you a great bed bath but no making eyes at her cos she's my wife, (I think that's why I'm allergic to hospitals).

32

Three days later Jude was sat at his garden table trying to piece together the jigsaw that Rosebud had given him.

'Well, aren't you the one?'

He turned and watched as Dexter did his usual one-handed leap into his garden.

'Don't mind me,' said Jude, he turned and grinned at his neighbour. 'Thanks, for looking after Spud. I owe you big time.'

'I know you do mate. Don't worry I won't forget. He was great company, really good fun, even came out with me on a couple of jobs.'

'Did he? He was okay?'

'Good as gold. Did exactly as he was told and he loves the Land Rover.'

'Glad to hear it.'

'Rosie helped too. She'll be glad your back, she's been worried sick.'

'Has she?'

Dexter nodded.

'Yep, underneath that tough exterior is a heart of platinum.'

'Platinum? Really?'

'Oh yes,' said Dexter. 'And now that you're back on your feet, sort of, we need to plan our next move.'

'Do we?'

'Course, we're a team remember?'

'Are we?' Jude said jokingly. 'I don't remember that.'

'Ha,' Dexter laughed. 'Must be the drugs they gave you; you know when you got cut.' He approached Jude, stared closely at his bandaged arm then poked it.

'Ouch!'

'Just checking,' said Dexter.

'What? What exactly are you checking?'

'That it's actually hurting. Now I need to know everything that happened. Every little detail.' He smiled. 'You see, so many reasons for me to visit, come and check you're okay.'

'And I need to know more about Nurse Isabella. You? Married? I had no idea.'

'To be honest mate, for the first three months neither did I,' he grinned. 'I was pissed up for most of it. It was a lifetime ago. Good swerve at changing the subject though.' He turned and went and sat on the grass. 'Besides, catching killers is far more exciting, you do realize you are now the local hero.'

'Am I?'

'Course,' Dexter scratched at his chin. 'Liking the beard thing going on by the way.'

Jude laughed, he hadn't shaved since it happened and his stubble had grown into a proper beard. He rubbed at his chin enjoying the feeling.

'I'm going to shave it off soon, and I need a haircut.'

'Make yourself office ready again.'

'I like to look smart.'

'Course you do, now come on tell me what happened.'

'Haha! With your contacts you probably know more than I do, you do realise I passed out.'

Dexter lifted his hand and copied him, rubbing his chin again but this time with a thoughtful look as if pondering the credibility of Jude's statement. A couple of seconds and he nodded agreement.

'I did hear you wimped out,' he stretched his legs out in front and rested on his elbows behind him. 'But I would like to hear the gory details from your good self.'

'How did you hear I wimped out? Who told you?'

'I have my sources,' he said tapping the side of his nose. 'Which, if I may remind you, in case you have forgotten that too, are available as we – Team Mumford - unite in our crusade for justice.'

'Oh you're good,' Jude laughed. He leaned over, picked up a glass of water with his unbandaged right arm and took a couple of sips.

'But reliable as my sources are,' said Dexter, 'it's always best to get the lowdown from the primary source. And that my friend, on this occasion, is you. We need to work with facts, don't we?'

'Indeed we do,' Jude nodded. 'I hope I don't disappoint.'

'Besides, I gave you Ivy's address in the first place. I sort of feel responsible for what she's done to you.'

'Don't be daft,' Jude laughed.

'I always knew that girl wasn't quite right in the head.'

'Well thanks for the warning, mate.'

'Oh come on! I did tell you she was one weird chick.'

'Weird is hardly the same as 'knife wielding maniac' is it?'

'Okay, okay, sorry you got sliced,' Dexter nodded at Jude's arm.

'Joking. I was joking,' said Jude, before adding in a more serious voice, 'so, did you know Ivy was Saffron's daughter?'

Dexter sat up straight, the answer to Jude's question clear in his expression.

'Bloody blimey no I didn't.'

'Or that Lawson Peterson was her dad?'

'Bloody hell! Didn't know that either. But, yeah, it makes sense, he was always hanging round her at school. We all knew it was only because her parents had money and to be honest Saffron knew as well, I'm guessing.'

'He raped her. It was when she came back from France for her mother's funeral.'

'Aha! The chatter was that something untoward went on,' Dexter nodded his head in understanding. 'And when they arrived back with a baby, that got the gossips going big time.'

'I bet it did.'

'But by the time I'd got back from travelling things had settled down. Olga had turned up and moved into the cottage with a baby and I'm guessing people thought it was the same one.' He sat up, pulled a tin from the pocket of his shorts, sorted banana skins and tobacco and started to roll a spliff.

'Do you have to?'

'Boss, may I remind you that you are no longer a copper, so unless you intend to grass me up,' he grinned. 'See what I did there?'

Jude watched him and as he did, memories of his five-month bender resurfaced. He kept silent though.

'So matey,' Dexter was really cheery. 'Tell me everything, exactly as it happened.'

'She came at me from behind,' he said. 'With a knife.'

'Bloody blimey.'

'I was gazing into the snug, fortunately I saw her reflection, in the stained-glass window.'

'Bloody, flaming blimey.'

'Otherwise, who knows... from what I gather a knife in the back seems to be her M.O.'

'You're back!' It was Rosebud, sunhat on, carrying a watering can which she put down. 'How you doing? You okay? You poor dear.'

'I'm fine, thanks.' Jude lifted his bandaged arm. 'Thanks for helping out with Spud by the way, very kind of you.'

'That's okay, he was great fun.'

'Fancy a puff, Rosie?' Dexter held out his spliff.

Rosebud shook her head. Dexter held it out to Jude; he shook his head as well.

189

'Help you relax mate. Make you feel better.'

'I feel fine, honestly,' said Jude. 'I've just got to wait for my arm to heel, then I'll be as right as rain.'

'Please yourself,' said Dexter. 'You know I still can't believe it, no murders for years then two in quick succession. Another couple and we could become the murder capital of the U.K.'

'I hate to think what that would do to house prices,' said Rosebud. 'Any idea when the last one was?'

'It was up at the Manor, before you moved here,' said Dexter. 'Bob Mann, he was the previous owner, the one before the now dead previous owner.'

'Two dead Lords of the Manor, both knifed in the back, sounds as if the place is cursed,' Rosebud looked thoughtful. 'The Murders at the Manor, that would be a great title for a book.'

'Great,' said Dexter, eager to join in. A Manor House that dishes out karma to any villains who live in it.'

'Very believable,' said Rosebud.

'A story of revenge dished out by a ghost walking the halls,' Dexter started to get way too excited. 'He, the ghost, met a horrible death and he walks the corridors of the Manor looking for villains to murder horribly.'

'He? Why not a she?' said Rosebud.

'Naaah,' said Dexter 'It should be a male ghost, more believable.'

'How sexist!' said Rosebud.

'I like to look upon it as a compliment to the female sex.'

Jude listened and watched his neighbours as they teased each other with an imaginary story that Dexter wanted Rosebud to write but that she made clear she wanted nothing to do with.

'Rosebud,' Jude interrupted their chatter. She paused, her eyes on him, questioning the interruption.

'Due to my enforced rest, I've been having a go at the jigsaw you leant me.' Jude heard Dexter laugh but didn't think anything of it. 'And guess what, I think you've given me the wrong pieces.'

190

'Have you counted them?' she asked, a wide-eyed look of innocence on her face.

'First thing I did.'

'And?'

'There are a thousand pieces, the problem is they don't match the picture on the box.'

She laughed so loudly it made Jude jump. As she quietened, her shoulders dipped and she let out an exaggerated sigh.

'You've not figured it out yet then?' she said.

'What's to figure out? Here, come and check.'

Earlier that day Jude had placed all of the pieces in their neat piles either side of the table.

'I've sorted out the corners, all of the edge pieces and they definitely do not match the picture,' he said.

Rosebud laughed again; this time Dexter joined in.

'I'll come round and put you out of your misery.' She headed to her back gate.

A couple of minutes later Rosebud and Dexter were stood one either side of Jude. They were laughing, he wasn't. Jude knew that they knew something that he didn't.

'Look,' he said. 'This picture in no way matches the jigsaw pieces.'

'You can be a cruel bitch sometimes,' said Dexter.

'Moi? Cruel?' Rosebud winked at Dexter and turned to Jude wide eyed.

'What?' said Jude. 'Tell me what I'm missing?'

'Have you read the instructions? Rosebud took the lid of the box from him, turned it upside down and showed it to him.

'It's a bloody jigsaw,' said Jude. 'Why would I read the instructions?'

'Because,' said Rosebud. 'This is not just any old jigsaw, and if you'd read the instructions, you would have understood that.'

191

'It's a picture of a room with a dog and a garden,' said Jude. 'And it's Christmas.'

'Correct on all counts,' she said. 'But that's not the picture you're making when you fit the pieces together.'

'Isn't it?' Jude screwed up his forehead, pulled at his beard.

'Nope,' she said, shaking her head slowly. 'You see this,' she turned the lid over to the picture side again and pointed to the dog sitting in front of the French windows staring out.

Jude nodded.

'Course.'

'Well, the picture you are trying to recreate is what the dog is seeing as he looks out of the French doors, it's his view. You've got to try to figure out what is in his line of vision.'

Jude stared at the front of the box and after a few seconds a slow smile showed his understanding. The longer he gazed at the picture, the more he thought about it, the broader his smile became.

'I get it!' he said eventually. 'What an ingenious idea.'

'I did it mate,' said Dexter. 'It's good fun.'

'You just have to put yourself into the position of the dog,' said Rosebud.

'Brilliant,' said Jude. He stared again at the picture, transfixed by the image. Rosebud and Dexter left him too it, not wanting to interrupt his train of thought. It was only when a doorbell interrupted the silence that Jude looked up.

'I think that was yours,' said Rosebud. She nodded to the box. 'Give it another go with your new found knowledge.'

'Excuse me a sec.' Jude got up and disappeared into his cottage. He reappeared a couple of minutes later balancing a tray with a jug of water and 4 glasses in his right hand.

'That was D.I. Jones,' he said, placing the tray on the table. 'She's on her way around the back.'

'Not letting her through the house then?' said Dexter.

'I made an excuse,' said Jude. 'Didn't want her to see my whiteboard.'

192

'Wise move,' said Dexter.

'And it gives you two a chance to buzz off,' Jude smiled at the horror on their faces.

'Why would we do that?' said Dexter. 'We're Team Mumford remember.'

'What he said,' said Rosebud.

D.I. Jones appeared through the back gate and was invited to sit at the table next to Jude. Dexter and Rosebud were both on the lawn, laying on their fronts facing them, resting on their elbows, their chins in their hands gazing at the detective and ex-detective as if they were the stars in a prime-time movie. All that was missing was the popcorn.

'I have news,' said D.I. Jones. She looked at Rosebud and Dexter.

'I guessed that's why you're here,' said Jude, he nodded to his neighbours, 'don't mind them.'

'Hi,' said Rosebud, giving a childlike wave.

'Watcha,' Dexter grinned. 'We're his assistants.'

'Assistants?' said D.I. Jones. She turned to Jude. 'You've got assistants?'

'He has,' said Dexter proudly. He pointed to Jude. 'He's like Santa and me and Rosie, well, we're like his elves. He gives us instructions, guides us, tell us what to do.' He paused. 'Only he's not the best at working as a team so we're having to teach him...'

'He's getting better though,' Rosebud interrupted, she turned to Jude. 'Aren't you?'

'What? What?' said D.I Jones.

'Don't mind them,' said Jude. 'They get a bit carried away.' He smiled at D.I. Jones. 'You were saying?'

'Okay, back to the real world,' D.I. Jones smiled and sat back. 'It's all good news. Thanks to you, I've ticked a few boxes this week.'

'Have you indeed?'

'So, I thought I'd come by and thank you personally.'

'I'm listening,' said Jude.

And so were Rosebud and Dexter.

D.I. Jones placed an object onto the table. Jude recognized it straight away.

'My wallet!' Jude grinned. 'Where did you find it?'

'On the river path, credit cards, even your cash, still in it.'

'Brilliant!' he picked it up and searched through it. 'Wow, thanks. It must have fallen out of my pocket.' He placed it back onto the table. 'But I'm guessing that's not why you're here?'

'That's quite correct.' D.I. Jones stared first at Jude then at Rosebud and Dexter. 'Ivy has been arrested for the murder of Lawson Peterson.'

'Christ,' said Jude.

'Any clues as to why she killed him?' Dexter shouted over.

'We are still investigating, but it appears she confronted him a couple of days earlier, told him she knew he was her dad, and apparently he laughed at her and made a few quite nasty comments. By the sound of it she went off and stewed for a bit then returned and, well, poor bloke, never knew what hit him.'

'Bloody blimey,' said Dexter.

'That poor child,' said Jude. 'It's all my fault.'

D.I. Jones, Dexter and Rosebud turned to him.

Jude returned to the day when he was in the cemetery, the day Ivy overheard the conversation he had with her mother.

'It was because of me; she overheard her mother telling me he was her father.'

'Don't be too hard on yourself,' said the detective, 'you weren't to know.'

'But she killed him because of me,' said Jude. 'Did she confess?'

'Not exactly, 'said the detective. 'I'm not sure if you're aware they have pretty tight security up at the Manor.'

'I did know,' said Jude. 'Was she caught on CCTV?'

194

'She was caught on their cat's petcam.'

'Blue!' said Jude.

'That's the one,' said D.I. Jones. 'Sat on top of the fridge and watched the whole thing calm as you like. Didn't do a thing – maybe they should have got a dog!'

'Their cat's got a webcam?' said Rosebud.

'On its collar,' said Jude.

'Wow! I might get one for Simmy.'

'I love CCTV, makes our life so much simpler,' said D.I. Jones.

'Hey Jude, maybe you should get one for the big man,' Dexter laughed and nodded towards Spud who was lying flat out further down the lawn.

D.I. Jones turned to Jude.

'It's a damn good job you spotted her reflection, else you would have gone the same way as Mr Peterson.'

Jude reddened and swallowed hard.

'Don't think that hasn't occurred to me.'

'And she is of course also being questioned about her attack on your good self.'

'Was my statement okay? Do you need anything else from me?'

'I'm going to need a statement about what happened that day in the cemetery,' said D.I. Jones. 'I've spoken to her mother but I need to hear it from you. She's been charged with aiding and abetting an offender by the way.'

'But she was upstairs, gaffer taped to a chair.'

'She knew what Ivy had done and instead of reporting it to us she tried to cover it up. But it all took a turn when they had a row.'

'I'm not surprised by any of that,' said Jude.

'Of course, she's standing by Ivy.'

'She's her mother,' Jude paused, 'so you'd expect her to. Any idea what's going to happen to Ivy?'

'She's in a secure unit being assessed. Personally, I think the mother was in denial, the girl has always been a bit strange apparently.'

'I told him she was weird,' Dexter shouted over, he turned to Jude. 'I told you that didn't I?'

'And as we have already established,' said Jude with a wink at Rosebud, 'that is hardly the same thing as being a knife wielding maniac.' He turned to D.I. Jones. 'So is that it?'

'Oh no, no, no,' the detective shook her head, a wide grin appeared. 'I've ticked way more boxes than that.'

'I…, I mean we, my team and I, can't wait to hear it,' said Jude sitting back.

D.I. Jones leant forward over the table. Her body language suggested her words were for Jude's ears only.

'We now know that it was Mr Peterson who attacked Chantal Dubois.'

'Was it? I thought Sasha – his wife – gave him an alibi?' said Jude.

D.I. Jones sat back, a satisfied grin on her face.

'She changed her statement. Says he forced her to provide him with an alibi. Terrified of him she was.' She lifted her arm and ticked the air with an imaginary pencil. 'So that's another box ticked.'

Jude could not summon up the enthusiasm D.I. Jones was displaying.

I think you're wrong, but I have no idea why.

'Well done,' he said.

'Hold on, there's more.'

'More?'

'Years ago,' said D.I. Jones. 'It was just after I'd become a detective, the previous owner of the Manor.'

196

'Bob Mann,' said Jude.

'You've heard of him?'

'I heard he was murdered. I understood he was Sasha's uncle.'

D.I. Jones nodded.

'Huge mystery at the time. He was a bit of a villain apparently, there were loads of suspects, few clues, we never even found the murder weapon.'

'I heard he was stabbed,' said Jude. 'In the back.'

'Correct,' she said. 'Same as Mr Peterson, knife right between the blades.' The detectives body shook in an exaggerated tremor. 'Poor bugger didn't stand a chance.'

'Well, Ivy couldn't have done that could she?' said Jude. 'She wasn't even born.'

'Very true,' said the detective. 'But we've got the murder weapon. It was found at the back of Mr Peterson's safe.'

'What? And it was definitely the knife that killed him?' said Jude.

The detective nodded.

'No doubt at all.'

'Bloody blimey!' Dexter shouted.

Jude and D.I. Jones turned around.

'Sorry!' Dexter reddened.

'Don't mind him,' said Jude.

'I won't,' said D.I. Jones. 'We're old friends.' She picked up her glass of water.

'By the way Beryl,' said Dexter, 'they know, I told them… …about your daddy… sorry.'

'Beryl?' said Rosebud and Jude together.

'What?' Dexter looked one to the other. 'That's her name.'

'No it's not, it's D.I. Jones,' said Rosebud.

'Excuse me you lot, I am here you know,' D.I. Jones glared at the three of them then turned to Dexter. 'Now, what did you go and do that for?'

'I'm a victim of circumstance, they got me drunk,' Dexter lowered his head and put on his sad face. 'Sorry mate.'

'D.I. Jones please do not concern yourself, your parentage secret is safe with us,' Rosebud turned to Jude. 'Isn't it?'

'Of course,' said Jude. 'I quite understand why you wouldn't want it to be common knowledge. Can we get on with why you're here?'

'Right, turns out it was him, he did it. Lawson Peterson killed Bob Mann.'

'Any idea as to why?' said Jude.

'He did it so's his girlfriend, the lovely Sasha, could part inherit the Manor. That way he could afford to buy it.' D.I. Jones sat back obviously pleased with herself. 'Bob Mann was a bit of a ruthless sod by all accounts. Anyway, after his death, his two nieces Sasha and Lottie inherited the Manor House. Lawson was going out with Sasha at the time and when she got her half, they got married and all he had to do to be Lord of the Manor was buy out the sister. Get it?'

Jude didn't get it. He didn't get it at all.

If Lawson Peterson killed Bob Mann why on earth would he stash the murder weapon in his safe?

33

Jude's whiteboard now resembled a work of modern art. It's boxes, lines and jottings could be interpreted by ten different people in ten different ways.

The previous evening he'd added a new name, Bob Mann – local gangster. He had no idea if there was a link between what had happened at the Manor House all of those years ago and what had happened to Chantal but he'd added it anyway.

His injured left arm was now on the mend, but his guilt at being the one to push Ivy over the edge to prompt her to kill her own father, weighed him down and reignited the previous guilt he felt over leaving Chantal to freeze to death.

It was worse after dark, his brain switched to overdrive and acted out one scenario after another and his crossover to sleep was flickering and fitful.

Experience had taught Jude that in order to tread the pathway of truth, he had to ask the right people the right questions. And that was causing him a problem. However, as his arm healed, so his mind cleared and one morning just as a gentle light spilled through the bare windows and across his bed, he opened his eyes and it dawned on him who he needed to speak to next.

Jude had still not remembered to oil his bike and the squeak had got worse. By the time he walked his bike up the gravel driveway to Eaststowe Manor, he didn't hear the rhythmic noise as the wheel turned, its pitch as tuneless as a child scratching a violin for the first time. No, he listened to the rhythmic message being transmitted to him, WD40, WD40, WD40. He had the newly purchased tin; it was biding its time on the shelf in his shed ready to anoint his bike with the gift of silence. But with recent events a squeaky bike wheel had not been a priority for him.

The skewbald pony was standing, head over the post and rail fence. It could have been the squeak from the bike wheel that brought it there but it was more likely to have been the owner of the dark blue Nissan hatchback parked alongside the fence. Jude rested his bike against a Silver Birch.

199

He was about to head up the steps to the front door when he heard shouting from around the side of the house. He recognized the female voice, it was Sasha's. Instead of announcing his arrival in the usual way, he turned and headed towards the kitchen garden.

He could hear another voice now; it was a man. When he got to the wrought iron garden gate, he peeked around it. He thought he had recognized the car on the driveway and a few feet from where he was standing, it was confirmed. Sasha's visitor was Dr Fernsby. A very angry Dr Fernsby. He and Sasha were facing each other, having a full-on row. They took it in turns to scream their grievances at each other. It was only Jude who stood his ground and listened.

Dr Fernsby: You called my wife! You had no right getting her involved.

Sasha: But I had to, I couldn't do it all on my own…

Dr Fernsby: You should have contacted me then!

Sasha: You're always at work!

Dr Fernsby: Then you should have contacted the police.

Sasha: No! Chantal, she was going to tell them about Lawson, what he did to Saffron. I couldn't!

Dr. Fernsby: You put us through this to save yourself!

Sasha: Not me! Charlie, he loved his dad. Look, I'm sorry, I suppose I should have contacted the police but…

Dr Fernsby: But it was an accident…

Sasha: There was an argument. She had a head injury you stupid man! You weren't there…

Dr Fernsby: No, I wasn't, because you…

Sasha: Because I took control of an impossible situation.

Dr Fernsby: And made things ten times worse. That Olga woman turned up on my doorstep telling me my Freya has been spreading vicious rumours…

Sasha: I had to deflect the blame somehow.

Dr Fernsby: Of course I denied Freya would do such a thing.

200

Sasha: Did she tell you anything?

Dr Fernsby: My wife told me everything, she broke down in front of me. How do you think that made me feel?

There was a short pause. When Sasha spoke again her voice was calmer.

Sasha: I'm guessing not as bad as if you were having to traipse up to the prison every week...

Jude stayed hidden and silent and when the shouting stopped and he returned to his squeaky bike, the questions he had come to ask Sasha Peterson had been answered.

34

Thursday night was curry night at 2 Willow Walk. Jude was updating his whiteboard when it arrived at just after 7pm. He loved his curry, but he was eager to continue his work so he ate his food in half the time it usually took him.

According to D.I. Jones three murders had been solved. Tick. Tick. Tick.

Tick 1: Ivy Kaine killed Lawson Peterson. She had confronted him about being her father, he had laughed at her and so she had returned and killed him. And Blue the cat had captured it all on his collar camera.

Tick 2: Lawson Peterson killed Bob Mann, the previous owner of the Manor. Lawson had motive because with Sasha's uncle dead, Sasha and her sister inherited the Manor House and he could inherit half of it by marrying her and buying the other half from her sister. Okay, that sounded feasible, except that he kept the murder weapon with his victim's blood still on it in his safe – why on earth would he do that?

Tick 3: Lawson Peterson killed Chantal Dubois. He apparently attacked her and left her for dead because she kept pestering him about what he did to her brother. Sasha had withdrawn her statement giving him an alibi on the night of the murder, so theoretically he had opportunity – but there was no actual evidence he did it, and anyway, why on earth would he kill her for being a nuisance?

As a result of his recent visit to the Manor, Jude now knew that Lawson Peterson was not responsible for Chantal's death. Sasha was involved and so was Mrs Fernsby. But how could he prove it? Lawson was disliked by most of the villagers and apart from his son Charlie, who apparently loved his dad in spite of his bullying ways, Jude could not think of a single person who was mourning his passing, so should he even try?

A knock at the door interrupted him. It was Sasha Peterson.

'A few minutes of your time,' the tone of her voice suggested that he had little choice in the matter. He opened the door slightly and she took it as an invitation to enter his cottage and sit down in the middle of his sofa.

'I take it that is your murder board?' She nodded to the whiteboard.

'I was just updating it.' He stood in front of it in an effort to block her view. 'What can I do for you?'

Spud, was standing by the kitchen door, he let out a low growl.

'Spud! Stay, it's okay boy.'

'Is it?' Sasha stared at Jude and pulled a pack of cigarettes from her jacket pocket. 'Okay?' She took a cigarette from the packet and placed it between her lips.

'I'm sorry, no smoking indoors,' said Jude. 'And what exactly do you mean?'

'You were seen,' she removed the cigarette.

'Excuse me?'

'The other day when you came to my house. Charlie spotted you.'

Jude reddened.

Blast that boy.

'What did you want?'

'I came to see you.'

'That's not what I asked. What did you want?'

'To ask you a couple of questions.'

'I'm here now. Go on, ask me your questions.'

'No need, you've already answered them.'

'I see. Who answered them?'

'You... and Dr Fernsby,' Jude paused, he stared at her. 'I heard you arguing. But I'm guessing you already know that which is why you're here.'

'So, you sneaked into my house and listened in to a private discussion.'

'No, I visited your house and overheard an argument taking place in the garden.' He cleared his throat. 'And I now know that you were involved in Chantal's death and so was Mrs Fernsby.'

She lifted her left hand and took her eyes off him to examine her perfectly shaped red nails. Jude did not take his eyes off her though.

'And why would you think something so silly?'

Jude scratched his chin; he had shaved off his beard a couple of days previously and he was beginning to miss it. He put his elbows on his knees to bend further forward.

'Let's just say, it's all a bit too convenient,' his eyes stayed on her as he spoke, looking for a hint, a clue, that he was getting under the skin of this woman. 'Now, at a guess, I reckon you're here because you want to know what I heard.'

She was still examining her nails. Her face gave nothing away so he continued.

'It was you who told Charlie to spread rumours about Olga and Chantal. And he told Freya and they were so nasty the other kids at school started giving Ivy grief. What you didn't count on was Ivy telling her mother.'

Sasha shifted uncomfortably and gazed at him with unseeing eyes.

'And her going around to confront Dr Fernsby,' said Jude. 'You know, I thought it was odd when I first met you. When we were in the garden and Lawson arrived, you told him I was a tennis coach.'

'I read it in the papers, along with hundreds of other people. It said you were a private detective who had come here to be a tennis coach. You see, there is a perfectly simple explanation.'

'The only simple explanation is the truth.'

She's on the defensive.

'The truth.' She turned her gaze to him. 'So tell me Mr Mumford, do you think your version of the truth matters?'

'Truth has only one version.'

204

'What I mean is,' her lips turned up to taste a smile, 'why aren't you at the police station, telling them your wild theories?'

Because...'

...because I have no real evidence and I don't want to tell the police where some of my information came from that's why.

'Your silence says it all,' she said. 'The facts are that you listened in to a private discussion on private property between myself and the good doctor and you imagined you heard some sort of argument which well... quite frankly is ludicrous.' She narrowed her eyes and stared into him. 'Are you still on painkillers? Maybe you're taking a few too many?'

'I know what I heard.'

'And I know what is the right thing to do. If you do go to the police, Dr Fernsby and I will tell them you got it wrong. They think they've solved the case, so who will they believe?' She stood up, snapped open her handbag, pulled out a lighter, lit her cigarette, took a long drag and blew out the smoke. 'In short Mr Mumford, you have no evidence, no witnesses, no nothing.'

35

I t was approaching midnight; Jude had been staring at his whiteboard for over five minutes. He was hoping inspiration would strike and as the midnight hour passed, a full blood moon rose over the Fens and it did. He got up and added a new name to his whiteboard; Lottie Armitage.

The following day at 1pm he was standing on Rosebud's doorstep. She opened her door, lunch plate in hand a gaping silk lemon dressing gown with a trim top and matching pair of shorts. She grinned.

'Hi, well this is a surprise.'

'Hi.'

'Come in. I'm just on lunch…'

'I know, that's why I knocked now.'

She went and sat on a tweed settee with a high back and nodded him to an oversized armchair.

'Thanks,' she said. She crossed her bare legs. 'I appreciate you not interrupting me during my working hours.'

Jude sat down and scanned the room. Shelves of books, plants, functional furniture pieces before his gaze settled on her. For a few seconds they looked at each other in silence, then both tried to speak at the same time.

'You work in your pyjamas?' said Jude.

'Excuse the jammies,' said Rosebud.

And both reddened up.

'Go on,' said Jude.

'Yes,' she nodded, 'if I'm feeling inspired when I wake up, I travel from my bed to the kitchen to feed Simeon of course, then straight to my laptop so that I don't lose the creative flow. She blushed again as she finished speaking. 'I guess that sounds a bit mad. Have you had lunch? Fancy a sandwich?'

Jude shook his head.

'I'm good thanks...'

'How's the arm?'

'Well on the mend thanks.'

'Not a good injury to have when you're sporty,' she grinned then stopped suddenly. 'Not that any injury is good, at any time, if you get my drift.'

Jude laughed.

'I do,' Jude laughed, 'Fortunately it's my left arm, still, I had to postpone my first two clients.' He paused. 'Now, remember you said you wanted to help?'

'Of course. Is that why you're here? I'm impressed you're starting to work as a team.' Rosebud put down her plate, brought her legs up onto the sofa and tucked them under. 'Team Mumford.'

'Well, I suppose it's more of a favour really,' Jude smiled at her eagerness.

'A favour?'

'Tomorrow, I need to go off out for the day.'

'Is it part of our investigation?'

'It is.'

'Where are you going?'

'Scarborough.'

'Can I come along? I've never been to Scarborough, and Dext too. He could come, we can both help.'

'No, neither have I been to Scarborough, and no.'

'Can I ask why not?'

'Sorry, I need to go on my own,' said Jude. 'But there is something you can do which will help me enormously.'

'What's that then?' She smiled her excitement.

'It's going to be a very long day and I'm not taking Spud.'

'I think I can see where this is going,' her excitement tapered off.

'I wondered if you wouldn't mind feeding him for me. At lunch time, and again in the evening,' Jude stared eyes pleading. 'Please, it really will be a great help.'

'Okay then. But what about his walkies?'

'He'll be fine, I'll take him for a long walk later and wear him out.'

'What's in Scarborough?'

'I need to see someone.'

'Who?'

'Lottie Armitage.'

'Who's that?'

'Sasha Peterson's sister.'

'Aha! The sister. So what's she got to do with it all?'

'That's what I intend to find out.'

'You've got some mystery thing going on in your head, haven't you?'

'I haven't figured things out yet, but I think she may be able to help.'

'Don't be a spoilsport, tell me.'

'I'm sorry, I can't, I have no evidence… yet. That's why I'm going to Scarborough. I'll tell you when things are clearer in my own mind.'

'You don't think it was Lawson who attacked Chantal, do you?'

'I know he didn't.'

'You know? Do you know who did?'

'I have a good idea.'

'So why aren't you at the police station, like any normal citizen?'

'I haven't got any evidence,' Jude shook his head.

'Let me get this straight. You want me to look after Spud while you swan off to the seaside to get evidence to prove that a person who you are not prepared to name attacked my friend.'

'That's right.'

'How could I possibly say no.'

That night in bed, Jude pondered his trip to Scarborough. But it was not just his next day adventure that kept him awake. Saffron had been constantly on his mind. She was a woman whose life had taken one tragic turn after another, and as each life blow struck, instead of bouncing back she sank deeper into a personal pit of despair. He fell asleep with her in his night thoughts, and when he woke just before 5am, his arm pain free for the first time, he knew exactly what he could do to help her.

36

The train was twenty-five minutes late leaving Eaststowe. Jude didn't mind because it gave him a chance to grab a black coffee from the station cafe. He gazed out of the window for most of the journey, fields, houses, shopping centres, industrial estates, more houses, then eventually, the sea. The view excited his bones, his heartbeat quickened as he watched the glistening ripples of the wavelets as they lapped the shore-line.

He was looking forward to his visit. He intended to make a day of it and visit the castle, the open-air theatre, the tramway and maybe even go for a stroll along the beach.

Apart from the slight delay to his journey, it was all going well, he felt upbeat, positive and as he neared his destination, he had high hopes the day was going to provide some of the answers he was searching for.

When the train arrived at Scarborough station he headed for the street to the sound of seagulls and the taste of salt in the air. He followed his mobile phone instructions to the Grand Hotel. And that's when things started to take an unusual turn.

The sound of seagulls got louder, the racket was interspersed with the screams and the laughter of small children, most of them off their faces on ice cream. And that is when he heard it. Somewhere a dog barked. At first it was background noise, but it barked again; nearer this time.

That sounds like my Spud.

His thoughts turned to his pet and he wondered what he was up to at home, whether he was indoors or outside in the back garden, basking in the sun, or maybe ogling Rosebud doing yoga in her garden.

His phone told him to turn left, he obeyed and the Grand Hotel appeared in front of him, he looked up to get a better view of the Victorian building but a bark made him turn. A large dog stood a few feet away from him. It bounded up to him wagging its' tail. Jude gasped. It was Spud.

'Spud! What on earth!'

Spud was whining, excited to see his master. Jude made a fuss of him but he was puzzled, he had after all left his pet at home under Rosebud's care. That was when Rosebud stepped out from around the corner, arms wide in greeting, a smile to match.

'Surprise.'

Dexter appeared next. No drama with the arms but a grin as wide as Rosebud's smile.

'Bet you didn't expect to see us.'

Jude stood aghast, looked from Spud, to Rosebud, to Dexter, back to Rosebud and back to Spud.

'Too bloody right I didn't.' He got down on one knee to make a fuss of Spud. It was also an attempt to hide his annoyance. 'What are you doing here?' he asked Dexter and Rosebud the question but his attention was still full with Spud.

'Do you remember that conversation we had about working as a team?' Dexter knelt down to pet Spud but it was also an attempt to catch Jude's eye. 'Well…'

As if it had been well rehearsed, Rosebud took up the tale of how the three of them had got there.'

'As Dext and I have never been here, we thought it would be a great day out.'

'Besides,' Dexter took over the conversation. 'I have to see the sea at least once a year and as I haven't seen it so far this year it seemed like the perfect opportunity.'

'But how did you get here?' Jude got to his feet and shook his head.

'In my trusty Land Rover of course,' said Dexter. 'Spud loved it.'

'And he was so good,' Rosebud added.

'I bet he was,' Jude turned to Rosebud. 'I left him in your care.'

'I beg your pardon. I hope you are not suggesting I have not taken care of him.'

Rosebud sounded annoyed, Jude couldn't tell if she was genuinely annoyed or if it was an act.

'You sort of kidnapped him,' said Jude.

'Hardly,' Rosebud burst out laughing. 'And if you want to split hairs, I could say you abandoned him.'

'Enough now team,' Dexter called for silence. He turned to Jude. 'Look, I know it must be a bit of a surprise…'

'Surprise? You can say that again.'

'Okay, so it's a shock, seeing us pop up like this, but try to look on the bright side.'

'There's a bright side?'

Dexter stood silent for a moment before jumping to attention and pointing at Jude.

'Course. You get a lift home.'

'Just think you haven't got to travel back on the bad, smelly old train,' Rosebud was keen to support the idea. 'It'll probably be late anyway.'

'That's if it's not cancelled,' Dexter added.

'Actually, I rather like train travel,' Jude was determined to sound at least a little annoyed by their antics, but his expression gave him away. 'And in my view, they're usually pretty reliable.'

'Bloody blimey,' Dexter turned to Rosebud. 'He's cracking a smile.'

The group headed for a bench overlooking the sea where Dexter and Rosebud did their best to persuade Jude to let them go with him to Lottie Armitage's house. But Jude was adamant he was going alone and it didn't take them long to realise he was not going to change his mind. He pointed out that she was expecting him to be alone and that she may be intimidated if the three of them went in 'mob handed.'

'What, even with Spud?' said Rosebud. 'How can anybody feel intimidated by Spudsy?' She leant across to stroke him and he jumped up and placed his paws on the bench beside her as if seeking out space to sit on her lap.

'Spud down,' Jude shouted at him. 'Okay, how about this for a plan? You go for a walk with Spud, and we'll meet up when I'm done.'

'Only if you promise to tell us everything about your interrogation,' said Dexter.

'Yes everything,' said Rosebud. 'Every little teensy detail.'

'Interrogation? It's hardly that, but I will tell you everything I can.'

'Fair do's,' said Rosebud. 'Will Spud be okay in the sea?'

'He'll love it. Best check first though, some beaches don't allow dogs.'

'Well,' Dexter grinned, 'we'll meet you back here in a couple of hours.'

***

Jude had recognized Lottie Armitage from her Facebook photos. She was the image of her sister. He had sent her a message and after a long internet silence she had agreed to see him.

She lived in the shadow of the Grand Hotel. A well-maintained Victorian town house with sash windows, red and gold curtains and a dark green front door.

She answered the door without a word and barely a smile, let him in and pointed him to the back room.

The home still retained many of its original Victorian features, like her sister, this woman had taste. She nodded him to a green chesterfield sofa. Jude sat and she did the same on a similar one opposite. Even now, as they watched each other, there were no polite questions 'How was the journey?' or even the offer of a courtesy drink. She sat straight backed and asked the first question.

'How is Sasha?'

'She's fine,' said Jude. 'Seems to be holding it all together in spite of Lawsons death.'

'I'm not surprised.'

'Are you not?'

'She's well rid of him, nasty piece of work.'

'I heard he had narcistic tendencies.'

She laughed.

'Huh! You make him sound like a political party.'

'I take it you weren't a fan?'

'At first I thought he was only after her for her money.'

'And you changed your mind?'

Lottie nodded.

'He was after her money but there was more than that, he was completely obsessed with her.'

'She's a good-looking woman. She looks like you.' He reddened. 'Sorry, that sounds a bit…'

'Don't apologise. You're right, she is beautiful.' She laughed.

'I could see you were her sister from your Facebook photos.'

'People do say we look alike. But I was lucky enough to get the common sense.'

'You really should secure your Facebook account a bit better by the way.'

'Cheeky!' Lottie laughed again.

Jude was relieved to see the woman opposite him relax a little. He sat back and crossed his legs.

'I don't suppose you could tell me a little, about their relationship?'

'He was a real bully,' she sighed. 'I could never understand why she stayed with him. In the end he treated her like a servant and she put up with it. It was as if he had some sort of hold over her.' She paused, sighed and looked directly him. 'When she married that bastard, she just exchanged one abuser for another.'

Jude uncrossed his legs and leaned forward.

'Can I ask what exactly you mean by that?'

She stood up.

214

'Would you like a cup of tea, or maybe I can get you coffee?'

She made him coffee, offered him biscuits and then told him exactly what she meant. It took her nearly two hours.

After their talk they said their goodbyes and parted on friendly terms. Jude was pleased, it had been a fruitful visit and he thought that Lottie seemed relieved to have a heavy burden lifted from her. A story previously untold. The trouble was, was it her story to tell?

He headed to the beach front, to the bench to meet Dexter and Rosebud. They were already there with a bag full of sandwiches, crisps, and drinks. Between mouthfuls Jude batted away their questions telling them he needed to think about everything she had told him before he repeated it. Dexter wasn't happy about it but Rosebud understood and supported his silence.

After lunch they walked along the beach, splashed about in the shallow sea, they visited the castle and ate ice cream - Spud devoured his own vanilla cone in one mouthful – then they went to a bar and ate and drank and readied themselves for the journey back to Eaststowe.

Jude sat in the back of the Land Rover with Spud. Dexter and Rosebud cracked jokes and sang songs, 'Ging Gang Goolie' (Dexter's choice from his scouting days) and 'I Will Survive' (Rosebud's choice because she had the words written down and pinned up on her wall at home after a disastrous relationship several years previously). They stopped off at motorway services for a drink and a toilet break (much to the relief of Spud) and when they piled back into the Land Rover Jude said he was 'dog tired' and to prove his point, rested his head against Spud and pretended sleep. It was not long before a genuine tiredness overtook him and he did exactly that. He didn't wake up until they turned into Willow Walk.

'Wakey! Wakey!' Dexter shouted. 'Bloody blimey mate, you could snore for England.'

It was just after 11pm. They swapped 'goodnights' Dexter and Rosebud hugged and they parted ways.

Jude went upstairs to shower and change. He was back down twenty minutes later. He grabbed a torch and Spud's lead from the kitchen and together they headed off out over the Fens. They stuck to the managed path, pausing only when he heard a rustling in the bushes to see if he could spot any creatures of the night. He recollected what D.I. Jones had said to him at the police station on the day he had found Chantal's body. *'It's a creepy place at night tis the Fen.'* In a way she was right, it was creepy, but night time wildlife, animal calls and rustling bushes held no fears for him. It was people, not animals that scared him the most.

37

After lunch the next day, Jude picked up the pot of fresh percolated coffee, the largest mug he could find and went through to the front room. His laptop, pens, sticky-notes and highlighters were placed alongside each other on the table, he was ready to start work. A picture was starting to emerge. It was like crossing a bridge from a barren wasteland into a garden. All he had to do now was dig out the weeds.

He picked up a red highlighter, went over to his whiteboard and was about to start writing when there was a knock at his front door. He walked backwards to it not taking his eyes off his whiteboard. He was still staring at it when he opened the door.

'We've come to say sorry.'

It was Rosebud's voice. Jude turned around. Rosebud and Dexter were stood side by side on his doorstep, each holding out their peace offering, a bottle of Dom Perignon (Rosebud) and a large bottle of cider (Dexter).

'It was wrong of us to follow you up to Scarborough,' said Dexter with his sad face. His eyes, wide in innocence, still sparkled mischief though.

'And it was wrong of me to drag Spud along,' said Rosebud. 'Even though he really enjoyed the day. It was a thoughtless, selfish…'

'It was my bad,' Dexter interrupted. 'I'm a bad person, it was a deleterious…'

'Oh stop it the pair of you!' Jude stood and stared at his neighbours. In truth he had long since forgiven their escapade. Spud had had a great day and – after the initial shock – he had too. He had learned a lot from Lottie, he had enjoyed his tour of Scarborough and his neighbours company. But he wasn't about to tell them that.

'We're forgiven then,' Dexter invited himself into the cottage, brandishing the bottle of cider in front of him as if it were a white flag. 'I hope so cos we need to plan our next move.'

Jude sighed and opened the door wide.

'I suppose,' he said. 'Take a seat, I'll get the glasses.'

'Top man,' said Dexter.

Ten minutes later, Jude was on the sofa watching Rosebud and Dexter as they stood in front of his whiteboard examining his work.

'Have you updated it?' said Rosebud. 'From yesterday?'

'I was about to,' Jude paused with another heavy sigh. 'But then a couple of clowns knocked on the door.'

'Funny,' said Rosebud.

'Un-bloody-grateful,' said Dexter.

Rosebud and Dexter examined every box, every line attempting to understand the connections and catch up with Jude's thinking.

'I must say,' said Dexter. 'There are a lot of lines going nowhere.'

'That's because I haven't finished making the updates yet. And that's because…'

'I know, I know, a couple of clowns knocked on your door,' Dexter grinned. 'You love us really though, don't you?'

Rosebud nudged Dexter.

'Best not wind him up.'

'Excuse me I am here,' said Jude.

'Sorry,' Rosebud turned to him and smiled. 'Be a love and pop open the champagne.'

A couple of minutes later, Rosebud was examining the whiteboard again, this time with a glass of champagne in her hand. Dexter was doing the same with his glass of cider and Jude was sitting on his sofa with a glass of champagne watching them.

'According to D.I. Jones it's all done and dusted, case closed.' Rosebud nodded to the board. 'Nothing on here suggests that.'

'D.I. Jones has got it wrong,' said Jude.

'You know that do you?' she said.

'Yep,' said Jude. 'I just need to get enough evidence to prove it.'

'Did yesterday help?' Dexter grinned. 'Come on, spill the beans. We're Team Mumford, remember?'

'Of course, Team Mumford,' Jude laughed.

'Come on mate,' said Dexter. 'Not feeling the love here.'

'What happened yesterday?' asked Rosebud. 'What's our next move?'

'The next thing I need to do is speak to Sasha again,' said Jude.

'We can come with you,' said Dexter. 'We could be like, good cops, that's me and Rosebud and bad cop, that's you of course.'

'Brilliant idea! But can I be a bad cop?' Rosebud turned to Jude. 'You can't say no.'

'Look at his face,' said Dexter. 'I've got a feeling he's gonna try…'

'I've got to go alone.'

'You can't,' Rosebud shouted at him.

'But, it's got nothing to do with Chantal's death. It's about her uncle.'

'The guy who was murdered years ago?' said Dexter. 'What about him?'

'He was abusing her, his own niece.'

'How awful!' said Rosebud. 'Is that what you found out yesterday?'

Jude nodded.

'The bloody bastard,' said Dexter.

'And that's why I need to go up there alone,' Jude sipped his champagne. 'She doesn't like speaking to me, she's hardly going to open up to all three of us, is she?'

'You're wrong you know,' said Dexter, 'You need us there.'

'Do I?'

'If she was involved in Chantal's death. How do you know she's not going to attack you?'

'I'll take my chances.'

'You do realise that if one of us had been with you when you went into Olga's house, you wouldn't have been cut,' said Dexter, he animated his words by holding out his left arm and slashing across it with his right hand just to make sure Jude fully understood him.

'You must admit,' said Rosebud. 'There's safety in numbers.'

'But we can't all go up there…' Jude tried to plead his case.

'Okay, I get that,' said Dexter. He sat and thought for a few seconds then beamed, first at Jude then at Rosebud. 'I've got a plan,' he said. 'And it's bloody brilliant.'

Rosebud was still sipping her first glass of champagne. Dexter was on his second glass of cider. Jude drained his glass, reached for the champagne bottle and poured his third glass of champagne.

Dexter explained that he was due a visit to the Manor to mow the lawns and check the vegetable garden. His suggestion was that Jude time his visit to the Manor so that they were both there together. He told Jude that she (Sasha) rarely invited anybody into the house so if she was prepared to talk to him it would probably be in the kitchen garden and he (Dexter) could lurk around 'in plain sight' (he used finger quotes to emphasis his words) and be both an observer and a helper if things turned bad.

'What about me?' asked Rosebud.

'Well, that might be a bit awkward,' said Dexter turning to her. 'Because I'm not due up there until next Friday,' he turned to Jude, mid-afternoon, three-ish is that okay?'

Jude nodded.

'And you'll have gone back to the smoke by then.'

'Bugger.'

'You should spend more time here,' Dexter winked at her. 'But I tell you what, if I can get near enough, I'll call you so that you'll be able to hear everything.'

Dexter sat back with a broad smile on his face, it wasn't to Jude or to Rosebud, it was a smug smile of self-satisfaction at coming up with such a brilliant plan. Satisfied it could not be improved upon he grinned at Jude. Jude half smiled back and reached again for the champagne bottle. He knew they had won; he couldn't say no to them.

38

At 8:50am the following Thursday Jude was sitting in his front room staring at Rosebud's Volvo. The door was open at the back and she was trailing backwards and forwards with boxes and cases and piles of clothes.

She'll be wanting her jigsaw back.

He had completed it the previous day. It had taken him nearly three hours and when he had finished it he had picked up his phone and took a photo as evidence.

After lunch he picked up the jigsaw box and went next door to return it.

'Afternoon,' Rosebud was at her front door.

'Completed yesterday,' he said offering her the box.

'Thanks,' she said. 'Fun isn't it?'

'It certainly is,' Jude nodded. 'The way you have to figure out what's within the dog's eye view. It's brilliant.' He held his phone with the photo out to her. 'And here is the evidence.'

'Very good,' she glanced at it. 'Well done. Shows you have observation skills. I've got some more at home. I'll bring a couple when I next visit.'

'I'd like that.'

Rosebud removed her Alice band, lowered her head and shook her hair forward. There was an awkward silence that lasted until Simeon decided to head for the open garden gate.

'Simeon!' Rosebud yelled.

Jude chased after him and grabbed him before he escaped. He held the hissing cat at arm's length and carried him back to his mistress. Once safely back in her arms he hissed at Jude. Rosebud laughed.

'Thanks.'

'Ungrateful!' said Jude talking to Simeon. 'I've probably just saved you from being run over.'

'He doesn't see it like that,' said Rosebud. 'As far as he's concerned you're just a nosey busy body who stopped him having a bit of fun.' She turned to her pet. 'Did the nasty man stop you having a bit of fun then.' She lifted her head and winked at Jude through strands of tumbled hair. 'Thanks. He loathes men and he hates strangers picking him up, so to him you're like a double whammy of despicable things.'

'Oh dear...,' said Jude. 'I didn't realise.' He stood for a moment unsure what to say. 'Anyway, take care and I hope you have a good trip back to Highgate.'

'Thanks, it shouldn't be too long before I'm back again. They'll be releasing Chantal's body soon.' Her eyes glistened sadness at the memory of her friend. 'And then of course there's Stefan, he's being cremated, I'll need to go to York sometime and pick up his ashes.'

'I'm so sorry.'

'I'll spread their ashes together, maybe at the pet cemetery, it's what Chantal would have wanted.'

'I'm guessing you'd have to get permission; from the new owners. Any idea who they are?'

She nodded and her eyes met his.

'Well,' she said. 'As of 10:15 yesterday morning, turns out it's me.'

39

The next day Jude set his alarm for 6am. Less than an hour later Spud had been fed and was out back with his bone and Jude was standing in his front room staring out of the window. Rosebud's Volvo was still there packed and ready to go.

A Land Rover with an animal trailer attached turned into Willow Walk. It drove to the end of the road, and did a three-point turn in six tries. Jude shouted goodbye to Spud and put on his waterproof jacket and green wellingtons. He slammed his front door shut as the Land Rover pulled up by his front gate.

The driver of the Land Rover leant across and opened the passenger door.

'Morning Dexter,' said Jude as he climbed in.

'Morning,' Dexter nodded to the packed Volvo. 'You do realise she'll be gone by the time we get back.' A banging noise in the back made him turn around.

'Oy you two! Stop it! Behave!' he turned to Jude. 'They've been like that all the flipping way,' he said. 'Little buggers! I had to stop twice.'

'Thanks for doing this,' said Jude as they turned onto the High Street.

'So did you say goodbye?' said Dexter. 'To Rosebud.'

Jude nodded.

'Yep. When I gave her back the jigsaw.'

Dexter laughed, but stopped sharp as a battered Fiat Punto in front of him decided to turn right without indicating. Several bumps from the trailer indicated movement.

'Sorry,' he shouted over his shoulder. He lowered his window. 'Arsehole!' he shouted to the free-wheeling driver who was fast disappearing along the lane.

'Did you?' said Jude. 'Say goodbye.'

'Of course,' said Dexter, 'last night. And I got my instructions for her garden while I was at it.'

They drove through the village, past the shops and Parish Council offices.

'I wish she'd spend more time here,' said Dexter.

'Maybe she would if people were a bit nicer to her,' Jude cleared his throat. 'Some of them really don't like her, do they?'

'Jealousy, I reckon. By the way, she's expecting us.'

'How on earth did you contact her?'

'I went and knocked on her front door of course.'

'I didn't think she ever answered her front door. I tried twice; I could see she was in but she wouldn't open it.'

'She only opens up to people she knows,' said Dexter, 'and likes.'

They pulled out onto the main 'B' road for the short drive to the edge of the village.

'You do know she doesn't like me,' said Jude.

'I know, I know, she threatened you with an axe,' said Dexter. 'But believe me after this she is gonna love you so much, she'll want your bloody babies.'

'Seriously?'

'Okay, sorry, bad taste. Trust me. After this she is gonna love you.' A banging noise from the trailer distracted him, eyes still on the road he half turned his head. 'Shut up you two!' He shouted. He turned to Jude. 'You'd never believe they're the best of buds.'

Five minutes later the Land Rover was bumping slowly up the pot-holed driveway to Saffron's cottage. Dexter stopped the vehicle metres from her front door. Saffron, wearing the same jacket and tie dye skirt Jude had seen her in on the day of their first meeting, was standing on her doorstep.

'After you,' Dexter nodded to Jude. 'You did all the work tracking them down.'

Jude opened the door of the Land Rover and stepped down just as another bang rocked the trailer.

225

'Hey,' he said. 'Calm down you two. You're home.'

Saffron ran towards him, gone was the sullen faced manic character who had previously confronted him, her expression, her body, her whole demeanor was a simple picture of pure joy. Jude stood his ground, waiting to greet her but as she neared, she veered sideways passed him by and headed for the back of the trailer. A few seconds, a clunk, a bang and the back was down.

'Sofia! Marigold!' She was shouting, crying, her joy. Her uncontrolled tears and emotional ramblings were her way of expressing her happiness at her recovered love.

Jude felt a surge of pride. He had done this. He had helped a woman who, overwhelmed by personal life events had turned inward and retreated into a world of her own.

The sound of a donkey clumping down the ramp made Jude step forward, but Dexter appeared next to him, put his hand on Jude's arm and shook his head.

'She'll be around in a minute,' he said. 'Hold on.'

Seconds later a tear-stained Saffron appeared holding a blue rope, at the end of the rope was a brown and white donkey. It looked around, then at the cottage, twitched its ears forward, opened its mouth and let out that noise that donkeys make.

'Here,' said Saffron, handing Jude the rope. 'Sofia, you behave now. Don't be spiteful!' She disappeared again around the back of the trailer and there was the clumping sound of another donkey being unloaded. This time the donkey was brown and smaller and wearing a yellow head collar.

Without a word she passed Jude, grabbed Sofia and, with a lead-rope in each arm, headed to the cottage. She was returning Sofia and Marigold to the home they had so cruelly been taken away from.

Both donkeys behaved like model specimens and walked obediently behind their mistress as if there were a quiet understanding as to who was the boss.

Just before Saffron disappeared around the back of her cottage, she stopped, turned to Dexter and nodded.

'I reckon the next time you come knocking at her front door, she'll answer it,' said Dexter. 'Come on, let's get back.'

'Is that it? Shouldn't we go and help her or something?'

'She's fine,' said Dexter as he climbed into the Land Rover. 'Isn't the internet a wonderful thing?'

'Indeed, it is,' said Jude climbing in.

Dexter started to turn the Land Rover and trailer around. It took him several minutes, edging forwards and backwards and Jude had to get out and move a random bucket, a broken wheelbarrow and a mooning gnome to avoid driving over them.

When the manoeuvre was done and they were facing the way out, Jude opened the passenger door and was about to jump in, but Dexter's attention was on his wing mirror. He turned to Jude.

'You're wanted by the looks of things.'

'Ay?'

'She's beckoning at us; I'm guessing it could be you she wants to speak to.'

Jude jumped down and slammed the door shut. He walked around the front of the vehicle and turned and faced the cottage. Saffron was standing on her doorstep. He headed towards her and stopped a few feet away.

'Hi,' he nodded and gave a half wave.

She stood, eyes on the ground, hands clasped in front of her.

'Sorry,' she said.

'What for?'

She stood silent still gazing at the ground.

'I presume you mean when I came to see you?' said Jude. 'Please, it's me who should be sorry. I didn't realise what you've been through.'

Jude turned to go but she called after him.

'That day.'

He stopped, turned back to face her.

227

'What day?'

'I didn't tell the police,' she said. 'But I'll tell you.'

'Okay,' said Jude taking a couple of steps forward.

She lifted her head for the first time, put her hands into her pockets and swayed gently from side to side.

'That day, out on the Fen...'

Jude hinted a smile; it was a look of encouragement.

'The first time I met you?'

She gave a short quick nod.

'I saw her, she wanted to speak to me.'

'Who?'

'Chantal of course!' she sounded frustrated, as if Jude wasn't keeping up.

'She wanted to talk to you?' said Jude. 'What about?'

'Knew if she'd come to the house, I'd take the axe to her.'

'What did she want to talk to you about?'

'Said she was sorry, wanted us to be friends again.'

'And what did you say?'

'I told her. I wasn't ever going to tell her but I did.'

'You told her what?'

'They think I don't remember but I do.'

'They? Who's they?'

'People, everyone...'

'And what do you remember? What did you tell Chantal?'

'I told her it was him,' she said. 'The one who did it, who hurt me.'

'Who? Who are you talking about?'

'Lord of the Manor of course. But he's dead now.'

'You mean Lawson Peterson? You told Chantal, he was the one who raped you?'

Saffron nodded then stood silent, her eyes on the ground, spilled tears still telling the tale of her pain.

'I bet she was shocked. What did she say?'

'She went mad at me. Said I should have told her before. Said she was going to help me; she was going to tell the police.'

'And what did you say to that?'

'I told her to go away. It's all done with.'

'I see. And did she go?'

Saffron nodded, this time several nods in quick succession.

'She was my friend once.'

'I heard,' said Jude. He could see her hands trembling. He wanted to walk up to her, comfort her in some way but sensed a nearness to her might have the opposite effect. After a few seconds he whispered.

'So, you just saw her the once, that day on the Fens.'

She shook her head.

'I went for a long, long walk in the snow,' she said. 'Come back in the dark I did.'

'Did you?' Jude spoke in a whisper. 'Did you see anything when you walked back?'

She nodded, vigorously this time.

'What did you see? Who? Did you see her again?' He waited for Saffy to say something and after several silent seconds she did.

'Lady of the Manor and her big car, and her, that kiddies mother, you know, the one whose pony got killed.'

'You managed to see them in the dark?'

'Course, I got my night time binoculars. I see owls and all sorts. By the trees they were….'

'And it was definitely them. You're absolutely sure?'

Saffron nodded several times in quick succession.

'Did you see Chantal?'

'On the ground.' She stood, eyes half closed, swaying slightly. 'That kiddies ma, she was by her, with a branch.'

'With a branch?'

'By her feet.'

'Why didn't you tell the police this?'

'No, not the police. No, I don't talk to the police.'

'Okay,' said Jude. 'Look, what you have told me is very helpful. But we really need to tell them.'

'No! Not talking to the police.'

'Okay, no problem. Sorry.'

'I need to go see Sofia and Marigold,' she turned went into her cottage and slammed the door.

Minutes later Jude was back in the Land Rover and they were heading for the road.

'What was all that about?' asked Dexter. 'You looked as if you upset her. How did you manage that?'

'I suggested she talk to the police about what she saw.'

'What did you do that for? She hates the police.'

'But why? What on earth has she got against them?'

'To be honest, I don't think it's the police exactly, I think it's people in authority she has a problem with.'

'Any idea why?'

'I think it stems from when she was in the hospital, institution, whatever it was... Let's just say I don't think it was the kindest of places.'

'Crikey, I didn't know.'

'No reason why you should. The place was closed down a few years ago. They used to lock patients in their rooms for hours on end, tie...'

'I get the picture, poor Saffron.' Jude sat in silence, deep in thought.

'So are you going to tell me what she said?'

'Not just yet.'

'Oh come on!'

'I'm sorry, I just need to think.'

'Bloody blimey mate, you do way too much of that, way too much.'

Jude put all of what he had been told by Saffron and then by Dexter to the back of his mind.

'She's quite a character isn't she?' he said. 'I'm glad we could help her. Sofia and Marigold are now back where they should be.'

'Well, I must say I'm bloody impressed you managed to track them down. She was devasted when they disappeared. Put her back years it did.'

'Must have been dreadful for her.'

'And the worst of it?' said Dexter. 'When they went missing Chantal was the one consoling her, 'helping' her through the trauma of it.'

'And she's the one who stole them! What a piece of work.'

'And Saffron knew it all along, but nobody believed her.'

'Well at least she's got them back now.'

'The way Chantal manipulated her after Mr Hill died was shameful,' said Dexter. 'But I'm guessing she knew there was nobody looking out for Saffy anymore.'

They headed back into the heart of the village, towards Willow Walk. The clouds had scooted off to the next village and the sun warmed the air.

'How did you find them?' asked Dexter. 'Sofia and Marigold.'

'It was easy,' said Jude. 'Chantal was an animal lover, so let's face it, if she was responsible for their disappearance, she wouldn't have let them come to any harm, would she?'

'Good thinking.'

'I contacted the animal sanctuaries. Every bloody one. The one in Devon, where you picked them up received the two donkeys

231

from a woman at that time, she used a false name but their descriptions matched, the donkeys and Chantal's. I suppose she wanted to make sure they weren't traced.'

'She certainly sent them far enough away.'

'The only reason the manager down there remembered her was because they had a common interest.'

'Which was?'

'France. He owned a property there.'

'Aha! Her downfall, Chantal never did lose her French accent.'

They turned into the High Street, passed the corner shop as Freya Fernsby and Charlie Peterson were going in. Jude watched them, turning his head as they drove past.

'Young love,' said Dexter. 'Isn't it wonderful?'

'For a short while,' said Jude.

'Oh dear, sounds as if you've been burnt mate.'

'Thanks again for picking up Sofia and Marigold. Let me know how much I owe you.'

'Oh dear, good subject swerve. Well, if ever you want to talk about it, we can swap heartbreak stories.' Now, about payment.' Dexter turned off the High Street and headed for the church. 'Would you be interested in a deal?'

'What sort of deal?'

'Well, I play a bit of tennis, I wouldn't mind having a few lessons.'

'No probs. You're on. My arm's nearly better, I could start you off in a couple of weeks. Thank God she got my left arm.'

'Yep, indeed. Could have been so much worse. Couple of weeks is brill.'

They drove on in silence.

'You enjoying village life then?' said Dexter.

'Love it.'

'You'll stay then?'

'That's the plan. I guess I'd better find somewhere to buy, I don't want to waste my money renting too much longer.'

'You'll be lucky buying a decent property round here, unless you like a new build, plenty of those.'

'I'd sooner stick pins in my eyes.'

It was Dexter who interrupted the silence that followed.

'If you're lucky, your landlord might consider selling.'

'I don't know who owns my cottage. I just deal with the estate agent.'

Dexter laughed.

'I had the same dilemma, but she sold me mine.'

'She? You had the same landlord?'

Dexter nodded.

'I may as well tell you; you'll find out soon enough anyway. It's Rosebud, she owns your cottage.'

'Rosebud!' Jude didn't attempt to hide his surprise. He said the words to himself, trying to understand. 'Rosebud is my landlord?'

Dexter nodded as he turned the Land Rover into Willow Walk.

'Yep. She bought numbers 1,2,3 and did them up. Made a good job of it as well, they were a bit wrecked before. She kept number 1 for her visits, obvs., and let out numbers 2 and 3. I rented number 3 for nearly a year, then we came to an agreement and I bought it.'

That's how she knew so much about me when I first met her. And of course, the matching hardwood front doors with the stained glass, tall stemmed roses in full bloom, one red, one yellow, facing each other nodding forward in greeting. The same doorbell.

'So that's why people round here are so jealous of her.'

'Probably. Anyhow, she was okay with it, selling to me, only stipulation is that I have to give her first refusal if I decide to sell.'

'And you're okay with that?'

233

'Course. Why wouldn't I be? It's my home. I love it, I'm not going to sell up.'

'I'm not sure if I'd be happy with that.'

'She's a very canny businesswoman, along with being a very successful writer of course.'

'She must be.'

'Have you ever read any of her books?'

Jude shook his head. I keep meaning to, I like crime novels. Just haven't got round to it yet.'

Dexter pulled the Land Rover up outside Jude's cottage.

'Crime novels? Where'd you get that idea from? She doesn't write crime.'

'Doesn't she?'

'Nope,' Dexter laughed, 'call yourself a detective man...'

'So, what does she write?'

'She's one of these what they call erotic fiction writers.'

'Erotic fiction?'

Dexter nodded.

'She writes about sex.'

'What!'

'And bloody blimey I have to say she's pretty good at it. The writing and the other stuff....'

'Other stuff?'

'The sex.'

'You mean you and Rosebud? You're a thing? Together?'

Dexter turned off the engine.

'No we're not together, not exactly, I suppose, helping her with her research would be a more accurate term to describe it.'

'But I thought, Rosebud and Chantal? I thought they were together.'

'Maybe, maybe not,' Dexter shrugged. 'There were rumours.'

Jude sat staring to front with his mouth open.'

'They may have been true, I never asked.' Dexter opened his door and jumped out.

'And you weren't curious?'

'Course I was, but bloody blimey I could hardly ask her, could I? It's not like we were together, together.' He grinned. 'Our Rosebud is a free spirit.' He winked at Jude. 'Like myself. Go on, buzz off. I've got to get this trailer back and get to work. My mortgage doesn't pay itself.'

40

'Didn't I make myself clear last time? What are you doing here?'

Jude had caught Sasha unawares this time.

'Can we talk?'

'I hear you've been doing a lot of that.'

'You've spoken to your sister then.'

'She called me. You do realise I could call the police, have you for harassment.'

I do realise that, but I'm guessing you won't.

'Go on then, call the police. I'm happy for them to hear what I've got to say.'

Please don't.

Her blue eyes bore into him, hinted fury. She stepped out, slammed the door shut behind her and head high, came down the steps towards him. They stood and faced each other for a few silent seconds, before she turned and walked around to the side of the house.

'Charlie not around?' he asked as they passed through the side gate.

'He's upstairs watching some chess match or other.'

She headed to the pergola, covered now by vines showing off newly formed bunches of purple grapes, it added an exotic feel to the garden. She sat on the bench and nodded Jude to the chair opposite. A glass flower vase of multi-coloured Foxgloves sat centre table and she shifted it slightly to one side so that they had a clear view of each other.

Jude sat back and crossed his legs. Over her shoulder, a few metres behind her Jude spotted Dexter, with a spade, a rake and a grin. He gave Jude a thumbs up.

'What exactly did you hope to achieve by speaking to Lottie?'

Jude turned his attention full to Sasha.

236

'We had an interesting conversation. I hear she didn't get on with your husband.'

'My husband got on with very few people,' she said. 'The exception of course is those people he could make money from,' she smiled her amusement. 'In which case he could be very charming.'

'I heard exactly that from her.'

'You had no right to speak to her.'

'She didn't have to answer my questions,' said Jude. 'But she was happy to.'

'She had no right talking to you about me.'

Jude took a deep breath, uncrossed his legs and leant forward. Gone was the timid, anxious lady who had greeted him with a nervous smile on his first visit. He no longer felt he needed to tread lightly around this woman.

'I just want to get to the truth.'

'You want the truth?' Her eyes misted over and her voice tapered off to silence.

'Lottie, she told me everything,' said Jude. 'About what your uncle did to you.'

'She said she told you.'

'Your uncle, he threatened you, didn't he? Not to tell. That's what abusers do.'

'It was all years ago. All best forgotten.'

'He isolated you from your friends, called you special, bought you presents…'

She sat silent, eyes glazed staring to front.

'I'm so sorry. It must have been horrendous.'

Out of the corner of his eye Jude could see Dexter edging along the vegetable border towards where they were sitting.

'I broke down one day,' Sasha nodded. 'I told Lawson what he did to me,' she started to shed real tears. 'We'd been dating a few months. Obviously he was furious.'

237

She reached into her jacket pocket, took out a packet of John Player cigarettes and a flip top lighter, seconds later they were on the table next to the vase and she was puffing away, her first few puffs in quick succession, before slowing as the combination of toxins calmed her.

'Uncle Bob was moving to Spain. Bastard was going to get away with it. Lawson didn't want that,' she wiped away a tear. 'He killed him for what he did to me.'

'Are you sure that's what happened?'

'Of course,' her gaze was unwavering.

'I think you're lying.'

Sasha didn't attempt to hide her anger at being doubted.

'Well excuse me but what you think doesn't actually matter. As far as the police are concerned the case is now, after all this time, closed.'

'I think it was you who killed your uncle. And I think Lawson helped you cover it up.'

Jude continued to watch her, waiting for some sort of emotion to expose her lies. But there was none. Dexter was much closer to them now; he gave Jude another thumbs up and lay his mobile phone down onto the grass.

'And I think what you didn't realise at the time was that yes, you'd killed one abuser, but you walked straight into the arms of another.'

'Why would you think that?' she looked up now, her eyes sharp. 'In those days, I loved my husband and he loved me.'

'He wanted to own the Manor, 'and he wanted to own you. I know he was obsessed with you.'

'Lottie again.'

'And he knew the only way he could do both was to help you and marry you. And you played right into his hands. If you had gone to the police and confessed what you'd done to your uncle you could never have inherited the Manor. This way, with the crime unsolved, you inherited, he married you and all he had to do was buy Lottie's half from her.'

238

'Oh well done Sherlock, have you just thought all that up?'

As a matter of fact, yes, most of it I have. And it's pretty good, I think.

'You see, what I really struggled with was,' Jude stared at her. 'If your husband did kill your uncle, why on earth would he keep the knife?'

'How on earth would I know something like that?'

'The other thing of course is that creeping up behind someone and stabbing them in the back doesn't seem to me like something your husband would do. I'm guessing he'd be more confrontational.'

Sasha laughed.

'How many times did you meet my husband?'

'A couple.'

'And you actually have the nerve to think you knew him?'

'I've known people like him.'

'Are you aware he was a narcissist?'

'Of course. I recognized the signs, from what people said about him,' said Jude. 'But that is not in question. What is in question is whether he was a murderer or not.'

'Why? Why are you saying these things?'

'You killed your uncle and Lawson kept the knife, as a warning to you, as a way of controlling you.

He thought he detected a slight nod.

'Why can't you just let things be and get on with your tennis thingy?'

'I just want to get to the truth.'

'I know, if you're really struggling for clients, how about I book in for a course of lessons.' She sat back and thought about it, let the impromptu idea take shape and as it did, she smiled. 'In fact, that is a brilliant idea. I could do with a new hobby.'

Jude didn't try to hide his surprise at her suggestion.

239

'Thank you but no thanks. I have several potential clients,' his eyes stayed with her. 'You could at least pretend to be a bit upset by his death.'

Once prompted Sasha did just that. She blinked; her eyes wetted, she pulled a hanky from her jacket pocket and patted away manufactured tears.

'Actually,' she said. 'I am upset. But the simple fact is I have to move on, for my own sake and for the sake of our son.'

'And that brings me to my next point.'

She sat silent, waiting.

'Do you remember the last time we spoke?'

She puffed cigarette smoke in his direction by way of acknowledgement.

'And I happened to say that I knew somehow that you and Mrs Fernsby were involved in Chantal's death?'

More cigarette smoke.

'And you told me I didn't have any evidence and that there were no witnesses.'

Her eyes bore into him. She dropped her cigarette, ground it out and without hesitation lit another one.

'It turns out there is a witness. A witness who saw your car at the scene that night.' At last Jude detected panic in her eyes.

She stared at him unblinking, stood up, unbuttoned her jacket, shrugged it off and placed it neatly on the bench beside her then sat feet square on the ground, hands clasped together in her lap like a prefect at an assembly.

'My husband killed Chantal. I'm a witness to the number of times he threatened her.' She shouted as if attempting to silence not just his voice but his thoughts. 'And of course our car was seen! He was there. He attacked her.' She paused, 'Who was it saw our car there?'

Her gaze focused on a Red Admiral butterfly as it hovered above the flower vase for a few seconds then landed on the leaf of a pink Foxglove. As it slowly raised and lowered its wings in readiness to fly off, she wished she could do the same.

Jude cleared his throat and scratched his chin.

'It was Saffron. She saw your car on her way back from her evening walk.'

'Saffron! That crazy hippy woman?'

'She's really not that crazy.'

'Okay, so, she's a witness to my husband being there.'

'She didn't see your husband,' said Jude. 'It was you she saw, and Mrs Fernsby.'

Sasha sat in thoughtful silence.

'I see,' she said. 'Can I ask why you haven't gone to the police with this so-called evidence?'

'Because…'

…because even if Saffron could be persuaded to speak to them, she would make a terrible witness and you know it.

'Once more Mr Mumford, your silence tells me everything I need to know.'

'You were there, why don't you just admit it?'

'Mr Mumford,' she turned to him with a gentle smile. 'Why are you looking for problems where there are none?' She paused, seeking a reaction from him. 'Sometimes in life things do just fall into place, don't they?'

'And that is what has happened here isn't it? Everything has just fallen into place for you. Very convenient.'

'Yes, you're right, it is convenient, for me, and for Charlie of course.'

'But it's not the truth.'

This time Sasha's laugh was loud, and it was real.

'You want to hear the truth? Well here it is. My husband was a bully. I'm glad he's dead! The fact is Charlie and I now have a future, and he can lead his best life, playing chess, sewing and not playing tennis.' She hinted a smile. 'This village is a safe place once more so why don't you just leave things be? You'd be doing everyone a favour.'

241

'But she died,' said Jude, his voice breaking. 'It was because of me, I left her.'

'Oh get over yourself! You're a detective. You must have seen loads of dead bodies.'

I have. But I've never been responsible for somebody's death before.

Jude couldn't hide his frustration, a new found energy harnessed his thoughts, manifested as anger.

'I didn't want this!' he placed both hands onto the arms of his chair and stood up towering above her. 'None of it! I just came to Eaststowe to be a tennis coach. I didn't know I was going to witness a killing, did I?'

Sasha sat straight, looked up, her eyes bore into him and a slow smile curved into her features.

'Strictly speaking,' she said, 'you didn't witness a killing.' Blue the cat appeared and jumped onto her lap. She turned her attention to him and stroked the purring animal as he snuggled into her and curled up, only then did she look up and acknowledge Jude again. 'But your dog did.'

'Spud! How would you know he was there unless you saw him!'

'Now please leave. I want you off of my property.'

'But… hold on a minute, you were there so you must have known she was alive. Of course you did! You left her there to die! How could you do that?'

'I asked you to go.'

What happened next took Jude completely by surprise. Sasha's expression transformed to panic, she turned her head and screamed.

'Dexter, help! I need you!' she shouted. 'Help!'

Dexter arrived beside Sasha within seconds, she stood up and screamed again.

'He's harassing me. He won't go away.'

'But…' Jude didn't have a chance to get a word in.

242

'Dexter, make him leave.'

'It's okay, now calm down,' Dexter placed a protective arm around her. 'Don't worry, I'll sort it.'

'He's been harassing me,' she shouted. 'Saying horrible, horrible things. Get rid of him now.'

'I'm afraid you're going to have to leave,' Dexter stepped forward, winked at Jude, squared his shoulders and puffed out his chest. 'You heard what the lady said.'

'Oh stop it,' Jude turned to go but accidentally brushed into Dexter.

'That's enough now,' Dexter shouted. 'The lady said leave.' He closed in on Jude and whispered, 'take one for the team mate.' And without any further warning hit Jude on the chin.

Under attack, Jude had to defend himself. He went into auto pilot. His first punch slammed into Dexter's right eye, his second, third and fourth punches, belted full into his ribs.

41

Later that same evening, as light dwindled into the secretive shadows of night-tide, Jude was lying on his sofa staring at the ceiling. He heard a car, got up and went to the window as Sasha's Range Rover pulled up outside Dexter's cottage. Sasha got out, went around to the passenger side and opened the door. Slowly and carefully, Dexter emerged, one arm rested on her shoulder, the other he held protectively against his ribs.

After beating Dexter, Jude had stood over his neighbour and stared down at him, horrified at what he had done. He had opened his mouth to say something, but a single whispered word was all he could manage *'sorry.'* He'd turned to Sasha, who, as she cradled Dexter's head in her arms had let rip a verbal attack of brute force, accusing him of being a thug who should be locked up. He couldn't disagree and when she returned her attention to comforting her injured gardener, Jude had fled the scene.

That night Jude slept fitfully, his mind replaying every punch, redrawing the shock and then the pain on his neighbour's face as he rained blows upon him.

At a time after midnight, a car pulled up outside Jude's cottage. He didn't hear it because, in his night-time dream he was revisiting his daytime nightmare blow by blow. It was only when the driver got out of the car and slammed the door he jumped awake. Freed from the visions that tortured his sleep, he crawled out of bed and went over to the window. From his place behind the curtain he spotted Rosebud's Volvo.

She's meant to be back in Highgate…

Rosebud was at Dexter's gate. As she pushed it open, she glowered at Jude's cottage and instinctively he retreated further into the shadows. He watched until she disappeared into his neighbour's cottage.

In one afternoon Jude had rewritten the story of his new life. His credibility was shot and his dream of becoming a tennis coach was trailing along behind it. After all, who would want to work with a thug?

244

Jude had rarely felt lonely in his life. Even after he moved to Eaststowe where - when he arrived - he hadn't known a soul. He had never felt isolated because he enjoyed his own company and of course he had Spud. But on this night he loathed the man he had become. A feeling of emptiness overtook him and for the first time he understood the feeling of loneliness. His only shred of comfort was the fact that Spud had not been at his side to witness his thuggery.

42

Three days after the attack, the sun was in top form, radiant in a cloudless sky, unlike Jude, who was hidden away in his cottage skulking in the shadows behind his drawn curtains.

'Spud, here boy.'

Concerned that his pet had not made an appearance, he went to the kitchen, stood just outside the back door and scanned the garden. It was unusual, Spud normally appeared as soon as he called him. But on this particular morning, although Jude kept calling, Spud was nowhere to be seen. He ventured out and headed to the back gate to check it was locked. It was. He started to fear for his pet, he called again and again. Nothing.

'Spud! Here boy! Come!'

'Woof!'

It was definitely his bark. Jude sighed his relief as he headed back up the garden path. A couple of seconds and Spud appeared, at least the top half of him did. He was in Dexter's garden, paws on the wall, he barked another couple of times as if to invite Jude over.

Oh shit. Still best get it over with.

Jude headed to their boundary wall. In the centre of Dexter's lawn was a child's paddling pool filled with water and laying immersed in the middle of the pool was Dexter.

Dexter wore sunglasses so Jude could not see his eye, but even from the distance of his own garden he could see his neighbour's bruised ribs all well on their journey to telling the tale of a brutal beating.

'I'm sorry,' Jude winced then swallowed hard. 'I'm so, so sorry.'

'So you should be. I'm off work cos of you.'

'Can I… come over?'

At least he's talking to me.

'Course.'

246

Jude used the same entry point into Dexter's garden as his neighbour always used when he visited. He placed his right hand onto the wall and leapt over. Spud greeted his master as if he hadn't seen him for days, jumping up, licking, whining and smiling with his tail.

'Down boy, down,' he headed for the paddling pool. 'Dexter, I'm so sorry.'

'At last!' Dexter raised an arm and splashed water towards Jude. 'You've come to visit me. Pity I had to take Spud hostage to get you here.'

'Hostage?' Jude let out a breath in a heavy sigh.

'Don't worry, he came willingly, but a couple of sausages from my breakfast helped.'

'I bet they did.'

'I had to get you here somehow.'

'I... I didn't think you'd want to see me.'

'You do realise I was messing with you; you weren't actually meant to hit me back.' He lifted his sunglasses. 'Look! Look what you did to me!'

Jude stared at his neighbours swollen and purple eye.

'I'm so sorry. I don't know what came over me.'

'Take one for the team I said. I did it so's I'd get her confidence.'

'I get it. Look, is there anything I can do?'

'Plenty. You owe me big time.'

'I'll come and help you gardening, you know, when you get back to work.'

'Huh! Whenever that is.'

'Is it really that painful?'

'Look! Look at me!' Dexter tried to lift himself up. 'Does that look painful to you? And that? And that?' As he spoke he pointed to a different purple patch on his battered torso. 'Mate, I can't even play my guitar.'

247

'Are we?' Jude raised his eyebrows, 'still mates.'

Dexter tried to chuckle but winced instead.

'Course we are. We're Team Mumford remember.'

'But what about Rosebud? I can't see her wanting anything more to do with me.'

'Don't worry about Rosie, she'll get over it.'

'You reckon?'

'Course she will. Look, she knows that that cloak you wrap yourself up in every day is just camouflage and that somewhere buried inside is a decent bloke struggling to find himself.'

'Find myself? Is that what she thinks?'

'It's what we both think,' Dexter lay back and splashed water over himself. 'Christ it's hot. And she knows, as I do, that one day you'll have the courage to bust yourself out.'

'You make it sound like a jailbreak.'

'Mate, lucky it was me you whacked, if it had been someone else you could be planning just that...'

Jude swallowed hard and turned his head away so that he could no longer see the injuries he had inflicted.

As if realising his master was struggling, Spud wandered over, sat, then lay down beside Jude and rested his head on his foot.

'You see,' Dexter nodded to Spud, 'he's there for you. He's one clever dog.'

'I know,' said Jude. He sat down next to his pet and stroked him. 'I saw Rosebud came back.'

'To see me, tell you what, between her and Sasha I'm being well...'

'Knock! Knock!' The back gate opened. 'Only me,' it was Rosebud, in a skimpy pink t-shirt dress.

'Rosie!' Dexter grinned and lifted his sunglasses again so that she could get a good look at his eye, then he half lifted his body out of the water so that she could get a close up of his bruises. 'Look at me, I'm turning purple.'

Rosebud neared the paddling pool and sat down beside it to examine Dexter's injuries.

'Well they look as if they're cooking nicely,' she glared at Jude. 'Did you have to?'

'Now then Rosie, it wasn't entirely his fault. I did sort of start it. To be honest I'm just grateful I'm still breathing.'

'As I said, anything I can do,' said Jude.

'Oh I've got a list mate.'

'You poor love,' Rosebud leant forward and kissed Dexter on the forehead just above his purple eye before glaring at Jude again. 'Well it's a bloody pity you didn't fight like that when Ivy went for you.'

'Good point,' Dexter nodded. 'That is a very good point indeed.'

'If I remember correctly,' Rosebud winked at Dexter. 'He had no defensive wounds at all.'

'Too bloody right,' Jude hadn't spotted the wink. 'Ivy had a rage and a flaming great knife and my arm was spurting blood like a Trafalgar Square fountain. I ran like crazy. I really thought it was the end of the party,' he swallowed hard. 'I thought I was going to die.'

'It's not the end of the party when you die mate,' said Dexter. 'The party, it still goes on, you just get permanently booted out of it.'

'Can we please change the subject?' Rosebud lay back on the grass.

'Sorry, sorry,' Dexter reddened, tried to shift and winced again. 'It's the painkillers, making me say stuff.'

'I guess you heard it all on your phone?' Jude turned to Rosebud.

'I did. Look, I don't know what your problem is but you seriously need to chill out.'

249

'You see,' Dexter winked at Rosebud then grinned at Jude. 'What did I tell you? We both know that deep down you're not actually a thug, not really. Besides we're friends, and friends forgive each other don't they? Everyone does stupid stuff occasionally.'

'Huh, what you did,' Rosebud narrowed her eyes at Jude. 'What you did was way more than stupid.'

'I know, I know, I'm sorry, it won't happen again.'

'As long as it not's a pattern of behaviour,' Rosebud turned on her side and rested her head against the side of the paddling pool.

'It's not,' said Jude. 'And thanks, both of you, for being so uncomplicated about it all, for not holding a grudge.'

They silenced their banter and as the three of them absorbed the heat of the summer sun they sheltered beneath the tree of their blossoming friendship.

It was Rosebud who broke the silence.

'I still can't believe you two actually had a fight. Are the pair of you ten years old?'

'I'm not the one in the paddling pool,' said Jude. But when neither of them laughed added. 'Sorry, too soon.'

This time it was Dexter's eyes narrowed into him.

'Yep, way too soon mate.'

'Let it be a lesson to you to never hit a policeman,' Jude paused, 'or an ex-detective.'

'Understood. Now go get us a six pack of cider from the fridge. I'm not moving from this paddling pool until tonight.'

'What, you're staying in there all day, what about if you have to, you know?' said Rosebud.

'I can piss in the pool.'

'Wonderful visual,' Rosebud sat up and pulled her dress up over her head revealing a bright yellow bikini.

'Nice outfit Rosie.'

'Of course. It's so flaming hot, why not?'

'You can join me in here if you like.'

'Tempting, but I'll pass on your kind offer.'

'Come on, where's your sense of fun?'

'Not in that paddling pool that's for sure. Not with what you've been doing in it.'

'Joking, I was joking.'

'Still no,' Rosebud lay back, closed her eyes and bathed in the sun.

Jude and Dexter did the same and even Spud joined in, he lay flat out, in the shade of a nearby apple tree.

'Dexter, I think now would be a good time to tell us about your wife,' said Jude.

'No... no... now is not a good time. The memories are way too painful. I need rest.' He lifted his head, opened his eyes and glared at Jude. 'Where's my flaming cider? Mate, you're going to have to learn to fetch and carry for the foreseeable if you want me to release you of your guilt.'

'Sorry. I'm on it,' Jude jumped up. 'Anything else while I'm there?'

Five minutes later they each had a can of cider and Jude and Rosebud were laid out either side of the pool.

'Amazingly there is an upside to this,' said Dexter.

'I can't wait to hear it,' said Rosebud.

'The Lady of the Manor thinks I'm bloody wonderful! I'm her hero, so if we need to get any info from her, I'm your man.' He gulped down his cider. 'So come on, are we any closer to figuring out who attacked Chantal?'

'First of all,' said Jude, 'I'd like to ask you both a question.'

'I'm listening,' said Dexter.

'As am I,' said Rosebud.

'If you knew person A had attacked person B but you also knew that person A would not attack again, should they be allowed to get away with it in certain circumstances?'

'Bloody blimey, what a question.' While he spoke Dexter was examining his bruises. 'You're the ex-detective, if you don't know, how'd you expect us to?'

Jude sat and thought for several seconds.

'I suppose it would have to depend on the situation, but who should judge the situation? Of course it should be a jury. But what if that was not possible? What if the case could not go to trial because there were no credible witnesses?'

'You're doing that thinking thing again aren't you?' Dexter laughed then winced.

'What thinking thing?'

'That thing where you talk but don't actually tell us anything. Enough now.'

'Sorry, sorry, force of habit.'

'Right,' said Rosebud. 'I'll try and answer your question. If there are no witnesses, there can be little or no evidence so the case would not be able to go to trial. Now tell us what you're on about.'

'I didn't say there weren't any witnesses. I said there weren't any credible witnesses.'

'So you're saying you've got a witness, but not a credible one?' Dexter's eyes lit up. 'I knew it! It's Saffron isn't it? That day we took her donkeys back; she told you something didn't she? I bloody knew it.'

'She can place Sasha and Mrs Fernsby at the spot where Chantal died.'

'Aha! Now we're getting somewhere,' said Rosebud.

'You'll never get her into the witness box,' said Dexter. 'Never in a million years.'

'And even if you did,' said Rosebud, 'the prosecution would make mince-meat of her.'

The three friends discussed whether or not Saffron should or could be a witness and then had a further discussion on whether she would even agree to it. Chantal was the woman who had changed the course of Saffron's life. The woman she had once loved, the one who had made her give up one of her babies and the only person who knew what had happened to the other. She had deserted her and then befriended her again and stolen her precious pet donkeys so that she could buy her land at a bargain price. Why would she, Saffron, care at all about bringing Chantal's attacker to justice?

'But Chantal's killer should be brought to justice,' said Rosebud.

'But she wasn't killed,' said Jude. 'She was attacked and left to die.'

'So that means Sasha and Mrs Fernsby, they're both to blame,' said Rosebud. 'They're both responsible for her death.'

'That's true. They knew she was alive when they left her there. But in a way I'm also responsible. I should have gone to investigate when Spud barked.'

'Don't say that,' said Rosebud. 'It wasn't your fault.'

'Pass us another cider,' said Dexter.

Jude leant over, grabbed a can, ring pulled it open and passed it to him. Dexter took a couple of gulps.

'Any idea which of them actually attacked her? And why?'

'Saffron said it was Mrs Fernsby beside her body,' Jude hesitated. 'The branch was next to her.'

'Well after what Chantal put that family through,' Dexter turned to Rosebud. 'Look Rosie, I'm sorry, I don't mean to speak ill of Chantal but...'

'I know what she was like,' Rosebud sat up, blinked back tears. 'But she was trying to make amends for what she did to the Fernsby's and to Saffron.'

'It sounds as if Mrs Fernsby decided to dish out her own karma,' said Jude.

'But she can't get away with it. It's not right.' Rosebud stared one to the other. 'Is it?'

'Rosie, Rosie, look at it this way,' Dexter placed his hand onto the edge of the pool to reach out to her. 'Love, you said yourself Chantal was trying to make amends. Do you honestly think that after what she put that family through that she would want to see Mrs Fernsby locked up? Think of the kids.'

A breeze whispered across the gardens and Rosebud turned away from her friend to face it. Dexter knew his words had distressed her. In truth he was feeling pain too, not just from his injuries, but from seeing a dear friend, a kindred spirit, suffering. He paused for a few seconds, but continued saying what he felt needed to be said.

'And do you honestly think she would want Saffy to go in the dock as a witness?' He struggled to sit up, couldn't quite make it so Jude went and helped him. 'Cheers mate. Rosie, you know as well as I do Chantal wouldn't want to put Saffy through that.'

The group sat silent again, a storm of thoughts blowing through each of their minds. Within minutes, each of the three friends were inhabiting a world of their own, the only sound, an occasional sigh and the gentle splosh of water when Dexter fidgeted in his pool.

'Rosie, are you good?'

Rosebud was lying down, she raised her head and wiped away a tear.

'You're right of course Dext. As usual.'

They sat silent again, but it didn't last long. This time it was Spud who interrupted their private thoughts with a loud yelp.

'Blimey, what's up with him?' asked Dexter.

'He's having a dream,' said Jude. 'It happens.'

'Simeon, does that,' Rosebud hinted a smile. 'I often wonder what he dreams about, he purrs and everything.'

'What do you reckon Spud dreams about?' asked Dexter.

'Bones probably, and chasing cats,' Jude turned to Rosebud. 'But not Simeon of course.'

All three of them watched Spud, sound asleep as he yelped at his visions. After a couple of minutes Jude got up, went over to the apple tree, sat down and brushed his hand over his pet's coat barely touching his fur.

'Hey Spud, you having a bad dream mate?' He paused and smiled down at him. 'I'd love to know what goes on in that head of yours.'

Spud opened his eyes and whined. He had been having a dream, it was the same dream he had had most nights since that evening, out on the Fen when he tried to tell his master that he had come across the body of a woman and two distressed teenagers.

He turned and licked Jude's hand, eyes gazing up at his master. If he could speak, he would have told him how he had seen a boy kneeling beside the body of a woman searching for signs of life. He would have told him about a girl holding a tree branch standing over them. And he would have told him that the girl was sobbing.

'Charlie what have I done? Is she ok?'

And the boy was doing his best to console her.

'She started it, she's a liar.'

'Those things she was saying about your dad…'

'They weren't true… we've got to get help. I'll call my mum; she'll know what to do. Come on, we need to get to higher ground.'

And Spud would have told Jude that when the girl turned around and spotted him she had become even more hysterical.

'Look! That dog!'

So Spud had returned to his master. And he would have told him all about it if he could have. He certainly wanted to.

But of course, although Spud was a very clever dog, he wasn't quite that clever.

Printed in Great Britain
by Amazon

58000052R00149